CAST SHADOWS

A

Jack

Blackmon

Trial

CHRISTOPHER C. BROOME

WestBow
PRESS®
A DIVISION OF THOMAS NELSON
& ZONDERVAN

Copyright © 2024 Christopher C. Broome.

All rights reserved. No part of this book may be used or reproduced by any means, graphic, electronic, or mechanical, including photocopying, recording, taping or by any information storage retrieval system without the written permission of the author except in the case of brief quotations embodied in critical articles and reviews.

This is a work of fiction. All of the characters, names, incidents, organizations, and dialogue in this novel are either the products of the author's imagination or are used fictitiously.

WestBow Press books may be ordered through booksellers or by contacting:

WestBow Press
A Division of Thomas Nelson & Zondervan
1663 Liberty Drive
Bloomington, IN 47403
www.westbowpress.com
844-714-3454

Because of the dynamic nature of the Internet, any web addresses or links contained in this book may have changed since publication and may no longer be valid. The views expressed in this work are solely those of the author and do not necessarily reflect the views of the publisher, and the publisher hereby disclaims any responsibility for them.

Any people depicted in stock imagery provided by Getty Images are models, and such images are being used for illustrative purposes only. Certain stock imagery © Getty Images.

ISBN: 979-8-3850-2767-5 (sc)
ISBN: 979-8-3850-2768-2 (hc)
ISBN: 979-8-3850-2769-9 (e)

Library of Congress Control Number: 2024912590

Print information available on the last page.

WestBow Press rev. date: 07/22/2024

To my children:

Cast your dreams on the winds.

Then let them sprout wings and fly.

Never let anyone tell you it is impossible.

Always keep striving.

ACKNOWLEDGMENTS

Thank you to my wife, Sonya, who supported me through this process. I would also like to thank my mother, Diane, who inspired me with her love of reading. God is good all the time.

ONE

Jack found himself in a chase as a warm breeze blew on his face. His thoughts fixed on capturing the man in front of him. He failed to realize the hot and hazy conditions in which he found himself. This day of all days was an excessively hot one in what was once the lazy South Georgia town of Moultrie. It was overcast and had a haze reaching down from what Jack thought was going to be a clear-skied day. Jack, an Atlanta homicide detective, had moved here after he found himself forced out of his once-promising career in Peach Tree City. His thoughts turned back to the chase and malice the man had shown his victim. He had brutally slain a beautiful, blond-haired southern belle with a bent toward ill-gotten behavior. She once was his accomplice, but that ended when her appetite for riches grew bigger than his bankroll was willing to give. This was the working theory, anyhow.

This case seemed so familiar. It drew him in just as it had years ago. The girls looked so much alike, and the circumstances were very similar. Both victims had beckoned him so strongly that he needed to search out the justice they deserved. Both girls were in their late teens, and both liked bad-boy types of men. They both had the opportunity in front of them but wanted it now rather than later. Their families both had money and influence and desired their children to finish college and then take part in the businesses they had created. Both girls, though, didn't want to work for that success; they wanted quick money and a good time. When Jack had moved to this small, quaint town, he had hoped to leave the past in the past. The past, though, wouldn't leave him behind; it almost seemed as if it hunted him down. The pull of the offense was too strong for him to deny. It drew him like a moth to a flame.

Sweat was rolling down Jack's face—a face that was beginning to wrinkle as he reached an age that not too long ago, he'd considered ancient. He felt his heart beating rapidly, and he thought he really needed to be on an exercise program. He had not been involved in a chase on foot like this since he left Atlanta. Just as he felt himself catching his second wind, he heard a strange popping sound. This led to a stinging feeling in his upper-right thigh. He suddenly began to tumble onto the grayish asphalt, which felt warm and somewhat sticky. As he slowly came to a stop, he eased into a strangely welcoming calmness. He thought this must be the shock caused by the wound he had just sustained.

As Jack lay there, hoping he wouldn't bleed out from the wound, he suddenly was surrounded by a small crowd of nurses from a long-term care facility, which was located due east of where he'd been struck by the lucky shot. He heard a very firm yet somewhat endearing voice say, "Call 911. I have checked the wound, and it looks through and through." He watched the gaunt, sullen-faced women wrap his leg in something white and stretchy. Through all his years as a beat cop and then a detective, Jack had never been shot or even shot at. He wondered how this could have happened. He thought back to all the warnings his superiors on the force had given to him in Atlanta. He then thought about the local sheriff and his warnings about pursuing the matter at hand.

As the wound in his leg ached with a burning pain, he thought, *I must catch this man.* Maybe he could be the one to stop him because someone had to. During the investigation now and back then, it was obvious that they were two of possibly half a dozen that had almost identical circumstances. He couldn't just lay there. He had to get up. He needed to catch this man. He tried to rise, but something unusual happened—his eyesight narrowed, and then it seemed oddly dark to him. He eased onto his back and closed his eyes as the face of the girl seared deeper and deeper into his memory.

Jack became more alert and looked around. The nurse whom he remembered wrapping his leg waved a strange-smelling concoction under his nose. It was an obnoxious-smelling potion, but apparently, it served its purpose in arousing him. His thoughts slowly returned, as well as the fiery sensation in his leg. Jack could only think of his failure to apprehend the man he had so desired to put behind bars. The gaunt nurse abrasively made the recommendation for Jack to lie back and relax.

"I do not want to see all my hard work going for nothing," the nurse said as she put her arm on his shoulder and pushed him back to a prone position.

"What is your name? Jack asked the woman.

"My name is Nancy. I work across the street at the nursing home," she said as she smiled at him.

Just then, he heard the ear-piercing siren of a late-model Ford Taurus patrol car coming down the sticky, tarred pavement. A slightly plump, middle-aged deputy eased out of the front seat, gracefully pulling on his gun-clad holster belt, which seemed to be weighing him down. Without any concern for the man with the dime-sized hole in his leg lying before him, he shouted at the small crowd to turn around and step out of the crime scene.

"Geez, Jack," Deputy Steve Maxum said, "I told you to knock this private-eye stuff off and stick to running backgrounds. Now I have to be out here checking on your hardheaded tail. Don't you realize it's just too hot for this?" The deputy scowled.

"Well," Jack quipped, "at least I didn't spoil your doughnut time."

"I see why you're the one lying on the ground with the hole in your leg," Steve said with a smirk.

Jack watched as Steve walked over to a nearby Honda Civic. He pulled his Old Timer pocketknife and a clear-plastic evidence bag from his pocket. Jack guessed that he had found where the bullet had lodged. This was confirmed when Steve remarked, "I will run this by the lab later and see what turns up." He then turned and put the bag in the patrol car.

"Well, you do that. I think I'll go get this scratch fixed," Jack said at about the time the ambulance was pulling up.

"OK. I'll come around later," said Steve.

Jack was given the once over, lifted onto a gurney, then roughly loaded into the back of the ambulance. As the ambulance started to move, Jack noticed the slightly nauseating smell of bodily fluid, which had been poorly cleaned from his ride. As the pain medicine started to work its magic, Jack reminisced in his drug-induced fog. He imagined the case he was working in Atlanta and the moment that in a similar ambulance with the same smell, he had escorted the young girl who had been assaulted. This, in fact, was the last case in which he would be employed as an Atlanta detective. He couldn't shake the fact that the current PI job he was working and the one that had gotten him ousted as a detective were eerily similar.

The young girl's name was Carly Evans. She was from the Evans family who had started and run a large brokerage firm in the Buckhead region of Atlanta. Emily Rygaard was from a well-to-do family in Moultrie. Both were blond-haired and blue-eyed. They both liked to walk a little on the rougher side of life at times. Jack left his thoughts as he arrived at the hospital emergency room. After being examined by the doctor, he was told that he needed surgery to clean up the wound. He waited nervously for some time, intermittently seeing the beautiful faces of the young teenage women. They seemed to haunt him now. Two orderlies walked in and let him know that they were taking him to the surgical suite. The last thing he remembered was the lights on the ceiling. He counted one, two, three, and then darkness

---

A loud clanging noise awoke Jack. Then he noticed a cold feeling. He deduced he was not wearing his clothes. In fact, it was a hospital gown, and the person who had caused the sound was a very beautiful nurse. He noticed a pan on the floor, which the woman had dropped. Suddenly, Jack became uncomfortable as he realized the situation he was in. He often looked down on receiving help, and this had taken him out of his comfort zone.

"Hello," the young and curious nurse said.

"Hello," said Jack.

"I bet you are trying to figure this out," she said.

"The last things I remember were the ambulance, its foul smell, being examined, and then the lights," he replied.

"Yes. The county paramedics are not known for their five-star-rated ride, but the surgeon is A-rated for sure."

She smirked. Jack pulled the sheet up and moved his gown so that he could see the bandage on his wounded leg. At that moment, the pain from his wound caused Jack's face to contort slightly.

"I think you may need a little more pain medicine," the young nurse said.

"Just not enough to put me into the deep sleep I was in before," Jack said.

"Just take this and relax." She reached out and handed Jack two little white pills. It wasn't long before he was in a comfortable glow again.

TWO

As Deputy Steve Windham was driving to the hospital to check on his old friend Jack, he received a call from Sheriff Jackson. "Didn't I tell you to make Jack back off and leave this silly notion alone?" the sheriff said angrily.

Steve had expected this call. After letting out a long sigh, Steve took a quick look in his rearview mirror as he changed lanes. "Well, Sheriff, Jack is like a bulldog going after a bone when his mind is made up," Steve said, turning off his blinker.

"I know Jack is your friend, and he showed you the ropes in Atlanta, but this isn't Atlanta. Everything isn't a grand conspiracy either. You need to get him under control, or I will have to run both of you out of this county," the sheriff said with an angry tone.

Steve paused and formulated his response carefully. "Sheriff, I know it seems like a stretch, but some of the math does add up. I know Jack is a bit wound up, and he has some abrasive ways, but he has solved many unsolvable cases because of it." Then there was a long pause.

"Just get him under control, and keep him from getting killed, deputy," Sheriff Jackson demanded as he ended the call. Steve was determined to do just that.

As the deputy entered the hospital room and saw his friend lying on the bed, he knew that no matter what, Jack wouldn't stop. The threat so long ago from the chief of detectives in Atlanta and the loss of his badge hadn't stopped him, and this hole in his leg wouldn't stop him. When he had first met Jack all those years ago, Steve had been a rookie beat cop in precinct three. Jack was the only person in the department who helped him after a rookie move almost ended his career before it had started. Steve missed a weapon during a routine pat down during an arrest of a low-level drug dealer. When Steve turned his back, the crook pulled the weapon. Luckily for him, he turned just as the man was starting to point the weapon. Steve grabbed the man's hands, and during the struggle, the weapon discharged. The stray bullet struck an innocent bystander, leaving a small flesh wound. Jack, who was the lead training officer of the station went to bat for the young cop, and he was able to save his job. Steve couldn't bring himself to the point where he would not help Jack.

"Are you here to grill me or gripe?" Jack asked when he noticed his friend standing in the doorway.

"I am here whether or not I gripe," Steve replied as he watched Jack wave him in.

"Well at least pull up a chair. I wouldn't want you to get tired standing there gawking. You act like you have never seen a victim of gun violence before," Jack replied with a half grin on his face.

"I am thinking that you aren't taking this seriously," Steve quipped. Jack heard the sound of a chair scraping across the floor as Steve moved closer. Jack realized his friend was more than likely there because of the sheriff. Jack had been told more than once to back off the Rygaard case. Jack knew that this conversation would not be the one he wanted to have. To know once again that he was so close to solving the case and then being told to back off was almost overwhelming to him.

"I am not here to be the bearer of bad news, Jack. I really am here to make sure you are all right." Jack smiled. Jack thought Steve's kind heart had betrayed him once more.

A beeping noise was coming from a square box with digital numbering on its screen. Then the beautiful young nurse walked in, smiled, and said, "You know, if you wanted me to come and see you, all you have to do is push the small red button at your bedside. Now sit there and think of something pleasant because your blood pressure is on the rise. If it doesn't come down, we will have to start you on blood-pressure medicine, and your stay with us will be longer."

"I might just have to run into more of these crooks, minus the guns, if this is the treatment I can receive," Jack said coyly. "What is your name?"

"It is Anna Lee," she replied.

"I really want to thank you and the rest of the staff for looking out for me today," Jack said.

"Oh, we are here just for people like you; you know, the ones who don't know they aren't quick enough to dodge a speeding bullet," Anna Lee said, smiling at Jack.

"I can't argue with that. I have skipped the last few CrossFit classes, and I have noticed my reflexes have slowed," Jack playfully replied. Steve squirmed awkwardly in the uncomfortably hard chair—not from the chair but from the schoolboy flirting that Jack was participating in with the pretty nurse. He knew the medicine must be good because Jack was usually more introverted than this around women, especially ones that looked like Anna Lee. The young, spunky nurse then turned, smiled, and told them that she would be back later to make sure everything was okay.

"Jack, we need to talk."

"Steve, I know there is pressure being put on you by Sheriff Jackson to shut this down. I need to know if you will be patient and hang in there a little longer."

Steve's face was downtrodden as he replied, "Sheriff Jackson has been good to me, Jack; he hired me after the debacle upstate. I was affected also. No one wanted to hire me after that, and the sheriff took me in. I don't want to ruin that, but I know how much this means to you. I will let this play out as long as I can." Jack looked over at Steve and thanked him. His kind heart didn't betray him after all. Steve sat there by his friend's side until Jack's eyes got heavier and heavier. Finally, he fell asleep.

Steve then rose, walked downstairs, and went through the exit doors. He continued walking into the parking lot and felt a strange sensation that someone was watching him. He stopped and scanned the parking lot, as well as the woodland past it. He didn't notice anything, but the strange sensation wouldn't leave him. He continued walking until he got back to his old Ford Taurus patrol car. He paused, looked around one more time, and opened the door. When he went to turn the ignition on, he could see something flash in the corner of his eye. I seemed like it came from the corner of the hospital.

Can this be the press taking pictures? Can this be someone with nefarious intentions? Because his friend was lying in a hospital bed with a gunshot wound, he decided to check it out. He got out and walked quickly toward it. Just ahead, he noticed a dark figure running away. He looked up and saw that the outside security lighting was not working. He continued, tripping on a crack in the concrete sidewalk along the way. Whoever had been there had quickly gone, and he had not even gotten a glimpse of the person.

Steve was back in his car now, finally pulling out of the parking lot. He thought of the strange occurrence that had just taken place. *What is going on*, he thought. *Has Jack stumbled onto something bigger than we realized?*

Jack had come into the sheriff's office a few weeks earlier while working on a case. He was hired by the Rygaard family to investigate the death of Emily Rygaard. He had made several visits to the office to dig for information in his PI role. He told Steve that the family members were concerned for their daughter. She was a senior at the local high school, and she struggled with life. She was struggling because of her mother's sudden death. She had planned to move to New York after graduation and study fashion. But the loss of her mother ended those plans. Her father, Thomas, told Jack that his daughter's behavior and attitude toward her future endeavors had radically shifted after the tragic event. Jack had been told something else: The change had come because of a young man she had gotten involved with. Her father tried to talk to her about him, but she refused to listen. She spoke of the man on occasion to her brother Tom, but he wasn't willing to share any details with her father.

Jack asked Steve to do a background check on a name he had come across during his snooping. The name of the man was Mikey

McGee. Jack thought this was an alias, and that premonition turned out to be true. There was no record of a man with that name in the department's file. He later found a small-time crook whose name was Johnny. He was the man who had spent a lot of time with Emily Rygaard. He was the boyfriend. Jack was trying to determine why he used an alias and why there was a hush-hush black-ops treatment. Jack almost caught the man coming into a restaurant, but he escaped. Then a chase ensued. And the pursuit ended with Jack lying in his hospital bed.

The next morning, Anna Lee came in early and let Jack know that the doctor was making his rounds and that Jack would be discharged later in the afternoon. She then asked some prying questions into the cause of Jack's injury. "I heard that you were chasing a man down the road in front of Regional Care Rehab yesterday, and he didn't take too kindly to that. Did he have something to do with Emily Rygaard's death?"

"I was, and he didn't, and the other is none of your business," Jack answered. He became curious about the reason for her interest. "He was double-parked and didn't like me trying to perform a citizen's arrest," Jack said.

Anna Lee didn't appear to like the response from Jack. He could tell from the look on her face. "Is that the way you respond to the woman who so tirelessly took care of you all night," she said.

Jack wondered if she knew something he didn't. "Is there a particular reason you are showing this much interest in this incident, Anna Lee?" Jack asked.

She then turned and looked at him squarely. "There is a very good reason. My boyfriend is Tom Rygaard, who happens to be Emily's brother. He told me last night during my break that an investigator his father had hired to find his sister's killer had been shot in the leg. So then I put one and one together."

Jack thought that the Rygaard's family members were very loving and that they just wanted to see the man who had ruined their lives brought to justice, but to involve someone like this young lady was going a step too far. "Anna Lee, I appreciate the care you have given me. I also appreciate the efforts you are going through to help your boyfriend, Tom. The idea of me giving you information and that leading to a bad outcome for him, though, is too much for me to think about. Please tell them I am on the case, and I will get my man." Jack watched the expression on her face change and knew he had gotten through to her. She thanked Jack and left.

THREE

The tall, tan man who was wearing a three-day-old beard walked away from the hospital thinking that he had taken too big a risk. He was young—in his early twenties—and muscular, but he walked with his shoulders pulled forward as if he were trying to hide himself. He considered himself lucky to have escaped the chase earlier. He couldn't imagine how the middle-aged man, who seemed to be too soft and out of shape, was able to keep up with him. He hadn't been that out of breath in a long time. The thought of a toy bunny trying to sell batteries and keep going and going crossed his mind.

He continued down the narrow street until he saw a small nondescript hole-in-the-wall bar. He stopped to look around the vicinity, and after checking for a minute, he felt safe walking in. He ordered the special drink of the day. This turned out to be a watered-down shot of Jim Bean. He looked at the dirty glass and then finished off its contents. It succeeded in the purpose it was created for. He felt himself calming a little. He needed to plan his next move. He was coming to the realization that he needed to leave this dump of a city.

Johnny Thompson had grown up in an average town called Albany. He tended to be a loner and disliked dealing with anyone. He was knocked around as a child. His parents were small-time crooks. His father worked part-time as a line cook, but his niche was being a pickpocket. His mother was a high-school dropout, mainly because she got pregnant at sixteen with Johnny. She was good at seducing unsuspecting older gentlemen into risky positions as Johnny's father videoed them. They would then threaten to show the videos to their wives unless they received a sizeable payment. This often proved profitable. They both seemed to regret having Johnny and showed their true feelings by abusing him verbally and physically. As a small child, they often locked him in the shed behind their small blockhouse with a small jug of water and no food to eat.

By the time Johnny reached middle school, he was following in their footsteps. He never fit in at school. Words that he tried to read in the books didn't make sense, and the more he tried to make sense of them, the more scrambled they seemed. The other kids around him seemed to know this. They often were cruel to him, bullying, ostracizing, and calling him names like stupid or moron. He figured that there was only one way to escape—enter the same lifestyle he had witnessed ever since he could remember. It was the only way for him to escape to what he thought would be a better life.

Sitting on a barstool opposite him, Johnny witnessed an older gentleman pull out a large roll of twenty-dollar bills. He got very excited. The sight of this money or any seemingly large sum of greenbacks always got his conniving side stimulated. He quickly formulated a plan to relieve the man of his money. He then got up and went to the bathroom. He walked into the unsanitary room and splashed water onto his face from the dirty sink. He then took a napkin and dried off the water. He twisted the handle on the greasy door, walked out, and sat down by the man he had spotted earlier. "Excuse me, pal. Can I buy you a drink?" Johnny asked.

"Who are you?" the smaller-framed man said to Johnny.

"Well, I am an undercover officer, and I need your help," Johnny replied as he motioned for him to lower his voice.

The man raised himself a bit off his barstool and snidely remarked, "If you are a cop, where is your badge?"

Looking around and then bending in toward the man, Johnny said, "Do you think I would carry my badge on an undercover assignment?" As Johnny watched the man's face, he could see his brain trying to work. "What is your name?" Johnny asked him.

"My name is Tim." At the same time, Johnny watched a burly man rise from a booth and walk outside.

"OK, Tim, I have a problem. There is a man who just walked out. I have been staking him out for a while. I think he spotted me. I need you to walk out the front door and see if he is waiting outside to jump me. I just need you to walk out and scan the parking lot to see if he is out there. When you finish, come back inside and tell me if he is out there. That is all I am asking you to do. After that, I will buy you a drink and will owe you a favor. Maybe I can help you out with a ticket or something."

"OK. If you will help me out with some tickets, I will do it," the man said agreeably to Johnny.

"Done," Johnny said excitedly. Tim, with a bit of effort, got up off the barstool and staggeringly walked toward the door.

A few seconds later, Johnny got up and walked to the back door. He pushed it open. He looked around. Witnessing no movement or anyone lurking in cars, he stepped out. He ran to the edge of the building and waited for the man to make his way closer to him. Johnny saw the man stumbling his way to the place where he had positioned himself. Preoccupied with the task he had been given, the drunken man walked close to the corner where Johnny was waiting. When he looked to his right, Johnny stepped out, swung, and watched the man fall unconscious to the ground. Johnny then took the money from the man's pocket, walked the way he had come, and hurriedly left.

A few minutes later, Johnny walked into a shabby house on the north side of town. He had been hiding there ever since his scheme to swindle his rich girlfriend's parents had gone sideways. The house was shabbily furnished with a small love seat and a few side tables. In the bedroom, there was a single bed with dirty sheets. He walked in and shut the door. The stench from the dirty house with take-out boxes and drink cans scattered around aroused his sense of smell for the worse. The heat from the un-air-conditioned house was almost unbearable. He suddenly felt like vomiting.

This was far from the future he had imagined as a child. There was no nice big house, fancy car, or large bank account. The only semblance of what he imagined was the occasional mark, who tended to be young, beautiful, and very impressionable. He sat on the love seat, sighed, and laid his head back, trying to think of a better scheme to help him get out of the situation that he was in.

At that moment, his cell phone rang. He heard the gravelly voice of the man who had turned him on to the Rygaard girl. He thought the scheme that had been pitched to him would lead to money in his pocket. He had worked cons like this before with the man—a beautiful girl whose family had money. The young beautiful girl had a wild streak. After gaining her confidence, this wild streak led to easy cash. Then the young girl got dumped. It had worked before without a hitch. This time, though, there was a big hitch.

"Johnny, my boy, where is my money?" Then there was an uncomfortable pause.

"I told you I couldn't follow through with the plan. The girl was about to rat me out to her parents unless I killed her ex-boyfriend."

The voice on the other end said, "Why didn't you just off the punk, Johnny?" Johnny wasn't afraid to kill. He had done it numerous times in the past, but the ex-boyfriend just happened to be Sheriff Jackson's grandson. He understood the seriousness of killing a family member of the lead law enforcement of the county. He didn't mind living the life of a drifter, but doing this with every law-enforcement agency in the state and possibly the country hunting him was unimaginable.

"I put a lot of work into setting these plans up, Johnny. I thought you were the man for the job, but now I am thinking that this was a mistake," the voice from the other end of the phone stated grimly. Johnny had been sure when this plan was presented to him that it could work with a little luck. He would then be able to rise out of small-time cons into something that would prove lucrative. He would be able to afford some of the desires that he had dreamed about as a kid—maybe a nice sports car, some fine clothes, and even a little cottage on a Florida beach. *This is not too much,* he thought, *for someone who has worked as hard as I have.*

He had gotten away from the street hustlers and wannabe wise guys; he couldn't lose it all now. The man on the other end of the phone seemed to be a key to his dream, and he couldn't afford to lose his trust now. "Wait. I know this hasn't gone as planned, but we can still ..." But before he could finish the statement, the phone went silent, and the voice on the other end was gone. Johnny sunk back into the love seat, thinking that all his work was for nothing and that this had been a waste of his time. He closed his eyes, and as these thoughts ran through his mind, he slipped off into a slumber.

A bright light shone in his eyes as Johnny awakened to the realization that his plan was over. It was a new day but not a new life. The all-familiar stench that lingered in the house reminded him of the direction that his life had gone in years ago. The only thing left to do at this moment was to get up and move on. He looked at the money he had pilfered from the drunkard on the previous night lying on the coffee table. It was around three hundred dollars. This would be enough for a bus ticket to a new town with new prospects.

He got up, splashed his face with water, grabbed his cell phone, and headed out the door. He was walking down the driveway when the gravelly voice he had heard the night before on the phone said, "Where do you think you are going?" He felt something stinging his neck, reached up, and felt the small needlelike object that had penetrated his skin. Then almost instantaneously, his legs gave way.

Groggily, he opened his eyes and wondered what had happened. He heard rubber driving over pavement, and it seemed to be at a slow speed. His arms and legs were tied tight behind him. It was still light because he could see small beams of it piercing the cracks of the hot, stuffy trunk in which he was trapped. This must be *him*. He must have sought him out to kill him for ruining the plan. He only knew the man by the name Oliver. He was introduced to him by a former cellmate named Justice. He knew Justice from doing a stint at the county lockup. Johnny wriggled around trying to free himself but soon found that a useless venture.

How could I have been so careless? It had all been going so well until that spoiled little rich girl had pushed him to a level that he hadn't been able to tolerate. He was prepared for the family and looks of disgust. He was even prepared for the scrutiny of the investigator that the family had hired. But when she talked down to him after refusing his request, tried to take over, and steal the money herself, it was the last straw.

She didn't have any time invested. She didn't do anything but take advantage of the station in which she was born in life. She went from a mark to help him accomplish his means to, unfortunately for her, a reminder of his past—the woman who had helped his father hold him down while beating him. She was supposed to put him first, but she made him feel unwanted. She always found a way to make him feel useless and unloved. Emily represented his mother at that time. She pushed him until he found himself fully engulfed in rage. She had to pay the price. He made sure that she did. Johnny realized that he had a price to pay as well.

The vehicle came to a sudden stop, and he heard the sound of a car door opening. Johnny felt the car rise as someone got out of it. Then there was a crunching sound of someone walking on grass that hadn't been rained on for days and that had suffered through one-hundred-degree heat. The trunk quickly popped open, and Johnny's eyes squinted from the bright light of the midday sun. A large, dark figure of a man appeared. He reached down, grabbed Johnny by the shirt, and drug him out of the trunk. He assisted him to his feet and pulled out a switchblade, popping it open.

Johnny screamed out, "Wait! It doesn't have to go like this. Please just wait. I don't want to die like this. Please! I can still help you. We can still help each other."

The large man gave an evil grin and said, "Yes, Mr. Johnny, you can still help me. That is why I am cutting the ropes off your hands and feet today and not your neck." The burly man bent over and with a flick of his wrist, cut the ropes from Johnny's legs. The man pointed to a dilapidated building in the middle of a dry hayfield. "Please, my friend, walk this way. I have prepared a place for you to rest up while I start the wheels turning on the next move in this thrilling game."

He hadn't realized it before, but now Johnny noticed something about the man's voice. He had talked with him many times on the phone, but now in his presence, it was very noticeable. It wasn't an accent or some sort of speech impediment. It was the sound of excitement, which could be heard in the voice of a hunter in the midst of stalking his prey. This, in turn, caused Johnny to feel a tinge of trepidation. He knew the man was dangerous, but if he played his cards right, there may be a payoff at the end.

FOUR

Jack was preparing for his release from the hospital. He eased himself closer to the edge of the hospital bed and slowly swung his legs off the bed and onto the floor. Jack winced as the pain pierced him. He tried to ignore it as he stood up. He had to get moving. He needed to get out and back to his mission to find the man. He made a promise to himself that he would not rest until justice was served.

He also had a feeling that bringing justice to this young girl's family would somehow lead him to finding justice and closure for the case that cost him his job all those years ago. He stood for the first time since being admitted there. It felt strange having to think about putting his leg forward instead of it just happening. He did, though, and after a little time, he found himself moving through the room collecting his belongings. Jack sensed someone and looked around. "Hey, my friend," he said when he realized it was Steve.

"Hey, Jack. You ready to blow this Popsicle stand?" Steve asked.

"I am, and I'm also ready for some real food! The meals they serve in here remind me of the food I was served in school as a kid—just bland and with a texture like cardboard," Jack said as he slowly walked toward his friend and exited the room.

As Jack walked down the hallway, he noticed the young nurse who had taken care of him. "What in the world are you doing? The doctor wanted to see you before you left."

Jack, looking disgruntled, said, "I am not working banking hours.

If he thought it was so important to see me, he would have been by already."

"Well, that may be so, but hospital policy states that I have to wheel you down in a chair." Anna Lee reached for the wheelchair and pushed it to Jack. She grabbed him by the arm and sat him down. "Sit back and relax. I will roll you down." She had surprised him with her quickness and determination as she had grasped his forearm and had gently pulled him down to a sitting position in the wheelchair.

"Well, Jack, it looks like you have met your match. I think if I were you, I would sit back and enjoy the ride." Steve snorted. She turned the wheelchair and headed toward the elevator. "Jack, I know I was a little too inquisitive last night with the question about Emily, but we have to find the man who killed her."

Jack understood this statement. He had been living with the same desire ever since Atlanta. "I promise I will stop by and talk to Mr. Rygaard after I have a little more time to sort this all out. I don't think bringing incomplete information and empty promises will accomplish anything at this time. I need to go back to the drawing board and rework my plan of action."

Before he could say anything else, Steve spoke up. "You need to take some time to rest and let this settle for a bit. It will do you some good and will keep the sheriff off our backs."

Jack didn't want to, but he agreed with him. "Anna Lee, tell Tom I will call his father in a few days to go over some details with him. There is no need for him or you to snoop any longer."

The elevator door opened, and Steve walked out to get the car. Anna Lee pushed Jack to the automatic door and helped him into his friend's car. Steve put the car in gear, and they left. "Where to?" Steve asked Jack as they were leaving the parking lot.

"Let's go to the diner. I told you I need some real food," Jack said as Steve smiled and turned in the direction of the diner. Jack's thoughts turned back to the case. He couldn't help but wonder what he was missing. There had to be a lynchpin that he could find and pull to break the quagmire and minutia he found himself in.

They pulled into the parking lot of the old rustic diner. Looking at the building brought Jack back to a simpler time. The diner looked like it was stuck in time. The outside of the building was covered with an old stucco veneer. The sign that hung at the top held the name "Bernie's Place" in faded red lettering. They pulled into a parking spot and got out of the old patrol car.

Jack was looking forward to the meal he knew awaited him. They walked up the cracked sidewalk to the double swinging glass doors and opened them. Jack was a little farther behind because of his limp caused by the gunshot. As soon as they walked through the doors, Jack looked around at the old familiar haunt that they had eaten at many times. He spotted a booth covered with blue vinyl on the left side and headed toward it. Jack looked at the walls on the inside of the building, taking in the four-foot-high wainscoting, which then turned into a rusty tin. The tin that covered the walls had come from an old tobacco barn where in years past, farmers had cooked the leaves off. They then sat and grabbed the menus.

"Well, boys, what will it be today? The special is chicken-fried steak with fresh, fried potato wedges, served with a little red-eyed gravy. Not too bad if I say so myself," a female voice said. Stacy Holcom was a tall, thin, middle-aged woman with auburn hair, who had been waitressing there for as long as Jack could remember. She was as much a staple there as the bacon burgers were, which drew a decent crowd most days.

"Give us a minute, Stacy. The smell that is emanating from the grill has my mind going back and forth from the special to the burger," Steve replied.

"OK, boys, take your time. What would you like to drink in the meantime?" she asked.

"I will take a sweet tea. You want a coffee, right, Jack," Steve said. Jack nodded, affirming the choice. They sat there silently looking at the menus. When Stacy came back with the drinks, Jack ordered the special, and Steve ordered the double bacon burger with the fresh fried potatoes.

"Steve, I just wanted to thank you for helping me out," Jack said. Steve looked at him with a funny expression. "Do you think I would do anything different?" Steve asked. Jack smiled and nodded in appreciation.

"Order up," Jack heard as Stacy slid the plates of food on the table before them. They both dug in as if it were the first meal they had eaten in days.

"Steve, has the sheriff calmed down any?" Jack asked.

"Let's just say he will not be sending you a birthday card, my friend," Steve replied and then laughed.

"Well, I guess it can't always be peaches and cream. Do you think he would consider letting me use the department's access to the FBI's criminal database to see if we can identify the man who shot me? I mean, if we do catch him, it will help him in the election coming up in a few months. He must know that the death of such a prominent family's daughter is not good for his image at this time, and he would likely lose a lot of votes if the man weren't brought to justice," Jack said, hoping his friend would follow this line of reasoning.

"I think the sheriff will come around with a little coaxing. He wants the man behind bars just as much as you do. He does not want the headaches he claims you bring when you fixate on your target, though, Jack," Steve replied.

Jack took a sip of his coffee and looked out the window of the diner and into the street, which was perpendicular to the spot where they had parked. He noticed something that seemed out of place—a car. It wasn't that the car shouldn't be there; it was that the car itself was out of place. The car was a mid-size Mercedes, was black in color, and had dark-tinted windows. This was not the type of car you saw on an ordinary day in this little town of poor-to-middle-class people.

He looked back at Steve and said, "I think we have been followed. Look behind you at the black sedan parked across the street." Steve had just finished his last bite of bacon cheeseburger. He looked at Jack incredulously and said, "Can't all the conspiracy and investigator business be put on pause at least until our food has settled?"

Giving him an angry stare, Jack said, "Just turn and see for yourself. I am not paranoid. It pulled up after we arrived, and it has just been sitting there. Let's walk over and see who is in there," Jack said.

"No. I will walk over there and see who it is, Mr. Conspiracy. It would take you longer to get up and walk to the door than for me to make it over to that car," Steve said as he got up. He walked out of the diner and headed to the car. Jack watched as his friend made it halfway through the parking lot. He looked over and saw the car's window slide down. A familiar silhouette was sitting in the car, and it pointed a gun at his friend. Jack then heard two loud popping sounds ring out. When Jack looked for Steve, he saw that he had taken cover behind a truck, with his gun drawn. The car sped off, and it was quickly gone.

By the time Jack made it to his friend, he was sitting with his head propped on the car. "You OK," yelled Jack.

"Yeah. Just a little shook up," Steve replied.

"Thank goodness. I don't think this town could have handled both of us wounded and lame. Did you get a look at the person in the car," Jack asked.

"No, it all happened too fast. I saw the gun come out of the window, and I took cover," Steve said and then took a long, deep breath.

Jack was thankful that his friend had not been injured. He heard sirens in the distance and knew that Sheriff Jackson was coming. The sheriff would have a lot of questions when he arrived on the scene. "Well at least I know now that there is fire because we are starting to encounter a lot of heat," Jack said.

"I believe you, brother, but convincing the sheriff is a different story. I have been working a drug-ring case, and he will probably think this is related to that and not the Rygaard case," Steve responded.

When the police cars arrived at the scene, Sheriff Jackson hurriedly walked up to the two men. "Steve, you all right?" the sheriff asked slightly shaken.

"Yes, I am fine. Just a bit shaken. It is not every day I get shot at, Sheriff," Steve responded.

Jack was just waiting for the sheriff to tear into him. "Jack, you OK," Sheriff Jackson asked.

"Yes. I was inside the diner when this happened. There was a mid-size Mercedes parked across the street. I think it followed us here from the hospital. Steve went out to see if he could make contact, but before he got to the car, the driver squeezed a couple of rounds off. He then sped off. I couldn't see the plates; I think the tag was removed," Jack told him. He was trying to shape the conversation, but he didn't think that it had worked.

Sheriff Jackson took a breath and then responded, "One shooting this week. Now a deputy is shot at. What in the Sam Hill is going on?" He paused. "I will have the CSI guys check the scene for evidence. Maybe we can recover a shell fragment or something else that we can use to find out who is responsible." He then looked Jack square in the eyes. "Jack, we can talk more at the office," he said as he walked to his car. He then looked back and motioned them to follow. Jack felt like the sheriff would have him locked up behind bars before the day was over.

Later at the police station, Jack found himself in the interrogation room awaiting Sheriff Jackson. He was thinking over the day's events and hoping to recall some detail that would help him break this case open. He knew it was all connected, but he couldn't put the pieces together. *There must be something*, he thought. The silhouette reminded him of the man who put the hole in his leg, but to say that was circumstantial was an understatement.

Sheriff Jackson walked in and sat down across from Jack, staring intently at him. "Jack, I can't deal with conspiracies. I have never believed in them. Something we found at the scene has changed that. The CSI guys found a bullet lodged in a tree trunk in the parking lot. The preliminary reports match it to the slug that caused the hole in your leg. That's worrisome," said the sheriff.

Jack looked at him and said, "I know you have your doubts about me from the stuff that happened in Atlanta, but I have always followed the evidence—even when it leads to places and people we wouldn't want it to. In Atlanta, it led to a dirty captain in the police department. But before I could connect all the evidence, I was set up. I didn't assault that suspect. He was beaten before I got there. Then I was quickly fired." Jack stopped to calm himself. "Sheriff, the events that led to me getting shot and then Steve being shot at are all related. Both girls were attempting to steal money from their wealthy parents. Both were slain. Both had slimeball boyfriends. The only difference is that in Atlanta, they were successful in obtaining the money; here, the money was never stolen." Jack stared back at the sheriff and awaited his response.

"I want you to know, Jack, that I have a friend who was in your department in Atlanta. He stood up for you when I inquired about you. His name is Simon Brooks."

Jack was taken a little off guard. Simon Brooks had come up in the force with Jack, and they had made detective together. Jack went to the homicide squad, but Brooks went to the major crimes' unit. They had corroborated on some cases over the years, but they rarely spent any considerable time hanging out.

"He told me you were a top-notch detective, and he believed you got a raw deal. He wouldn't elaborate any further. He was holding something back. Jack, I can't get involved with what went on up there, but after today, I believe events are lining up, which will lead us to stopping a criminal. If you are as stand-up as Brooks says you are, I am willing to work with you." Jack finally felt like there was a chance to catch the man who killed Emily.

FIVE

Thomas Rygaard Sr. was an astute businessman. He graduated at the top of his class after earning his MBA from the University of Georgia. He met a beautiful and charming woman named Stephanie, who was an aspiring law student at Mercer. After a short romance, they were married. He interned for several years at Goldman Sachs, and after finishing her law degree but never taking the bar, Stephanie became a mother.

They moved to a small town after having the first of their two children. Thomas quickly grew a good-sized clientele in his investment company, which he had founded. They had their second child, a girl, soon after he had built them a plantation-style home with considerable acreage to go along with it. Life seemed like it was a fairy tale for Thomas and his wife.

Tragedy suddenly struck his small family, though, when his wife died in a car accident. After a short time, he focused all his efforts on grooming his son to take over his business empire. Tom, his eldest, was always smart. He had shown potential in leadership ever since grade school. He was president of the student council, he nearly won the spelling bee when he was in the sixth grade, and he was an outstanding athlete, which earned him a swimming scholarship to his father's alma mater. He showed great potential for business as he earned his MBA just like his father had. He was well on his way to taking over Rygaard Enterprises.

Emily Rygaard was not her brother. She had no interest or any normal drive in her after losing her beloved mother. She showed little interest in academia and less interest in any sport. She always seemed defiant to her father. She rejected the role that he had planned for her. He wanted her to join Tom in running the family business. She totally rejected this.

From the earliest days after his wife's death, it almost seemed as if Thomas's beautiful daughter lived every day to spite any plan that any person made for her life. When she was in high school, she started hanging out with guys most would deem the bad-boy type. Her father insisted that she straighten up and fly right, or she would suffer the consequences and learn to live life without his money. She countered that with her new beau, who fit her usual type. She brought him home one night from what she explained was a hole-in-the wall bar on Smith Street. She enjoyed watching the disappointment on her father's face when she stumbled through the front door with the man.

That night, Thomas realized that his daughter had taken her defiance to a new level when he met the man whom she called Mikey. There was something different about him. All the other men whom Emily had dated did not usually make it to his home and definitely not in the drunken state he showed himself. He later tried to talk to his daughter about what he thought would happen if she pursued the relationship, but she wouldn't listen. She even seemed more driven to pursue this man after her father cut her allowance off.

Tom loved his sister despite the disrespect she had shown their father. She was often Tom's sounding board when he felt the pressure to live up to his father's expectations. He was the support that she needed in dealing with the sadness of life without her mother. He warned her that she was carrying this relationship to a level where she should be careful, but she was determined to hurt her father. No matter how much therapy or love was shown to her by her father or sympathy from her brother, she always seemed to blame her father for the tragedy that had struck the family. Mikey was going to be the vehicle for her to drive the deepest pain she could think of into her father's heart. She was going to help steal his fortune and ruin his business.

Johnny couldn't believe his good fortune when he was guided to a hot and rich young lady. He introduced himself to her by the alias Mikey. He had gotten involved with a group of small-time criminals after meeting a man called Justice when he was doing a small stint in county jail for armed robbery. Justice was what he called himself because he felt he was doing just that—robbing the upper classes of their wealth because he didn't have their opportunities.

Johnny soon learned that Justice was just the middleman. There was another man behind the scenes. This man introduced himself to Johnny via the phone as Oliver, after Johnny had earned the trust of Justice by performing smaller jobs. Johnny was young and handsome, so he would be perfect for the scheme. Emily was the mark whom Oliver had been spotted weeks ago. Johnny had been brought aboard by this man to work the mark. He was instructed on how to approach Emily at a party, where she was slumming it. She thought she was out to toss a few drinks back and maybe score some weed. Then she saw him. He was tall and dark. Something emanated from him that reminded her of a man with a sharp edge. Johnny played the part like an Oscar-winning actor. She fell for him, and soon, she was seemingly under his influence. Little did she know that he would be the mistake that cost her life.

Tom was unfortunate enough to be the one to find his sister's lifeless body. Her wound had been caused by a knife. He found her in his father's study. The blood that flowed from her would always be burned into his mind from that day forward. Her hands and feet were bound with zip ties, which cut into her skin. His poor sister hadn't been able to defend herself. She had been at the mercy of a merciless person. A picture that had been hiding the safe was moved from the wall, but the safe was not opened. The desk had been rummaged through.

Later, they were told by the sheriff that Emily had been beaten before her death. It was apparent that she hadn't been willing to give up the combination to the safe and that someone had tried to beat it out of her. Tom couldn't understand why his sister didn't open it up; she had many times in the past. Then it struck him that along with some cash, his father had kept his late wife's jewels in the safe: the diamond wedding ring she wore to signify the vows her mother had committed to, the diamond necklace the family bought her for her birthday, and the string of Tahitian pearls inherited from her mother.

Unfortunately, the investigation that the sheriff's office had conducted did not turn out to be fruitful, and the trail turned cold. Thomas Sr. and his son were told about a private investigator, who had formerly been an Atlanta detective and who had proven to be very effective in finding people who didn't want to be found. A meeting was arranged by some clients of the Rygaards, who had made the recommendation of the detective.

When the two men first laid eyes on Jack, they weren't too impressed with the middle-aged man who was wearing a pair of dirty khaki pants and a sports jacket that appeared to have been slept in. This made him seem out of place in the classy Italian restaurant. After engaging in conversation with him, though, it became very apparent that what was lacking in personal appearance was made up for in his mental acuity. His mind was sharp, and he had a gleam in his eyes, which grew brighter as he listened to their story.

In fact, this story piqued his interest because it was one that he had heard before. It summoned feelings in him that he thought he wouldn't have to deal with again, and he became determined to take the case. It was almost the same MO as the Evans case, and certainly the same person had planned it out. Jack was sure of it.

When Thomas Rygaard left the meeting, he knew that seeking justice for Emily wasn't the only reason that he had hired the man. He wanted revenge in the darkest way. He would let Jack find the man, but he knew deep down that the man wouldn't make it to see the inside of a prison cell. His would be the last face the man would see in this world. Just as he had taken the life of his daughter, Thomas would take the man's. He had fixated on this plan as soon as his daughter's coffin was put into her last resting place. He started missing work, which he never did. He would spend hours upon hours sitting in darkness in his office. Life, which once seemed to be so great, had turned on Thomas. He had lost his wife, whom he loved so dearly, and now his daughter was gone too. He vowed that he would have his revenge and that every moment from her death forward would be dedicated to obtaining the result he had promised himself.

Tom had sensed his father drifting into a dark abyss, and he was in a poor state of mind too. There had to be some way and some thread of hope he could find to save what was left of his family. He had just started dating a young lady. She was smart, kind, and easy to look at. Her name was Anna Lee, and she worked at a local hospital as a nurse. Over the next few weeks and as his father became more obsessed with finding the killer, Tom drew closer to the young lady. They spent all their free time together and slowly fell in love. He had to find a way to extinguish the idea his father had of taking personal revenge on the man who had taken his sister's life.

One morning while reading the newspaper, he read that someone had shot the detective they had hired while he was pursuing a man connected to a crime he was investigating. He was surprised because Jack hadn't communicated the progress of his search, and now, he had been wounded. He persuaded his girlfriend, who was a nurse at the hospital where Jack was being treated, to see if she could be assigned as his nurse. Then he wanted her to prompt Jack to give her some information that could help him uncover the killer's identity. If he could learn that, he could figure out a plan that would stop his father from fulfilling his thoughts of revenge. The hope of this was short lived though. When he had dinner with Anna Lee, she told him that Jack wouldn't bite on her inclinations.

SIX

The morning after Jack was released from the hospital and Deputy Steve, his friend, was shot at, Jack received a call from Tom Rygaard, requesting a meeting. Tom suggested that they meet at the Grey Owl coffee shop. He accepted and drove there to meet him. After he walked in, he looked around and saw Tom Rygaard sitting in a booth tucked away in the back of the building. The coffee shop was dark, but it had a modern motif with upscale furnishings. It was a spot that would fit right in, in Buckhead, a place where Jack had spent time while he was in the Atlanta police department. He walked toward the man, noting that he had picked a secluded spot where they could speak privately.

Tom rose as he saw Jack approaching. "Good morning, Jack."

Jack replied, "Good to see you, Tom. Will your father be joining us today?" He then took a seat across from Tom.

"No, this meeting is just going to be between us today," Tom said and then ordered a black coffee.

Jack's mind wandered as he thought back to Anna Lee, who had started asking prying questions while taking care of Jack in the hospital. "Tom, before we get started, I want to take a minute and tell you how displeased I was when I found out you put your girl up to asking me those questions while I was being treated in the hospital. That seems like a move of desperation." Then he looked at the man across from him with disappointment on his face.

"Well, Jack, honestly that was out of desperation. The situation with my father is not great. Thomas is spiraling out of control. He is separating himself from his business. He is avoiding me and all the people he knows. He isn't eating. The only thing he can focus on these days is you catching the man who killed my sister," Tom explained exasperatedly. "I am more focused on you. I presume that you were shot by the man who killed Emily, which means you got close to him. Can you tell me anything that I can bring back to my father?" Tom asked and then took a second to drink some of his mocha latte.

"I know I haven't told you or your father many details, Tom, but I have a bad feeling about sharing too many details with your father." Jack exclaimed.

"What do you mean by a bad feeling, Jack?" Tom asked.

"Tom, be honest with me. Is your father wanting to take matters into his own hands?" Jack asked curiously.

"Jack, I told you my father is in a dark spiral. I am afraid that when you give him the man's identity, it will be the end of the means for my father. He has expressed to me that he wants to end this man's life," Tom replied, looking down sadly and then taking a sip of his coffee.

"All the more reason for me not to tell you any more than I already have, which is the man's name and a little information on his past." Jack then paused and looked at Tom with concern. "Whatever happens from here on out, we can't share any more information with your father than necessary. Taking another human's life isn't going to bring your sister back or give your father his happiness back. It won't accomplish anything but bring him more pain," Jack said compassionately.

"You may be right, Jack, but it is what my father wants to happen, and he is a man used to getting what he wants. You must hurry up because my father has friends in the sheriff's department, and if something gets leaked, my father will know," Tom said with an air of concern that Jack could feel.

"I understand your concern, and I will go back and redouble my efforts. I will also have a talk with Sheriff Jackson about keeping a tight lid on these matters. You go back and try to keep an eye on your father. Also, Tom, please don't use any more sophomore antics like using your girlfriend to try to pry information out of anybody else," Jack said, trying to discourage the man. He then got up and walked out of the coffee shop.

Jack opened the door to his vehicle, sat down, and took a deep breath. He was rerunning all the investigative work he had put into finding the man who had killed Emily and put a hole in his leg. He had interviewed some of Johnny's fellow cellmates, who had told him that he had become a favorite of Justice, an ironic nickname for Earnest Wheeler. He had been running a small-time racket of hustlers and con artists when he had been arrested for petty theft. He was serving a two-year sentence in the Colquitt County jail. That was where he had come to know Johnny, who was serving a twelve-month sentence for stabbing a man with an Old Timer knife while he was trying to relieve him of a few hundred dollars.

The two became thick as thieves. Jack perceived that this was where the two had conceived the plan to steal all they could from the Rygaards. Jack had searched Justice's old hangouts and last known address for days, until he got lucky and spotted a man fitting the profile of Johnny. When he tried to approach him, the man fled on foot, and for some foolish reason, Jack ran after him. The result ended in a bullet wound and a stint of time in the hospital. *What steps do I now need to take to get back on the trail of the two men?* Just as he started his car, his cell phone rang, and the name on the caller ID flashed "Steve."

"Hello," Steve said. "Jack, where are you?" he asked cautiously.

"I just finished a meeting. What is going on, Steve? Is everything all right?" Jack asked.

"Not really, Jack, we just found a body on Highway 37 East. It is about five miles out on the right-hand side. You will see the flashing lights. Sheriff Jackson would like you to be on the scene. Can you come out, Jack? We could probably use you for this one," Steve said with some apprehension in his voice.

"Is everything all right, Steve? Is it bad? Why does—"

"You have to see this for yourself, Jack. Head over as soon as you can. I guarantee you want to be involved in this one," Steve said.

Before Jack could respond, the phone went dead. Jack sat in his car, and he couldn't think of a good reason he needed to assist them. His friend stated that Sheriff Jackson asked for him specifically. Jack knew that he was a good homicide detective, but Steve and the Sheriff himself were also. He snapped his seat belt in place and turned the key on his steering wheel. Then he turned left out of the coffee shop's parking lot and headed toward the crime scene.

After driving through town, Jack headed down Highway Thirty-Seven. Along the way, he passed the area where he had been shot. It looked like a bland and sleepy place. He was starting to think that he would never have peace in his life. There was always a case and always a crime. He thought, *Why me? What brought this craziness to me?*

When Jack was a few hundred yards out from the location, he noticed something unusual for a small town. There were some unmarked cars parked along the highway that he recognized as the Georgia Bureau of Investigation Special Crime Unit. He had worked with members of this unit in the past when there were special circumstance homicides. This could range from murders of state officials to the level of brutality used to commit the crime being investigated. He pulled up and parked in the driveway. He noticed a cotton field and an older barn that looked as if it were abandoned. There seemed to be a beehive of activity with several county deputies, his friend Steve, the coroner, Sheriff Jackson, and a couple of GBI agents. He could only imagine the gruesomeness that awaited him.

Sheriff Jackson and Steve walked his way. Sheriff Jackson stuck his hand out to shake Jack's hand and said to him, "Thanks for coming out, Jack. I know that you haven't been on a scene like this in years, but I think we have a mutual interest in this. I also think that with your homicide experience and because you have worked with the GBI investigators, I thought that your presence would be welcome here."

Jack walked toward the barn, but Steve grabbed his shoulder and said, "Hold on a second. I think you need to know that when you walk in there, you will find a gruesome scene, which I know you can handle. You also need to know that it is a scene you have witnessed before." Jack looked strangely back at Steve and tried to figure out what he was trying to communicate to him. "Just be prepared for what you are about to see, Jack," Steve warned.

When Jack took his first steps into the barn, he noticed that the area he walked into wasn't in as poor of a condition as the outside was. The area had a dirt floor, which looked like it had been cleaned. No trash was on the ground, and the area looked like it had been raked over. The light that the GBI had set up showed off the walls, which looked like someone had staged pictures. Furniture was set up. A love seat and a recliner were arranged around the area as well. Jack had seen this before; he just couldn't put together the pieces yet. When he walked into the adjoining room, he found a bed covered in a pink duvet and some dolls on it. Then it suddenly struck him: This was a replication of the crime scene he had worked on in Atlanta. This was, in fact, a replicated scene of Carly Evan's murder.

He walked further into the room and noticed that a man had had his hands and feet bound to the bed frame with zip ties—the same as the young girl in Atlanta. Someone was toying with them. He knew that the events surrounding the Evan's and Rygaard's murders were connected, but this showed a higher level of planning and ruthlessness. When he approached the bed, he seemed to recognize the dead body, but under the South Georgian heat and humidity along with the rats and other varmints that had wreaked their havoc, it was hard to tell.

Upon Jack examining the body, he did notice puncture wounds along with some superficial cuts. One of the GBI special agents approached Jack and rudely snapped, "You need to move away from the body and back out of my crime scene, sir."

Jack turned and stared at a young man who looked no older than thirty. His hair was cut short on the sides with thick wavy locks on top. His dress for such an occasion was out of place. He wore a dark, pressed suit like you would see in the business district of Atlanta and a light-blue tie with thin stripes. "I am Jack Blackmon. Sheriff Jackson called me in to advise him on this matter," Jack responded.

"I am Special Agent Jamie Johnson, Mr. Blackmon," he said while looking Jack up and down with a high-browed expression. "The sheriff said he had someone that had experience in these matters, but you do not fit the profile I imagined."

A few choice phrases started running through Jack's mind when he heard a welcome voice. "My goodness, if it isn't Jack Blackmon. I haven't seen you in years." As Jack turned, he noticed an older man with graying hair, who was thin with recessed eyes.

"Danny Strickland, you old curmudgeon. I thought you would have retired by now," Jack quipped back. The two men walked toward each other and shook hands.

"Jack, this is special agent Jamie Johnson. I have been trying to teach him a few tricks of the trade. Don't let his forwardness bother you." He then turned to his partner. "Jamie, this is my old friend Jack. I worked with him several times up north. He is a standup investigator. Sheriff Jackson asked me to let him advise us on this matter, and I agreed." The younger agent looked at them. He looked frustrated but held his tongue.

"So after looking at this mess, what would you assess it as, Jack?" the lead GBI detective asked.

"Well, Danny, it is about as strange a scene as I have witnessed in quite some time. There was some planning involved in this for sure." Jack turned, walked toward the bed, and looked at the stab wounds on the man's torso. "I do have a theory that might sound unhinged, and it might take some imagination to realize it."

Before Jack could get his next words out, the junior agent Johnson remarked, "There is no time for these theories. We need to look at the facts in front of us and make clear, concise decisions."

The comment brought a quick response from his mentor. "There needs to be room in these investigations for conjecture and thought, Johnson. This crime isn't your normal crime of passion or corner drug dealer vindictiveness. In all my time in this job, this scene reaches the top three I have worked at. Go ahead and speak your mind, Jack."

Stepping back a few feet, Jack replied, "When I worked a case a few years back, there was a girl who was murdered in this same fashion. The bed is made up similarly, the stab wounds are almost identically placed, and the extremities have been tied in the same manner. The outside room has similar paintings, and their placement on the walls is very close to the ones from that scene."

Danny put his hand to his chin and started rubbing his graying beard. "If I remember correctly, wasn't that the last case you were involved with, Jack?"

Jack winced as if in pain and looked at him after hearing the question. "You are correct. It was the Evan's case. Pressure was put on the captain after a few weeks of me working up leads. I was onto something or someone who didn't like where the investigation was going." At that moment, the coroner walked in.

"What was the approximate time of death," asked Danny.

"It is hard to tell. Judging from the rigor, maybe three days. The body must have been frozen. The temperature is way too low, and the decomposition process is out of whack. When you gentlemen are finished, I would like to go ahead and take the body back to the morgue," the coroner said.

Jack walked out and looked around at the farm and barn. He looked up at the clear sky and noticed the stars shining. Somehow, he had to make sense of this. Somehow, he had to find the light at the end of the tunnel. The end of the tunnel, though, seemed as far away as the stars in the sky.

SEVEN

The next morning, Jack was awakened by a nightmare. It was the first dream that he had had like it in a long time, but it was familiar. Jack could remember running into a building and trying to save a woman from the clutches of a tortured, distorted figure. When he was about to reach her and free her from her kidnapper, the footing of the floor beneath him gave way. It seemed as if he was being sucked into a dark abyss. Before he could be fully engulfed in the abyss, he awoke. He then came to his senses and realized that he was fully drenched in sweat.

His phone rang, and he picked it up and answered, "Hello."

There was a gravelly and tired voice on the other end that replied, "Good morning, Jack. This is Thomas Rygaard. I am calling to see if there is any new information you can update me on about Emily's death." There was a pause, and then he said, "Jack, you need to give me something. I cannot take not knowing anything. Please, Jack, I need this." Jack sat up in bed, rubbing his tired eyes.

"Thomas, why don't we meet for breakfast? We can meet at the diner in an hour." This, he thought, would give him some time to figure out how to handle Thomas. He remembered the conversation he and Tom Rygaard had had the day before. Jack had to find a way to make him turn his current train of thought away from the revenge he was seeking.

"No, Jack. We can meet, but we need to meet at my house. Be here in thirty minutes. I will have breakfast prepared when you get here."

The line then went silent. Jack rose from bed, took a quick shower, and dressed. Then he headed out to the Rygaard house.

Jack pulled up the long asphalt drive, which was lined by sycamore trees, and noticed how well manicured every inch of this estate looked. He had a thought about the man who had created all the well-maintained beauty he was looking at. He would not stop until every detail was perfectly wrapped up with a bow on it. He pulled to the end of the drive and stopped at the wooden double-doored entrance. Before he could knock on the doors, one side suddenly opened, and there stood Thomas. He looked as bad as he sounded on the phone the night before. He hadn't shaved, and his hair was not brushed. His clothes looked slept in. This was not the man he had met with when he was hired for this case.

"Come in," he said as he turned and walked down the long hallway. As Jack followed him, he noticed the beams of light shining on portraits of the Rygaard family. He noticed the striking resemblance of mother and daughter. Jack thought of the suffering the death of his wife and daughter must have wrought upon Thomas. "In here," the man grumbled as he walked into the kitchen and sat down at a sturdy and handsomely stained oak table.

"Thomas, I think—"

"Did you see the portrait of them when you walked down the hallway?" Thomas sadly stated.

"Yes, I did," Jack answered sympathetically.

"They are all I think about now. They were both so beautiful. Emily was the one person I could look at and see the face of my wife. She reminded me so much of her mother. She was a handful. She always blamed me for her mother's death, or at least, I was the outlet for her anger," the man said with a sadness in his voice.

"She was your daughter. That is all that counts. No matter what else happened, she knew you would be there," Jack responded.

Thomas, with tears starting to run down his cheeks, said, "I don't know if I told you. I cut her off from her allowance right before she was killed. I think that is the reason she brought that man over the night she was murdered. She was going to steal what would have been hers and run off with him. It's my fault," Thomas said.

There was an awkward moment, and then Jack said, "I have seen a lot of death in my time, and the truth is, Thomas, that the person doing the killing is the person at fault. Family and loved ones are left with the guilt of arguments and words not spoken, but guilt is for those who are guilty. I know and you do too that you're not guilty of anything but trying to protect your daughter." The two men sat silently. A man appeared with a tray of eggs, bacon, and biscuits. He set it down on the table between them, stepped back toward the counter, and grabbed a pot full of coffee. He poured the two men a cup of the steaming liquid and walked away.

"I want to get you up to date, Thomas. I believe you already know Johnny put a hole in my leg, so I won't bore you with those details. I do want you to know how much more fluid and dangerous the situation is becoming though. You know my friend in the sheriff's department, Steve Maxum, right?"

Thomas looked at him with interest. "Yes, I met him on an occasion when I needed help on some, let's say, indiscrete matter when Emily was alive."

Jack said, "I was dining with him the morning I was released from the hospital. A man followed us in a dark sedan and subsequently shot at Steve. Also, there has been another murder—a man connected with Johnny. He was known as Justice. He was killed in a rather gruesome and staged matter."

Thomas looked dumbfounded. "What are you trying to say? That we have someone trying to resolve the matter by killing the ones who killed my daughter?" Thomas asked.

"No. Thomas, your son alluded to the depressed condition you have sunken into over the last couple of weeks. I presume you are thinking of your daughter and maybe revenge on the person who killed her. I want you to know that the killing of your daughter is just one on a larger scaled plot. Now we have the sheriff and GBI on board. I need you to know that we are going to get Johnny. I also need you to promise me that you will not use any of your influence to pursue your wish to rid this world of him. This matter needs to be resolved legally," Jack said, pleading with him.

Thomas pushed his chair back from the table a bit and stared at Jack. "I have been eaten up inside, Jack, with all this sadness and grief. I need resolution, and I will get it one way or the other. The legal system failed to keep the monster off the street, but in the end, I will not. Thank you for coming by with an update, but please excuse me now. You can show yourself out."

Jack looked at Thomas in empathy for his situation. He could only imagine the grief the man was going through. He then got up and walked back through the long hall, again gazed at the portraits of the Rygaard family, and exited the house. He resolved to do whatever it took to get to the bottom of the case and stop anyone else from feeling the misery this family had.

Jack was driving away from the Rygaard's house when he received a call from Steve. "Hello. What's happening now," Jack answered.

"The ballistic reports just came in from both shootings, Jack—the one that left the hole in your leg and the one intended to scare me in the parking lot." There was a short pause. "Here is something that may surprise you. The bullets are not ones that you can buy from your local gun store."

Jack pulled his car over to the side of the road. "What do you mean, Steve? If they can't be bought by the average Joe, then where did they come from," Jack inquired.

"That's the rub, Jack. These bullets are made specifically for law enforcement."

Jack couldn't believe what he was hearing. This didn't add up. *What would a person like Johnny be doing with cartridges intended for law enforcement?* "Steve, I think this case has just gotten bigger than we thought it ever would. Let's meet later and get Sheriff Jackson to come along as well. We may need his help." Steve agreed and suggested the station.

EIGHT

Johnny did not know what to think of the current situation that he had found himself in. He was comfortable with the struggle of the day-to-day and trying to find a way to survive. He didn't mind doing the things it took to survive, but he never thought it would lead to the fortunate opportunity of his current state. It was only a few short days ago when he had been tied up and put in the trunk of a car. He had thought that the person who had done that to him was going to end his life. He found a different end to the predicament. He was offered an opportunity, which if successful, could end up leaving him with the biggest financial windfall he could ever have imagined.

The person was tall and had a scar located on his cheek under his left eye. He spoke with an Australian accent. Johnny only knew him as Oliver, a name he had read in a book once as a young boy. His old friend Justice had introduced him months ago. Oliver was the man who set him on the course he was following. Oliver offered him the chance of quick money when he turned him and Justice on to the scheme of fleecing the Rygaards. Now Johnny was in his clutches and afraid for his life.

Oliver was an intimidating man. He had a serious look, and you could tell he was not someone to take lightly. Johnny had been expecting the worst regarding the situation he found himself in. But then there was a surprise move that caught Johnny off guard. Oliver made Johnny a series of offers. The first was a quick death if he refused the kindness of the proposal. The second was a more acceptable offer. Oliver proposed that Johnny come aboard his crew. He would be employed by him to do whatever he asked. If he failed, the consequence would be a dirt nap. Johnny did not think twice and cast his lot in with the man.

He was told to stay put until matters were arranged, and then Oliver would be back. Johnny did not know what matters were being arranged, but he was not confident enough in his new role to inquire. Oliver walked over and got into the car where Johnny had previously been a prisoner. He opened the door, turned, smiled back at Johnny, said, "See you in a bit," and then left.

Johnny did think of running when the man left, but he knew there wasn't any place he could run to. He was being hounded by a private detective and sought by law enforcement for killing that spoiled, little rich girl. *No, Johnny thought, I will not run.* He would somehow bide his time and ride out whatever fate awaited. Besides, this Oliver looked like a man of means. After all, he was dressed in a perfectly tailored Italian suit, which was freshly pressed, and he drove a very expensive German-made sedan.

When Oliver made it back later that day to the barn where he had left Johnny, he brought a new set of clothes and a meal. The meal was eaten quickly, as Johnny was famished; he hadn't had a proper meal since he had run from the private detective. When he was finished, he dressed himself in the clothes and realized that they were the finest he had ever worn. *Now this is a life a street thug could get used to,* thought Johnny.

"I want you to listen to me and understand. You are about to take part in a journey—one that you will not fully understand. I will have you perform certain tasks without a full knowledge of the reason why. I will not tolerate boorish questioning or any variation of the plans I give you. I only want you to fulfill the task set before you. If you can manage to stay alive, you will be rewarded in a manner that you have not been accustomed to in the past. Here, you will need these." The man handed Johnny a stack of hundred-dollar bills and a handgun. Johnny took the money and put it in his pocket. Then he took the gun and examined it. No markings or serial numbers were on the gun, and it had a large clip with no ammunition.

"You think I want to shoot the man who offers me such a deal?" Johnny asked as he reached out his hand toward the man for the box of cartridges.

"I have a job for you. I will drive you to a car like the one I have waiting outside. I need you to go to the hospital and stake out the private eye who was chasing you before he was shot. Collect all the information you can on him. What shape is he in, how long will he be there, and who visits him? Then bring the details back to me," Oliver told him.

"Would you like me to finish the job I failed to complete the other day?" Johnny asked.

Oliver turned quickly and stared at Johnny intensely. "I told you what to do. Do what you are told and no more. Besides, you didn't put that bullet in his leg; I did."

Johnny looked crestfallenly at him. "You mean, you were there?"

Oliver walked to a nearby chair and sat down. "What you don't realize is that I have been preparing this plan for some time. Do you think you met Justice as a matter of fate while serving the time that the criminal system handed you? You need to realize I play three-dimensional chess and not checkers, mate." Johnny was amazed at what he was hearing, and he humbly nodded at the man.

When Johnny arrived at the hospital, he bypassed the usual parking lot and drove down to a darkened area behind a nearby store. He got out of the car that Oliver had given to him and walked up to the side of the hospital where a light was out. *The darkness of this night will serve me well, he thought.* He scanned the area and entered the hospital, avoiding anyone he could so that he would not to be recognized.

He walked by a nurse's station and put on a white coat that was lying there. He wanted to make people think that he was employed by the hospital. He walked to the floor where surgical patients were recovering and found the name "Jack Blackmon" scribbled on a whiteboard hanging in an open room where nurses were gathered around several computers, typing. He found an unused room, went in, and waited.

He witnessed a sheriff's deputy enter the room. Later, a nurse and then a doctor went in. He thought that the nurse was quite beautiful and decided to speak with her when the opportunity arose. When the time came, he approached her. "Excuse me, nurse. I am looking for the charting room. I am new and need some directions. By the way, what is your name?"

The nurse looked up and said, "My name is Anna Lee, and you will find the room around the corner—first door on your left."

Johnny decided to push his luck and said, "Maybe we could have lunch sometime, and you could help me learn the ins and outs of things around here—or something like that anyway."

Anna Lee snapped back, "Find someone else. I have a good man. Besides, I have seen your type many times."

Johnny stepped back, not expecting that reaction. He then asked, "Well, who is the lucky man?"

She looked at him with a scowl and said, "His name is not your business. All you need to know is that he is the best thing that could have ever happened to me. So move on and find a nurse with less experience with you flirty docs."

Johnny responded, "Excuse me," and walked away. When he was on his way down, he noticed the deputy that was in the room with Jack. The man was leaving, and he needed to not be in the area when that happened.

He rushed down the stairs and went to the sidewalk that had poor lighting. He stopped in the shadows and watched the deputy walk out and enter his car. He didn't know why, but for some reason, he noticed the man look his way from the car. The man then exited the car and started walking his way. He flashed back to the earlier incident of being chased by the PI and decided to be safer than sorry. He took off down the dark alley and hid in a nearby thicket. He waited a few minutes and decided the plan had worked. The man who had chased him was gone. He gave it a few more minutes and walked back to where he had parked, got into his car, and left.

He drove to an address given to him by Oliver. It was a ranch-style house about fifteen minutes out of town. He walked up to the front of the house, which had low lighting. Johnny took a key out and opened the door. He flipped the light switch on and found a fully furnished house. Then he walked into the kitchen, opened the refrigerator door, and found it fully stocked. He pulled out some sandwich meat, found some bread in the cupboard, and made a sandwich. He replayed the events of the night and found it oddly energizing. He pulled out his phone, pressed the preset number, and relayed all the details to Oliver.

"I want you to send a message, Johnny. I want you to wait for the release of our friend in the hospital. Follow him and let him notice your presence. If you get a chance, I want you to send a round in his direction. Don't wound the man. Just let him know that he is being hunted. Make sure the bullet is left in a place where it can be found."

Johnny didn't really like this idea, but who was he to question the man. "Will do," he replied.

A day later, the opportunity arose. He watched Jack leave by way of his deputy friend. The two men left the hospital and headed toward town. He pulled in behind them—not close enough to be obvious but close enough to watch their movement. They stopped at a diner where he assumed they were going to eat breakfast. He pulled to a side street where he was sure to be spotted and lowered his window. After some time had passed, he saw the deputy walk out of the diner, through the parking lot, and in his direction. He performed his instructions to a tee. He pulled out the gun he was given, pointed it in the deputy's direction, aimed at the trunk of a small tree, and fired. He started the car and sped off, noticing the deputy hiding behind a car in the lot. He drove off smiling with exhilaration.

He left the city and returned to his country hideout. This time, he parked the car in the garage around back. The law would have a heightened presence after the shooting at of one their own, and he didn't want to chance getting spotted. He went inside, sat down on the sofa, and tried to think of the reason he was told to not kill the man. He left the sofa, went into the bedroom, and lay down for a nap.

About an hour later, he was awakened by the ringing of his phone.

He looked around in a daze. When he came to his senses, he answered on the phone, "Hello."

"Nice job, Johnny. I heard the call on the scanner as it went out. Go to the wall to the left of the bathroom door. Then take the picture down."

Johnny did as he was told. When he took the picture off the wall, he noticed a small safe there. "OK, I see a safe," Johnny replied.

"Punch in ten, nineteen, and twenty-seven and take your reward," Oliver said. Johnny found more of the hundred-dollar bills like he had received earlier. "Take a trip tonight. Go down to Florida to a nondescript beach for a few days. When it's time for your next job, I will call you." Then there was silence on the line. He had ended the call before Johnny could get his words out.

Johnny got dressed, got into the car, and headed down backroads to avoid any police. It would take a little longer to get out of the county, but what difference did it make to him? He had a pocketful of money and a very nice car to drive. When that was accomplished, he found I-75 and made his way past the state line.

He suddenly had a thought. How did the man know he needed to roll over and open the drawer. He thought about that for a few miles and finally came to the only conclusion. He was being watched through cameras inside the house. *What else does Oliver have access to? Is the phone bugged?* Johnny started to realize that whatever happened, he was in this up to his neck. He wouldn't be able to slip off into the night like he had many times in the past.

Several days later, as Johnny was sitting on a white-sand beach south of Tampa and having a drink with an umbrella, he received a call on his cell phone. "Hello."

"It is time to come home, Johnny. Be here tomorrow," and the phone went silent. He sighed and then wondered what would be asked of him now. He finished his drink, walked back to his hotel room, and packed. He sat in the hotel room after collecting his belongings and looked around. This room was nicer than any apartment or rental house where he had lived before. He then reaffirmed to himself that no matter what, the payoff from his current employer was worth anything he would have to endure to continue the relationship.

The next day, Johnny drove down I-75 and took the exit toward Moultrie. He followed the same back roads that he had used to exit the location. He then pulled into the drive of the house. As he pushed the button to raise the garage door, he saw Oliver waiting for him inside. He pulled in, switched the car off, opened the door, and greeted him. Johnny was immediately drawn to the Italian-leather suit the man was wearing. If there was one thing Johnny noticed, it was that this man had style.

Oliver looked Johnny over, smiled, and said, "It looks like the vacation has suited you well. Glad you decided to come back." He then rose and motioned Johnny inside the house. The two men walked inside and sat at the dining-room table.

"Thanks for the vacation time. I really enjoyed it. I believe it was the first time I saw white-sand beaches and crystal-blue water," Johnny said.

Oliver obliged the statement. "I am glad our arrangement suits you. Now we have further business to complete. I want you to go to the location I have written on this paper." He then handed Johnny a slip of paper. "I want you to complete all the instructions I have given you, and when you are finished, call me." Oliver got up from the table and left.

The next day, Johnny traveled several counties over to pick up the items on the list in a rented U-Haul truck. He found himself searching for odd paintings, furniture, and a bed. He loaded them in the truck and drove them to a cotton field in the middle of nowhere. He pulled up to a barn that looked as if it had seen better days. He went inside and started cleaning up two rooms. After he placed the bed, furniture, and paintings in their prescribed places, he made sure to follow himself and remove any evidence that he was there. He got back into the truck and left. On his way back, he called Oliver and told him the preparations were ready.

The next day, Johnny watched the local news channel. He noticed the reporter standing in a field of wilting cotton. He noticed the barn where he had set the stage in the way he had been instructed. At first, he was confused why she was reporting from the local cotton farm.

"What in the world do these reporters have to go through to make a living," he said. Then when he noticed the reporter focusing on the barn, he turned the volume up and paid closer attention.

"A person was found murdered according to local law-enforcement officials," she said. "The name of the victim has not been released officially, but off the records, it is rumored that it was a local man who had served time in the penal system for robbery and petty theft," the reporter revealed. He was surprised by that statement. This seemed odd to him—a man who had served time. This couldn't be right.

NINE

Oliver was back in his exclusive residence in Buckhead, which was better known as Tuxedo Park. It was a very upscale neighborhood with picturesque mansions. Oliver owned a very impressive three-story, plantation-style house with three acres of well-manicured lawn. He felt reassured in his location, which sported security for the inhabitants of the area. This was much better than the hick town he had recently left behind. He was resting in his sunroom outside the library and basking in the glow of his latest conquest.

He couldn't imagine having a better life. There were no children to weigh him down and wife to nag him. Now all he wanted to do was wait for his plans to come to fruition. He did need to talk to his newly acquired asset, Johnny. He laughed a little. He thought that it was kind of rude of him to think of another person as an asset, but truly, that was how he operated in this world. His wishes were surely of the utmost importance. If others didn't realize that, they would suffer like every person who crossed him. He picked up his burner phone and pressed the nine, which was preset to his lackey's number.

"Hello," a seemingly timid voice on the other end said.

"Johnny, my boy, is everything all right?" Oliver asked.

"Yes, sir. Just sitting here awaiting your instructions. Is there anything I can do for you today?" Johnny asked.

"Tell me what you are thinking, Johnny. I like to know how my people are mentally." Oliver paused and waited for Johnny's response.

Johnny stammered, "Well, sir, there is a story on the local news about a man found killed in the barn that I set up per your instructions. They said that it was a former inmate. I just assumed that the barn was set up for a kidnapping or something."

"No, Johnny, there was a problem with your friend Justice. I had to take care of him." Oliver took a breath and then asked, "Is there a problem, Johnny?" Then there was another pause.

"Well, sir, I don't much care if he is dead, but they could tie him back to me and—"

"They already tied him to you. He was the reason the former detective was chasing you the other day. I just made sure that he couldn't talk to them further." Oliver paused a second to let Johnny speak.

"That no-good son of a, good riddance. I always wondered why he got off so easily from his charges. Now I know he was a rat. What is next, boss?" inquired Johnny.

"Let's lie low for a little while. I am working the plan out as we speak," Oliver said.

\- - -

Jack, Steve, and Sheriff Jackson were in a conference room at the station, meeting with the GBI investigators. They were discussing the circumstances of the recent murders. Jack was laying his case out as to why the killings were connected to the case in Atlanta from years past—the case that had caused him to become a former homicide detective. There were old crime-scene photos, which Jack had illegally appropriated and brought with him, of Carly Evan's death spread on the conference table. Alongside of them were pictures from Emily Rygaard's murder scene. They also had those of the most recent murder scene of Earl Stanaland, who was better known as Justice. The three victims had their hands tied, and they were killed with a blade from a knife.

Carly was killed in her bed. She was tied to the bed and lying on a pink duvet. Justice's killing was staged in almost the exact manner, even down to the pink duvet. The difference was Emily Rygaard was killed in her father's office.

"I believe the same man committed the first two murders," Jack stated. The other men in the group agreed—all but Agent Johnson.

Special Agent Johnson chimed in, "The Rygaard girl's case has some of the same characteristics but looks like it was a botched robbery. Then it was clumsily staged in a manner resembling the other two."

Sheriff Jackson sighed. "Two murders in this short of a time frame; we have never had this before. I want this over and people in jail."

Jack looked at the sheriff and told him, "We have Danny Strickland on the case now, sheriff. I think we have very good odds that it will happen sooner rather than later."

Danny smiled and said, "Jack, as I recall, you have solved more cases than anyone in this room. Why do you think I allowed you at our scene the other night?"

The door of the room opened, and a younger, well-dressed woman walked in. "Hey, Shelly," Steve said.

"Good morning, Steve," she replied. Steve explained to Jack and Danny that Shelly was a recent graduate from Florida State University and that she had her degree in forensic pathology. She continued, "I found something odd from the scene the other night. There was no trace of DNA; the place was wiped clean. Someone was very careful. I did find a single strand of long blond hair though." They all looked at one another and then back at her.

"Is there any match on file for the hair?" the sheriff asked.

"No, sir," she replied.

"Why would someone who prepared a scene so well like that leave a single blond hair lying around?" Johnson asked.

"I don't know. Maybe someone is trying to send us a message or maybe they are toying with us," Jack said.

"None of this makes any sense," the sheriff said as he sighed and sat down.

"My life hasn't made sense since I received the Evan's case in Atlanta," Jack replied.

"Jack, I think everyone in here, minus Ms. Shelly, needs to sit down and hear everything from the beginning," Danny said, waving at the young lady to leave the room.

The other men sat down at the table, and Jack started from the beginning. "I was called early one morning for a case. It was odd from the beginning. It happened on a lot that was under construction in Buckhead. First off, there weren't any major crimes happening there at the time. When I reached the lot, a few local officers were there, and they had broken protocol by traipsing over the scene. The house was dried in, and its walls were up.

"I walked up the stairs to where her body was located. I noticed the smell of death as I walked in the room. It made shivers go up and down my spine. She was tied to the bed's frame and stabbed multiple times. A look of fear was forever etched on her face. As I looked around, I noticed the room was staged. There was a bed with a pink duvet. Pictures were hanging on the wall. There were chairs and a love seat, as if someone was living there. The scene was remarkably clean—like a team of pros had gone through and gotten rid of everything. I worked every angle I could think of and came up empty.

"Then I talked to one of the officers, whom I instructed to set up the perimeter. I started shooting the breeze with him when he said something that caught my ear. He noticed an odd car in an abandoned lot. It stuck out like a sore thumb. I walked out and went to the lot. When I got close, the car peeled out, spinning its wheels as it left."

The group was silent, and then Danny asked, "Did you get a license plate number or any distinguishing marks from the car?"

"Yes, I did get some partial plate numbers," Jack replied.

"This is where I enter the story. I was the one whom Jack asked to run the partial plates. It came back with three possibilities. I ran down two for him that led nowhere. Now this is where it starts getting weird. When I ran down the third, it came back to Oliver Stansby. I then gave it to Jack," Steve said.

Jack cleared his throat and spoke up. "I proceeded in a normal manner. I ran him in the system and really didn't get any hits. I researched him and determined that he was from Perth, Australia. He received his master's in business from the University of Melbourne. He made it to the States when he was in his late twenties and brought a considerable amount of wealth with him. We couldn't fully ascertain where his money came from, but I did determine he had some shady roots in the down under."

Agent Johnson asked, "What happened then?"

"Then I went and questioned him about that day and the reason his car was close to the scene."

"What was his answer? "Jack heard Danny ask.

"He told me he was there looking at some investment property," Jack answered.

"Anything suspicious about that?" Danny asked.

"Not at first, but after some research there wasn't any property for sale in that particular area," Jack said. "I went back to re-question him but got blocked by his lawyer."

Sheriff Jackson commented, "Is that when things started to turn bad for you, Jack?"

Jack took a deep breath and then replied, "To say the least. The next day, I was in the captain's office and told that without any doubt, Oliver Stansby was to be left alone and dropped from the murder investigation." Jack then took a long deep breath.

"Let me guess: That is why your career ended up in the graveyard." Jack shook his head, affirming the sheriff's comment.

"I never thought I would be in the hot seat in Captain Smith's office. It was not long before I knew which side he was on in this matter. Mr. Oliver Stansby was a bigger player in the politics of Atlanta business than I could have imagined." Jack paused, taking a deep breath.

"What happened next, Jack?"

Jack looked back at the sheriff. "Well, of course, I didn't listen to him. I had to go where the truth led. I tailed the man for days and learned that he had people on his payroll who were less than desirable. Nothing I could prove in court, but it was obvious."

Jack looked down at the table. "I became persona non grata around the office. I felt that when I was watching Oliver, he was watching me, and he took his findings to Captain Smith. A week later, I found myself with a couple of uniforms serving a warrant on a small-time drug dealer, and I was accused of taking some of the money. The uniforms all pointed the finger at me. I went before the review board and was fired without criminal charges being filed." Jack walked to the window and peered out in silence for several minutes.

"I think it is time we start to put the pressure back on Mr. Stansby," Danny said. All the men in the room agreed with him.

"Well, I think the place to start is with Johnny. We attribute two of the three murders to Oliver, but the Rygaard murder is different. The MO for that one, though similar, is different," Steve stated as Jack turned back from the window and looked at the group.

"I agree. That one was rushed. She was tied up and stabbed like the others, but the scene was different," Danny commented.

"I think Johnny was playing with only a piece of the game plan and then discovered the man who was handling him in the barn, tied to the bed, and with holes in him," Jack proclaimed.

"Well, how to get Johnny is the first step in our plan then," Sheriff Jackson said, walking over and patting Jack on the back.

"Yes, we need to run all leads and shake the bushes on our friend, Johnny," Steve stated excitedly. Jack looked at him and smiled, loving his enthusiasm.

Jack left the conference room to get coffee and a honey bun. When he took his first bite, his friend Steve, who had followed him, laughed. "You would think that after the chase and subsequent shooting, you would take better care of yourself."

Jack put what was left of the creamy breaded snack in the trash. "Yes, it is time, Steve, but old habits are hard to break." Just then, Jack had a premonition of how to proceed with the investigation. "I think I am going to the funeral for Justice tomorrow. Maybe someone there will lead us to where we need to be."

Steve nodded his head and said, "I will be there with you. The time for you being a lone wolf is over."

Jack looked at him perplexed. "What do you mean, buddy?"

"I was talking with Danny, and he wants you to help him with the GBI task force, Jack. He told me he was going to his boss and recommending that he hire you. Until then, though, I have your back," Steve said as he picked up his own pastry.

Jack looked astounded at this revelation. He had just assumed that after his terrible experience in Atlanta that he was destined to be a low-rate private investigator. Now he was going to be asked to join the state's most prestigious investigative unit.

When Jack and Steve walked back into the conference room, Danny took him aside and confirmed what Steve had told him. He was authorized to hire Jack as a GBI special task force agent with his years of service taken into consideration.

"Thanks for putting in the good word for me, Danny. Outside of Steve, no one has believed in me lately. I appreciate and accept your offer," Jack said with a smile.

"Wait a few days before you thank me, Jack. The work is long, hard, and exhausting. The bureau needs a man like you, though, Jack. Let's get back to the matter at hand. I want to nail this killer and everyone associated with him," Danny stated, turned, and walked back to the conference table.

"All right, let's lay out our plan," Danny said.

"Steve and I are going to Justice's funeral tomorrow. I think maybe we can shake out a few leads there," Jack replied.

"Well, I think Agent Johnson and I will start by tracking down the hair fiber that was left at the scene and go from there," Danny said.

Sheriff Jackson looked at them and said, "Well, I have been in this business for the better part of my life, and I have acquired a lot of friends in this business. I am going to contact several of them from the Atlanta area and see what I can find out. First, though, I think we all need to go home or to our hotel rooms and get some rest. It may be a while after tonight before we can do that again." The men agreed and left the station.

Jack arrived at his apartment and reflected on events up to that point. He had witnessed the darkness of life many times. He had seen what one human could do to another human in moments of anger. In fact, he had incarcerated many people who had let their passions get out of hand. What he had experienced with this case was different.

Jack let his mind flash back to a simpler time. He was trying to decide his major in college. He wondered if he should choose a criminal-justice degree or something more suited to a nine-to-five station in life like business or engineering. Jack was never much on nine-to-five gigs, and besides, he had been trying to solve mysteries his entire life. His father had died when he was seven. He was struck by a vehicle. The person driving was never found. It was a classic hit-and-run. When Jack was a few years older, he put his entire effort into finding the person who had ruined his childhood and set his life on the path of criminal justice. He had no more success than the detectives who had preceded him, but it somehow made his purpose in life seem clearer.

There was a man who intentionally inflicted pain on others simply for the enjoyment of it. The man was powerful because he overwhelmed his victims. He was tall because the knife marks left on the bodies were from a downward angle. This was a step above what his experience had afforded him. He knew that with his new position of being a GBI special investigator, he would experience many more people with this same bent. He would encounter monsters who enjoyed inflicting pain on other humans. He thought, *Am I ready?*

The thought that life was merely cheap to another person was almost overwhelming to him. *Will I be able to meet the standard that is expected of me?* Up to this point, his life had pretty much been in a shambles—no wife, kids, or anyone to really share the moments that meant something. He had accepted a new job. *But is it really the right thing for me to do?* It had been many years since he had worked in a formal law-enforcement setting. He was older and knew he was rusty. He was left with many doubts running through his mind. The only answer he could muster for now was that he needed to sleep on it.

TEN

He was running down a dark alley in pursuit of a large dark figure. It was hard to tell what kind of clothing the person had on due to the darkness of the stormy night. He stopped to listen and look. All he needed was a suspect getting the jump on him. He could feel the sweat running down his brow and wiped it with his shirt sleeve. Suddenly he heard a noise from behind the dumpster. He pointed his weapon in that direction and approached it slowly. When he got close to it, he noticed something covered by a plastic canvas. When he pulled it back, he saw her.

Jack sat straight up in bed, covered in a thick sweat. *Another nightmare*, he thought. The more he worked on this case, the more frequent these nightmares became. He got out of bed and jumped into the shower. He got out of the shower, wiped the fog from his mirror, and started shaving. The same thoughts he had experienced last night started weighing him down again. "What a life," Jack whispered. He finished shaving and got dressed. He looked at his watch and realized that Steve would be there in about twenty minutes to pick him up. They would then head to the funeral home. Justice's wake was that day, and they needed to work the crowd for answers.

Jack heard a car pull into the drive. Then he heard a horn blow. He looked out the window and saw that it was Steve. He walked out of the house and got into the car. The plan was to leave early enough to stop by the diner and grab some coffee. The ride to the diner was awkwardly silent. Jack seemed focused on something other than the task of the day. When the two arrived at the diner, they walked inside and grabbed a booth.

"Good morning, guys. It is good to see you both back."

Jack looked up and saw the smiling face of Stacy. She was the waitress who had served them when shots were fired at Steve in the parking lot. He noticed that she had changed her hair color to blond. "Is it really that good, or are you overly chipper today?" Jack asked.

"Well, someone woke up on the wrong side of the bed this morning," she replied.

"Yes, I suppose I did. I apologize. How are you today, Stacy?" Jack said with a half-smile on his face.

"I am doing well, as you can tell. What can I get you guys today?" She then pulled out her order pad.

"Just two black coffees, and I like the new color," Steve replied.

She smiled, then walked to the back, and came out with two coffee cups and a pot of coffee. "I will leave the pot. I think you guys need it." She turned and walked back to the counter.

"What do you think we are going to find out today at the wake?" Steve asked as he studied Jack.

"I don't think there will be any great epiphany, but there will be some small thing—maybe a person or a phone number—which will lead to the next step. That is where a detective earns his stripes," Jack said with resolve.

"This is the Jack that I knew in Atlanta. Where have you been all this time?" Steve said.

"I have been in a hole for the last several years, but I think getting shot and the recent events have made me realize something. Exactly what the whole something may be, I don't know yet. But there is fixing to be a change. I can feel it, Steve," Jack said.

"Change is always perceived as bad in the average person's thoughts. I think change is always good if we want to make it good," Steve said and then sipped his coffee.

Then Jack looked at Steve and told him it was time to go. They got up, and Jack laid a twenty-dollar bill on the table, looked at Stacy, and said, "Keep the change." They walked out and got into the car. They drove down some nondescript roads for about thirty minutes and then arrived at the chapel where the wake was taking place.

Jack got out of the car, walked up the sidewalk, and stood outside the doorway for a minute to scope out the other cars. He was specifically looking for any foreign-made sedans, but he did not spot one. Then he decided to walk inside. When he entered, he noticed a hodgepodge of family and friends from the streets. Several men at the wake had served time with Justice. Jack looked at each group and knew that before this was over, he would have a lead to follow.

Jack turned, entered the parlor, took a seat at the back, and noticed several men gathered in the front. Jack remembered one of them from the time he had questioned Justice when he had been trying to find Johnny. He would talk to him after the service. There were some old hymns that were sung, and then a couple of the family members shared some memories from their childhoods. Jack's brow furrowed when Justice's God-given name was mentioned—Delbert Earl Stanaland. It was such a strange name for a man with a criminal record like his. Apparently, his mother was expecting a college graduate with a degree in computer science, but sadly, she got what she got. Jack sat and listened to the heart-wrenching tale of the sacrifice his mother had made to raise him and his two sisters. This caused a spring of sadness to rise up in his heart.

This further made Jack's introspection more prominent in his mind. He thought of it all again—no wife, no kids, and few friends. He was truly alone in this world. He then started thinking about the love this man's family had for him, but he was about to be lowered into his grave. The love he was shown had had an insignificant effect on his life. Jack knew he had been put here to help people. He reflected on all the people he had helped along the way. But love, well it had escaped him.

Steve elbowed his side as if to wake him out of his fog. The wake was coming to an end, and people started gathering in a side room. Both men stood up and started circulating around the crowd. For a while, they came up empty regarding information. Then Jack noticed a strange man sitting in a chair beside one of Justice's sisters. This man had caught Jacks eye earlier in the evening. He was dressed nicely, but an appendage on his left side was missing. He also had a noticeable limp. Despite this, he perused the crowd with an air of confidence, which seemed misplaced on him.

He walked over and introduced himself to the man. When he reached out to shake his hand, the man looked at him, and there were several seconds of uncomfortable eye contact. Finally, the man raised his one good arm and shook Jack's hand firmly.

"How did you know the deceased?" Jack inquired.

"Now that question was asked as if you are a lawman. Are you a lawman?" Jack was at first taken aback, but he thought, *Let's just go with it*. "Yes, I am. I got to know Delbert, or Justice as I referred to him, while doing some investigating of a recent murder." Jack paused to see how he responded.

"That seems about right. Justice was bad at staying out of trouble but was an expert at finding a man such as yourself to give information to so that he could help himself out of it," the man said with a smile coming to his face. "I taught him that back when I was living the same life. I thank God that I was shown a new way—one that took me away from the streets, with all its trappings," he replied.

"Were you related?" Jack inquired.

"Cousins," he replied. The man looked at Jack and then turned away. It seemed as if he wanted to talk but he was reluctant.

"Where are you from?" Jack asked.

"From Atlanta—specifically the Oakland City neighborhood. Justice and I grew up there. I gave him that nickname after he helped me get out of trouble with a local drug dealer," he replied to Jack.

"I am looking to solve his death. I think it is related to some other cases I am working. Could you help me with any information? Anything unusual happened to him before this?" Jack asked.

"Why should I help you?" the man asked as he turned back to look at Jack. There seemed to be more tension in his face now, and the shoulder with the missing limb was noticeably raised.

"Well at least give me your name," Jack said.

The man nodded. He took a long breath and exhaled. Jack looked and noticed the armless shoulder drop as the man seemed to relax. "Greg," he responded.

"Well, Greg," Jack said, "there are at least two other people in the grave stemming from whatever Justice was involved in, and anything could help, no matter how small." Jack handed a handkerchief to one of the sisters who had started crying profusely.

"The only thing I can tell you is he was meeting some guy from Atlanta. That is all I know. Now please excuse me; my family needs my help," Greg said.

Jack walked back into the chapel and sat on one of the teal-cushioned pews. He reflected on the events of the last few weeks and the thoughts of life he was having.

"Hello," a deep but soothing voice said. Jack turned and found a tall man with a medium build, white cloudlike hair, and piercing blue eyes staring at him.

"Hello," Jack responded.

"You look like the weight of the world is on your shoulders, friend. Can I help you? I am a good sounding board," the man said softly.

"You are the preacher who performed the service, aren't you?" Jack asked.

"Guilty," the man stated with a smile.

"Well, I think you led the service well. It is always sad when a family loses a loved one, no matter how bad they lived their life," Jack commented.

"Yes. I agree, but what about you? Were you a friend of the deceased?"

Jack then peered at the man. "No. I am an agent with the GBI and here for an investigation I am working on. I hoped to find some answers tonight, but I didn't really get many of those," Jack said wryly.

"Well maybe the answers you are looking for are not those of the investigative nature. Maybe God placed you here for another reason and different answers than you thought," the preacher responded. Jack paused because he didn't know how to respond. He felt as if he needed to walk away, but he couldn't. He somehow felt drawn to the man.

"Jack, I know the struggles of life myself. I lost my son to a drunk driver ten years ago. It sent me into a tailspin. Looking back, I know that God used that situation to help me be sensitive to times like these and people who, like me, need deeper understanding of the bitterness of life. That has been my purpose since then," the preacher stated.

Jack looked at him and knew he meant what he said. "What is your name?" Jack asked.

"Marvin Shiver," he responded.

Jack felt a pull toward the man. He wanted to ask him so many questions, but having this conversation at this moment would prohibit him from finding answers to the case he was working on. "Marvin, I would like to have this conversation, but I do not think this is the right place. Can I have your phone number and maybe call you later?" Jack asked.

"I will be glad to give my phone number." The man wrote his number down and handed it to Jack.

"Please don't wait until you find yourself in a spot where the walls come crashing down. I am available anytime," Marvin said. He shook Jack's hand and walked out of the chapel.

Steve walked in from mingling with the crowd and asked Jack if everything was OK. Jack nodded. "Let's go. I think we have gotten all we can from here," Jack said, and Steve agreed. The two men exited the funeral home.

When they reached the car, they got in, and Jack sat there looking out the side window. "I repeat the question, are you OK?" Steve asked.

"Well, two things are on my mind. First, I spoke to a cousin who grew up with Justice; his name was Greg. He relayed to me that Justice met with a man from Atlanta before his death," Jack stated. "I think this may be our friend Oliver."

Steve asked, "What is the second thing?"

Jack looked at him and said, "I think I met someone who may help me change things for the better in my life."

Steve had a confused look on his face. "What do you mean by change your life for the better?"

Jack looked at him and smiled. "I will let you know more when I know more." He turned the ignition on, pulled out of the parking lot, and headed back to the station.

ELEVEN

Johnny was anxiously waiting in the hideout house. He had been there for several days, and he was about unhinged. He thought that he needed to get out and get back into the action, but he knew he was being watched. The more he sat, the more he could hear everything—the birds chirping outside and the house cracking as it settled—and this was getting to be a problem. He hadn't been this bored even sitting in a prison cell. He needed to be in the game. *There has to be something more than this*, he thought. Then he heard the sound of his burner phone ringing. He picked up the phone in anticipation.

"Johnny, my boy, how is life today?" Oliver asked him with a chipper tone in his voice.

"I am getting frustrated sitting around in this house. Do you have a job for me, sir? I need to do something," Johnny replied expectantly.

"Well, I do need something, but I will need to meet you in a little town named Warner Robins. There is a military museum there. Do you know that place?"

Johnny smiled and answered. "Yes, it was the only trip my parents took me on when I was young."

Oliver told him, "Go there and meet me in the building with all the old jets. Leave tomorrow and be there at three o'clock." Then there was silence. Johnny put his phone down and planned his route.

At the station, Jack and Steve walked inside. They were going to meet with the sheriff. As they walked into his office, the sheriff was sitting at his desk. His elbows were on the desk, and his head was in his hands. When they entered, he sat back in his seat and looked at the two men. The stress poured from him, even though he tried to hide it.

"Where is Danny and Agent Johnson," Steve asked him as he walked over and poured a cup of coffee from the pot sitting on a small table in the corner.

"They actually got a hit off the DNA trace on the hair that was found at the scene. They are following up on it," he responded as he rubbed his eyes.

"That is a lucky break. Did they get a name?" Jack asked as he sat in a chair across from the sheriff's desk.

"You guys want some?" Steve asked after he took a sip.

"No. Thank you," Jack said as he turned up his nose and shook his head.

"No thanks," the sheriff replied and continued. "Anyway, it wasn't a 100 percent match, but there was someone in our county who was similar. I think her name was Stacy Holcom," Sherriff Jackson said.

Jack and Steve looked surprised. Steve asked him, "Do you mean Stacy the waitress at the diner, sheriff?"

The sheriff thought about it for a second as he stood and stretched his shoulders. "You know I don't visit the diner very much, but I think so. The agents said they were going there. Should we be worried, guys?" the sheriff asked.

"Nothing to be worried about yet," Jack answered.

"How did things go at the funeral home? Any leads?" the sheriff asked.

"I think we need to go to Atlanta. I talked with one of Justice's cousins. He stated that Justice met with a man from there a day or so before his death," Jack replied.

"Did he say it was Oliver Stansby?" the sheriff asked as a noticeable trio of wrinkles appeared on his forehead.

"No, but it is too much of a coincidence though. I want to go and put a little pressure on him," Jack said with passion in his voice.

"Jack, you work for another agency, and I can't stop you, but I do not think it would be wise of me to send my deputy with you."

Jack nodded in understanding. "I think that is fair. Besides, I can be stealthier alone," Jack answered.

Steve, who had been turning red in the face while the two men had been conversing, asked, "Well, what I am I supposed to do now. Go back to writing tickets? And furthermore, who is going to watch your back up there, Jack." He walked over and took a seat at the table.

"Steve, I want you to work in the county. I want you to look in every nook and cranny you can find because Johnny must be around here somewhere," the sheriff told him.

"I believe that he will be the key to unlocking all this muck in the end, Steve. So the sheriff is right. Find him," Jack said.

⁂

The agents drove to the location they were given after receiving the results of the DNA from the hair. They turned off the main highway and onto a dirt road that led to a trailer park. As they looked at the trailer park, they noticed the houses seemed to be stacked on top of one another; they were so close. They entered a dirt drive to the left of the road they were traveling. As they drove the pothole-filled drive, they had trouble finding the right address. As they continued driving, the trailers seemed to spread out. After passing a few dilapidated, dirty trailers, they found the one they were searching for and turned and parked in the front of the house.

They got out and knocked on the door. There was no response. Agent Johnson walked around back and looked in a window. To his surprise, the house looked empty. He turned the door handle, and surprisingly, it opened.

"Agent Johnson with the GBI. Is anyone here?" he shouted. There was no answer. He made the announcement once more. There was still no response. He walked in, went to the front entrance, and let Agent Danny inside. The two men started searching the premises. There was no sign of the girl. As they continued to look, they noticed that her clothes were gone and that things seemed scattered like she had left in a hurry. The cabinets were open, and dishes had fallen as if someone hurriedly searched through them. Furniture had been moved and looked out of place. It was obvious that she had left in a hurry.

Agent Johnson came across a hairbrush on a sink in her bathroom and bagged it. He thought to himself that he could compare samples from the brush with the hair they had recovered from the murder scene earlier.

<hr />

The two men arrived back at the station. They went in and noticed Steve, who seemed angry, Sheriff Jackson, and Jack in the conference room. They walked in.

"Hey, gentlemen," Agent Danny said calmly. "Steve, you look like you have lost your best friend," he continued.

"Well, Jack has decided to travel to Atlanta—alone," Steve replied in a frustrated tone.

"That might not be a bad idea," Agent Danny replied. "In fact, that just might be what we need to shake things up," he continued. Steve just shook his head.

"You guys find anything out?" Sheriff Jackson asked.

"Well, we found out that Stacy hasn't been at her job at the diner in several days," Agent Johnson replied, walking over and taking a seat.

"And it appears she has left town. We went to her residence, and no one was home. We searched her house, and her clothes and other personal effects were gone," Agent Danny added.

"Wow. That just doesn't sound like Stacy," Steve remarked. "She has been at the diner for a couple of years. She has as much of an attraction there as the chicken-fried steak," he continued with a concerned look on his face.

"Do you think she is in trouble or somehow got mixed up in the mess we are working on?" Agent Johnson asked. They all paused and quietly pondered on this remark.

"I hope not," Jack replied.

"Jack, you need to take Johnson with you," Agent Danny stated with conviction. "He is a native to Atlanta and has a bunch of contacts there; besides, this just seems to get bigger, and the stakes are higher."

At first, Jack thought this wouldn't be a tenable situation but then took a deep breath. He looked at the senior agent's face and realized there was no refusing his request.

Agent Danny continued, "I will stay here, and if it is OK with the sheriff, I would like to have Steve help me. We can try to tie up the loose ends here, especially with the new development of this waitress, who apparently could now be a missing person."

The sheriff looked at Agent Danny and said, "You have Steve and any other personnel that can help. This is turning into a nightmare, and we need resolution."

Johnny was now on the road to Warner Robbins. At this time, he had left Moultrie, and he was driving up I-75, excited to be back in the game. He was about two miles from his destination when he received a call from Oliver. "Hello," he said with excitement in his voice.

"How far out are you?" Oliver asked.

"About two miles out."

Oliver paused for a second and then said, "There is going to be a change of plan. We are not going to be able to meet face-to-face. When you get to the museum, go to the east parking lot. There will be a blue Toyota Camry with the tag WAZ275. The key will be in the ignition. Take the Camry and drive on to Atlanta. I will have directions preset in the GPS. Take your time; don't get pulled over while speeding. You need to be very careful. You will be delivering an especially important package to me. Do you understand these instructions?" Oliver asked.

"Yes, sir. I will make sure your package is delivered with care," Johnny said confidently.

"Good boy, Johnny," Oliver replied.

Jack and Agent Johnson had picked up their go bags, and they were headed to Atlanta. Jack was driving with a very heavy foot. He was weaving in and out of traffic and passing other cars as if they were standing still. He was driving like he was determined to get to his destination in record time. He noticed the man next to him put his hand on the dashboard to steady himself but also not saying a word. Jack asked, "Can you tell me about yourself, Johnson?"

He looked at Jack. "What do you want to know?"

Jack heard the apprehension in his voice. "Well, for starters, what is your first name? Calling you Agent Johnson all the time gets kind of awkward."

Agent Johnson smiled. "It's Erick."

"What is your background, Erick?"

"Well, I graduated from Mercer prelaw and decided I was not cut out to be a lawyer. Then I went through the police academy. I spent three years in Atlanta, walking the beat. Then I worked narcotics. I met Danny, and he encouraged me to apply to the bureau. I have been training with him for about three months."

Jack looked at him. "Danny is a good agent. I have worked with him on several occasions, and he hasn't stopped surprising me with his dogged determination and skill."

Erick laughed. "He has definitely beat that into me over the last few months."

All of the sudden, an all-points bulletin was put out on a blue Toyota Camry with the plate number WAZ275 from the emergency channel on the car's police radio. "The car was last seen in the Warner Robbins area suspected of trying to get on I-75 going north. The person or persons of interest should be approached with extreme caution," the voice on the radio screeched. Jack and Erick looked at each other.

"I wonder what this is all about?" asked Erick. Before Jack could answer, there it was—the blue Camry with the license number that had been reported.

Erick picked up his mic, called out his credentials, and said that the car was spotted by them. Dispatch called back and informed them that the local police, as well as the state police, were headed to their area. Further instructions came in not to engage until the other units were on the scene.

Jack looked down and noted that he was driving at a rate of seventy miles per hour. He made sure to drop back far enough so that they would not be spotted. The time seemed to be moving slowly, and the person in the blue Camry didn't seem to realize that it was being tailed. Erick was the first one to spot the bluish Charger that had pulled alongside them. It was the car of a state trooper, and it had a black grill guard, which was used for pit maneuvers. Jack then called out two local units behind them. Erick called out on the radio that they were about to light the Camry up. Anticipation gripped the two men as Jack reached down and activated his lights and sirens.

At first, the car seemed to not notice the lights of Jack's car. Then finally, Jack noticed that the man started driving like he knew he was the one being pulled over. The car in front's speed increased. In a moment, he found himself in pursuit, traveling at speeds of over one hundred miles per hour. I-75 seemed to come to life for Jack. More cars started filling the highway, which meant more chances of hurting an innocent driver. Jack used all his training to keep up with the fleeing Camry while trying not to develop tunnel vision. He also did not know that the man they were chasing was someone he had pursued before.

Jack told Erick to call the trooper and ask him to take the lead, as his car was failing to keep up with the demands of the chase. The blue Charger passed him and took the lead. The cars ahead swerved in and out of traffic in a manner that Jack couldn't imagine. *How do the two cars avoid the other cars?* he thought. The state trooper couldn't be shaken off the bumper of the Camry, no matter how evasive the Camry became. Just then, the Camry attempted to exit from the interstate. Jack noticed that the trooper moved in for a pit maneuver. Jack noticed the lights first, as they swirled around multiple times. Then as soon as he realized the pit maneuver was successful, the Camry slammed into a guardrail.

Jack pulled to the side of the Camry. He and Erick jumped out of the car with guns drawn. The man in the Camry jumped out, leaped over the guardrail, and sprinted toward the wooden area at the side of the exit. Erick was in front of Jack as the two men ran after him. Jack noticed the pain in the leg that had recently healed from the gunshot wound. He was significantly slower than Erick was, but he kept up the pace. Right before the driver went into the woods, Jack noticed him turn with his arm outstretched and before he could yell out, "Gun," there was a loud popping noise.

"Erick!" Jack shouted. He noticed Erick falling forward, landing awkwardly on his face, and sliding. Jack aimed and squeezed off two rounds. He then watched the man fall. One of the troopers ran up, checked the man, noted he was still breathing, and put him in handcuffs.

Jack then ran over to Erick. He noticed a wound in his chest. He pulled off his shirt and applied pressure to the wound. "Erick, hang in there. It's going to be OK. Just stay with me." The young agent's eyes looked at Jack as if they were crying out for help. He tried to speak, but he couldn't seem to form enough breath to do so. "Erick, come on, you fight. Don't give up!" Jack screamed. The young man's eyes closed, and his last breath went out of him with a weak gasp. Jack laid his head down and began to cry. *This can't be real. What just happened?* It was all a quick blur.

Jack got up and looked in the direction where the trooper had handcuffed the man he had shot. He then heard the sirens of an ambulance approaching. He walked over to the trooper and asked him if he was all right.

"Yes, I am good," the trooper replied.

"How is your partner?" the trooper asked Jack. Jack turned and looked back at Erick as the paramedics started to work on him.

"Not good," he replied. He walked closer and suddenly noticed that the man lying there with two wounds—one in his left leg and one in his abdomen—was Johnny. Jack tried to gather his thoughts. Erick the young agent was dead, and Johnny was handcuffed and on his way to the hospital. Jack walked over to the Camry as the troopers started to search for further evidence. There was nothing there though. Jack heard a strange banging noise. "Hey guys, there is a noise coming from the trunk." They all drew their weapons and surrounded the trunk in such a way as not to draw crossfire. Then in an instant, the trunk was open. They discovered something they were not expecting. Lying there tied up with a rag stuffed in her mouth was a young blond-haired lady.

Jack looked at her and realized that it was the young waitress from the diner. "Stacy, are you OK?" Jack asked as he pulled the rag out of her mouth.

She looked at him with gratefulness in her eyes. "I, uh, I think so." Then the realization and emotion of it all hit her, and the tears started coming like a waterfall. "What just happened? Why has this happened?" the young lady cried out. Then she shut down and curled up in Jack's arms.

TWELVE

Jack was taken to the Warner Robins GBI field office and was debriefed on the events of the night. He recalled to the review team the details of the chase and shootings that had transpired. The investigators cleared Jack of any charges from the night's events pending an official review. He was finally able to make the call he had been dreading. He picked up his cell phone and called Erick's partner and friend, Danny. He dialed the number and there were two long rings from the other end.

"Hey, Jack," a saddened voice answered.

"Danny, I know that you have been contacted, but I wanted to call and tell you that I am so sorry for the way things went down. Erick was trying to apprehend the suspect. In the fog of the situation, it happened so fast. Before either of us could react, he was shot. I then fired on the man and wounded him. We were able to place him in custody. He's wounded but alive." Jack took a deep breath.

"Erick was a good man, and he was living his dream. Jack, I know it all happened fast, and there was nothing you could do but what you did."

Jack thought about this for a second. Inherently, a question arose in his mind. *Did I do everything I could?* "Danny, maybe if—"

"No maybe, Jack. Life happens sometimes. I know you and the person you are. You performed your job well."

Jack was interrupted by a trooper whom he recognized as one

of the men who was at the scene with him when the wreck and subsequent shootings happened.

"Sir, Trooper Bates. I wanted to let you know I have gotten word about the suspect from earlier tonight who was shot ..."

Jack told Danny that he needed to go and hung the phone up. "Go ahead, trooper. I have been waiting on some news."

The trooper gave him a grim look. "He has expired." Jack took a deep breath and dropped his head.

"Before we go any further, sir, it wasn't your shot that caused his death. His wounds, though serious, were survivable."

Jack looked at the trooper with confusion. "Then tell me what caused his death."

"It appears that someone snuck into his room while he was recovering from surgery and injected him with poison, which induced a heart attack."

Jack immediately went into detective mode and asked a series of questions about staff and video footage. The trooper informed him that no one witnessed anything and that the video footage from the time was missing.

Jack walked away with some trepidation about all the events that had happened that night. There were too many coincidences for this not to be connected. He could only think that Oliver Stansby was somehow the fulcrum point in all that had happened. He had to be the one pulling all the strings. He needed to get back to the station and meet with his team. He picked up his cell phone and called Danny again. He informed him of what had happened to Johnny.

"Jack, tell me about Johnny. Did you have any idea that he was even around that area?" Danny asked.

Jack, still thinking about the death of Erick, refocused his mind and answered, "No, we were just helping on an emergency callout. I had no clue who was in the car."

Danny thought for a second. "What do you think the odds are that the ballistics from the gun Johnny used tonight and the slugs from your leg and the diner will match?"

Jack thought for a short time. "I would bet the farm that they are the same," he responded.

"Do you think Oliver Stansby had Johnny killed?" Steve asked.

"I can think of no one else, Danny. His hands have been in all this from the beginning, and we haven't even scratched the surface yet. I think we are going to have to go back to the drawing board and reset." Danny agreed wholeheartedly. "Danny, I will be transporting Stacy back tomorrow after she gets out of the hospital."

"It is a miracle she did not get hurt herself."

"That is a miracle, Danny. She had a few bruises, and she is shaken up from being kidnapped, but otherwise, she is OK. I will see you sometime tomorrow, Danny." The two men said their goodbyes, and Jack headed to the hospital to talk with Stacy.

When Jack walked into the hospital, he went to the nurse's desk to ask about the young waitress. The nurse confirmed that there were no physical injuries but noted that she was suffering from PTSD after the incident. He asked if he could talk with her, but the nurse recommended that she rest. She had given her the ordered sedative and wanted it to take its full effect. Jack walked down the hall. He noted that a uniformed officer was guarding her room. *Nice move*, he thought. He then turned, went into the waiting area, laid his head back, and then fell asleep.

It was dark, and there were neon lights highlighting figures walking by. He had an odd feeling like someone was watching him. Jack spun around trying to get his bearings, but he couldn't seem to do the thing he was trying so hard to accomplish. He felt something wrapped around his legs. Then it was pulled him, and he fell onto hard concrete. He tried to unwrap his legs, but he was unable to. Something started to drag him across the rough concrete. He felt cold sweat run down his forehead, and shortly, his entire body was covered in sweat. He had to get away. He had to break free, but the more he tried, the tighter the wrappings became. He looked toward the area in which he was being dragged and noticed an orange flickering light. The temperature had become warmer and warmer. He heard a strange manic laugh. *Can this be it? Can this be the time when I, like many others, fear?*

Jack then felt hands lying on his shoulders and someone shaking him. Then he opened his eyes.

"Are you all right?" A short-statured man with a full beard stood next to Jack.

"I will be," Jack responded as the man peered at him strangely. After a few seconds of silence, the man walked out of the waiting room. Jack found himself covered in sweat. The dreams were becoming more frequent. He looked at the small window and noticed the bright rays of light shining into the room. As he looked around, he noticed another person in the waiting area. The man glanced at him strangely, got up, and walked quickly out of the room. *I seem to be having that effect today,* he thought. *Conveniently, finding myself alone.*

He collected his thoughts and decided to call Thomas Rygaard. He wanted to give him an update on all the events that had happened. He thought that at least he would be giving someone some welcome news. He picked up his phone and dialed his former client.

"Hello," Jack heard from the other end with an unexpected, excited tone.

"Hello, Thomas, this is Jack."

"Hello, Jack. I have heard through the grapevine that you are going to tell me some very welcome news."

Jack was stunned at the cheerfulness in his voice. He knew Thomas wanted revenge, but to hear him this happy was almost frightening. "Yes, it could be viewed that way by some. Johnny is dead, Thomas. There was a short chase, and at the end, Johnny gave us no choice, and he was shot. He later died." Jack left the part about Johnny being poisoned out.

"Well, Jack, all that matters is that he is dead, and my daughter is avenged."

Jack got a strange feeling from this conversation. Something just wasn't right. "Who told you this news, Thomas?" A pause ensued.

"No matter, Jack. The deed is done. I know this isn't going to bring Emily back, but it makes me and Tom able to live and function just a little bit better today. This is the first time in a long time, I woke up ready to take on the day."

Jack's thoughts went to a place that he didn't want them to go, and he had to ask the question. "Were you involved with what happened to Johnny, Thomas?" There was a moment of decision that Jack had purposely presented to Thomas, and he eagerly awaited his reply.

"Jack, what kind of question is that to ask me? I didn't shoot him; that was you," Thomas said smarmily.

"I know you have been suffering, Thomas, but if you were part of this, please tell me now, and I can help you." Jack waited as Thomas paused.

Then he answered with a little spite. "I know that what happened last night has taken a toll on you, friend. Please don't equate my feelings now with more than happiness that a terrible chapter in my life and my son's life is over. But again, I didn't shoot him."

As Jack listened to the man, he felt sick. *If Thomas had something to do with Johnny's death, was he any better than him?* "You may think it is over, Thomas. For you it may be over, but there are other people and victims who were tied to this man and this case. What happened to Johnny last night has significantly impacted their lives and maybe even the outcomes for them. He could have led us to other people. He could have given us information." Jack stopped. He felt a surge of anger swelling in his body.

"Jack, I am sorry you lost a lead or some information. But the monster is no longer around to hurt anyone else. Now I must go. Good day." Suddenly the phone went dead.

Jack sat there thinking that the case just kept getting more and more twisted. He got up, went to the concierge station, and poured himself a cup of coffee. The caffeine started to clear some of the morning's fog. He then decided that he needed to go and check on Stacy.

When he arrived at the hall where Stacy's room was, he noticed that the guard was still posted. He was sitting outside the room reading the daily newspaper. Jack walked up, nodded at him, showed him his credentials, and then went in. Stacy was sitting on the side of her bed. When Jack approached her, he could tell that she was still scared and frightened by what had happened to her. Her blanket was pulled up to her face, and she kept glancing at him with fear in her eyes.

"Good morning, Stacy." She turned and looked at him with red and swollen eyes. "Jack, what are you doing here?"

He walked closer and gave her a warm smile. "Well, since the last time I saw you, I have accepted a job with the GBI."

She looked confused. "The GBI. What do they have to do with what happened here?"

Jack motioned to her and asked if he could sit. She agreed, and he sat down in a half-cushioned chair at her bedside. "Stacy, could you tell me what happened to you?"

Her eyes darkened, and she looked as if she were staring right through him. "Well, honestly, I don't remember much. I met a man online, and we really seemed to hit it off. We had been talking for a couple of weeks. I agreed to meet him four nights ago in person for the first time. When I agreed to meet him at a restaurant, it seemed fine. When we went to leave, I started feeling strange and passed out. When I woke up, I was tied up in the back seat of a car." Tears welled in her eyes and started running down her cheeks.

"Could you give me a description of the man? Do you think you would recognize him in a lineup?" Jack asked.

"I don't ..." She paused.

Jack noticed the panic setting in on her face and decided to change the direction of the conversation. "I noticed you changed your hair color; blond looks good on you."

She smiled slightly, knowing what he was trying to do. "Thank you, Jack. I thought it would help me shake things up a little. I have been in a rut lately, you know."

Jack smiled. "Yes, I know, Stacy. Sometimes life starts to swirl a little, and we can get stuck in a pattern. I have had my own struggles with the proverbial rut."

Stacy sat up and looked at Jack. "I need to make it back home. Can you help me with that, Jack? I need to be in a familiar place. I need to see familiar people. I need to be back in Moultrie!" Jack smiled and assured her that he would.

There was a knock at the door, and they looked in that direction. The doctor came into the room and introduced himself. He looked like he had just graduated from high school. His white coat even looked like it had been purchased before he came to work. He introduced himself as Dr. Dan.

"I think you have had a rough couple of days," he stated bluntly.

"We were just talking about that, doctor. When can I get out of here?" Stacy asked.

"I am Agent Jack Blackmon from the GBI. I will be transporting Stacy when she is ready for discharge."

The doctor surveyed the room, and Jack noticed a look that only a doctor could give—assured doubt. "I don't think she is ready for discharge just yet. You have been through a terrible ordeal." Jack watched as he picked up the chart attached to the end of the bed. "Your labs look fine. Tell me how you are feeling emotionally?"

Jack turned to Stacy and watched her give a heartfelt response. "I know I have been through the ringer. I thought I was going to die. I know I will have to deal with this event for the rest of my life. But if I don't get home with the people I know and can't be back in my normal place, I believe I will just wallow in fear and grief. I can't let that happen. So emotionally, I will survive."

Jack watched as Dr. Dan scratched his head and noticed his facial expression soften. "OK. Just promise me you will follow up with your doctor in a few days. I am also recommending some counseling for everything you have been through." Stacy nodded.

"I will make sure she gets the help she needs, doc," Jack assured him. "I will follow up with her over the next few days and weeks."

"I will go put in the discharge orders and get you out of here as soon as possible," the doctor stated. He then shook their hands and left to do just that.

"I will go and wait in the hall, and you get dressed. We can get a start on our trip when you are ready." Jack walked out of the room and waited for her. When the order came in and Stacy had gotten dressed, the nurse arrived with the wheelchair, and the three of them traveled down the elevator with the posted guard in tow. They went down to the ground floor. When they exited, Jack heard Stacy gasp as she looked in the lobby.

"What's wrong? Are you OK?"

Stacy lifted her hand and pointed her finger. "That is him! That is the man I met at the restaurant." Jack looked in the direction she was pointing and witnessed a medium-sized, middle-aged, dark-haired man turn and run out of the front of the building.

Jack turned to the officer and said, "Stay here with her." He then ran in the direction the man had just been spotted. When he got just out of the doorway, the bright sun made him temporarily blind. When his vision settled, he ran further into the parking lot. He saw several older people leaving but no one resembling the man. He went to the side parking lot and saw the man get into a black Lincoln town car. Jack ran in that direction to see if he could at least get a license-plate number. As the man sped away, Jack noticed that the plates on the town car had been removed. He then picked up his cell phone and called the state troopers' post. He put out an all-points bulletin on the car.

As he made it back to Stacy and the deputy, he relayed the details to the officer. The deputy made a similar call to his station and repeated the instruction Jack had given.

"I need to get my car, and we need to go," Jack said. "Can you stay and keep an eye on her while I do that?" Jack asked the deputy.

"Yes. No problem. Go get it," he replied.

Jack got his car and drove to the front entrance. Jack helped Stacy get into the car. As they were leaving, Stacy looked at Jack. "I don't understand all of this. I just wanted to live a little. Now everything is spinning out of control, Jack."

Jack looked over at her. "Stacy, I know it seems that way now, but I will not let anything happen to you."

Jack started driving and got onto I-75 south. He entered the middle lane and put his cruise control on eighty-five miles per hour. He checked his rearview mirror, but he didn't notice anyone following them. He looked over at the scared young lady and told her that he thought they were in the clear. He noticed that the anxiety lessened from her expression and her body relaxed.

"Jack, what happens when we get back?"

He glanced at her. "We will find a safe spot for you and put you in protective custody."

She looked at him with apprehension. "Well, can I at least stop by my place and get some of my things?"

He had failed to mention to her at the hospital that her belongings had been taken from her trailer. He didn't want to upset her any further. "Let's worry about that after we get you settled in the safe house."

The two rode in silence for about an hour. From time to time, Jack peered into the mirror, continuing to check for a tail. Stacy sat in silence looking out the window.

"Stacy, can you tell me anything about the man you met at the restaurant?"

She looked over at him. "Well, when I first started communicating with him through the website, he seemed like a gentleman. He would speak of sophisticated things like fancy restaurants and taking exotic trips to islands. He seemed like a man with means. I guess that kind of got my hopes up that he could be the man who could take me from my boring life. I should have known that he was too good to be true." She started to tear up, and then small tears ran down her rosy cheeks.

"Well, there is nothing wrong with having hope, Stacy, especially a young beautiful girl such as yourself." Jack then gave her a warm, fatherly smile.

"I should have known better, Jack; the world doesn't work like that." She turned away from him and was silent.

"What can you tell me about his appearance?"

She furrowed her brow and looked back over at Jack. "He was an average man—probably around six feet tall with brown, curly hair. He was wearing a nice suit and expensive leather shoes. I was really sucked in by his appearance."

Jack knew the story. It was the same as the other women. "That is nothing to be ashamed of. We have all had people who have had the same effect on us. Is there anything unusual about the man?" Jack asked.

She thought for a minute. "Well, there was one thing, now that I think back. It seemed as if he was being very careful about his speech," Stacy said.

Jack turned the blinker on to exit from the interstate. "Can you explain that comment a little further?" Jack asked.

"It seemed as if he was trying to talk in a way he wasn't used to—like he was trying to hide his accent or something."

Jack thought about this. "If you could describe that accent, would you say it was Australian?"

"No, I don't think it was Australian. It was more like European."

Jack looked puzzled. "Anything else?"

"I don't think so. It's just so blurry right now."

Jack watched her hands start shaking. He reached over and held her hand. "That's all right. It will come back to you. Take as much time as you need. We can talk more later." They drove in silence for the next few hours.

Jack picked up his cell phone and speed-dialed Steve's number.

"Hello, Jack. Where are you?"

Jack was glad to hear his friend's voice. "I have just gotten back into the city limits. Can you call the sheriff and Danny? Then let's meet in the conference room at the station in about an hour. We need to discuss what has happened. I also want a safe house for Stacy and a twenty-four-hour guard on her," Jack stated and pulled into a local fast-food joint.

"I think that is a wise move, Jack. I will get moving on calling the team," Steve said. The two men said goodbye, and Jack went through the drive-through and ordered some burgers for them.

THIRTEEN

By the time Jack arrived at the station and walked in, the sheriff, Steve, and Danny were in the conference room talking. Jack walked Stacy into an area used for deputies to rest when they pulled double shifts and left her on a couch to rest. He walked back to the conference room and shut the door. He looked at the gray filing cabinets, as their drawers were open. The men were viewing case files and copies of reports as they sat around the small conference table.

"Jack, I am glad you're back safely," Danny said.

"Danny, I am glad to be back also, and I am sorry about Erick."

Danny's countenance dropped. "He was a good man, and he was going to make a great agent. He had a strong instinct for detective work." Jack noticed a sad expression on the man's face, which he had not noticed before.

"When is the service going to be held?" the Sheriff asked.

"I was told he will have a full-honors memorial service next week. He had no family, so I don't think any private service is planned. In fact, he was a product of the foster-care system. He had an incredibly hard time growing up. He told me he liked to be a loner; he wanted the bureau to be his life," Danny somberly answered.

"Well, if you think about what we must do for our jobs, the people we deal with, and the ugliness of it all, that really wasn't a bad plan," Steve said.

"If we are not careful, life will pass us by, and when we are old, we will be left with nothing but bad memories and unsolved cases that won't leave our thoughts," Jack said with a tinge of bitterness.

"Come on, guys, let's focus back on the matter at hand. We will have time for all of this later," Danny responded.

Sheriff Jackson pulled a file from the table and pointed to it. "Our ballistics from when Jack was shot and the bullet we pulled from the tree at the diner," the sheriff said as Jack walked over, picked it up, and began to read.

"Here is the expedited report from the GBI crime lab from the incident in Warner Robbins. Notice anything?" Danny said as Jack picked up the second report.

Then a dumbfounded look came upon Jack's face. "This isn't right, is it?" Jack then laid the second report on the table.

"What did it say?" Steve asked as he looked at Jack.

"If this is right, then the whole case just expanded," Jack said as Steve started to read both reports.

"The bullet from Jack's leg wound does not match any weapon in our system or the federal database. The bullet from the diner and the one used last night do. There must be a mistake, guys," Steve remarked.

"I was chasing Johnny, and he turned and shot. I didn't hear a second shot." Jack turned and looked at Danny. "The report did say the two bullets were of the same caliber. The same type but different guns were used according to the rifling pattern. Someone else was there, Danny. When I was shot, someone other than Johnny pulled the trigger. Someone has set this whole thing into a freewheeling motion, and we have been chasing his tail the whole time." The men looked at one another with blank expressions.

"We thought Stansby was involved, but it was not to the level I think so now. We thought he might be the big fish, and he may well be. But now I think he was involved with the day-to-day details also." Jack sighed as Sherriff Jackson made this remark.

"If he is, then we need to think what his end game in all this could be," Steve said.

"Well, it all seems to have started with the girl in Atlanta. That is where Jack started to play a factor in this. I think Jack needs to go back there like he originally intended. He can shake the trees a little more," Sheriff Jackson said and then looked at Danny, seeming to beg for affirmation.

"I agree, sheriff. This time, I will go with him. I will also have several more agents so we can cover more ground up there," Danny said.

"I think you both are on the right track," Jack replied and stood up. "We need to do something first though. This morning, I called Thomas Rygaard. He seemed to have already known that Johnny had met his demise. I got the feeling that he had someone poison Johnny last night."

"I don't think that is a good idea, Jack. Thomas is a good man, and I know the death of Emily has been tough on him, but to kill someone, I can't believe that reasoning," Sherriff Jackson stated.

"Sheriff, I do not think he was the one who put the poison in his vein, but I think he may have paid someone to do it. I would like your permission to take Steve and go question him further about the conversation we had earlier," Jack said, walked over to the window, and looked out, deep in thought. He saw a sudden gray flash, which darted toward him, and a large black bird. He realized it was a mockingbird dashing and thwarting the flight of a larger crow. The crow was known for finding and raiding other animals' nests, including mockingbirds, and eating their unborn eggs. He couldn't help but think this caused the smaller bird to get so angry that it provoked it to such great recklessness in attacking the scavenger.

"Go ahead and take Steve to go talk with Thomas. I hope he was not involved. But if he was, no matter how bereaved or sorrowful, taking a life is crossing a line that I will not defend," the sheriff stated as Jack looked at him.

"As the ones who investigate these crimes, our lot is not an easy one. Danny, go ahead and arrange our plans for Atlanta. I will take Steve and go have that conversation with Thomas. When we get back, I will call you," Jack said.

Jack and Steve left the station and got into Steve's old Taurus patrol car. Jack had a smile on his face as they eased out of the parking lot.

"What in the world do you have to smile about?" Steve said with a stern voice.

"I remember when I was a rookie cop in Atlanta, driving a car in about this shape. I hated it. I thought that if I could work hard enough stopping bad guys and helping people on their bad days, I would be able to make detective. Then I could get higher pay and a better car. I realize now that those were the days when I had it the best. All I had to worry about were street punks and making moves to catch them and take them off the streets."

Steve looked at him strangely. "You don't have to drive this rust bucket every day, so don't reminisce too much about the good old days."

Jack laughed. "Think about it, Steve. We are heading out to question a man who possibly killed his daughter's murderer. He has had his life turned upside down, and if he was responsible, it is our job to put him in jail. I never thought I would have to do that back in the early days," Jack told Steve as he shook his head with the absurdity of his comment.

They arrived at the Rygaards' residence and drove down the drive, looking at the well-manicured yard and picture-perfect house.

"How do you want to go about this, Jack?"

Jack thought for a minute. "Well, we will start out easy by telling him about the events that led up to Johnny being hospitalized. Then hopefully, we can get him to somehow talk about Emily. That's when an opening will come available." Steve took a deep breath and nodded.

When the two men made it up the stairs at the entrance and before they could ring the doorbell, a man who Jack recognized as the butler opened the door. "Mr. Rygaard has been expecting you. Come in." The two men entered the home, caught off guard by the quick response of the butler. "Mr. Rygaard is in his study and is awaiting your presence there."

Jack looked at Steve and noticed the same look of uncertainty that he himself was expressing. When they crossed the threshold of the study, they heard, "Mr. Rygaard, the police officers that you were expecting are here." The two walked in and found Thomas at his desk with files in front of him.

He quickly closed the files and got up. Then he greeted the two men with a handshake. "Jack, how are you today?" He looked toward Steve. "You are Sheriff Jackson's deputy, Steve, right?"

Steve finished shaking his hand. "Yes, sir. Sorry to have to see you under such circumstances."

Thomas waved the two men toward chairs across from his desk. Jack walked over and motioned for his friend to sit beside him. Thomas looked at the two men like a fox looking at the chicken coop.

"How can I help you two today?" Thomas said as Jack crossed his legs and leaned back in the chair.

"I wanted to come by and talk about the events that happened with Johnny and his subsequent death."

Thomas leaned back in his seat, matching Jack's ease. "Jack, all that really matters is that he is dead. I don't really want to know the circumstances that led him to that state."

Jack looked at Steve with a surprised expression. "Thomas, I have to say I am a little surprised at your reaction to all this. The last time I was here you seemed to be on the point of major depression. Not knowing any details of what was happening with the investigation seemed to be driving you mad. Now it seems as if it doesn't matter," Jack stated as Thomas smiled.

"It really doesn't anymore. He got what he deserved."

Jack got up from his seat and walked toward a picture that Thomas had painted of his daughter when she was about thirteen. He looked at it, turned to Thomas, and said, "She looks like her mother in this painting. It almost matches the one in the hallway of your wife. It was such a sad thing—her life being taken at such a young age." Jack watched as Thomas flinched a little.

"Yes, she wasn't a perfect child. She had her problems, but to be murdered when she was just truly starting to live caused a lot of sadness."

Jack watched as the man talked. *No tells*, he thought. *He must be a good poker player.* "Well, we did get Johnny, but he wasn't the person who had planned everything, Thomas. The fact that he died really has impeded our investigation. He was the man who committed the act, but we would like to catch the mastermind."

"Honestly, Jack, I am happy he is dead, and he deserved what he got. I do feel better today that he is no longer around, but I had nothing to do with his death."

Jack seemed to believe what was just spoken, but he just couldn't reconcile how Thomas knew Johnny was dead. "Thomas, I want to believe you, and I do not like sitting across from a man who has lost his daughter to question him about her murderer. Thomas, how did you find out so quickly? How did you know when the information hadn't been made public?"

Thomas looked as if every cog in his head was turning as Jack was questioning him. "Jack, I," he said, paused, and then continued. "To be honest, I received a call last night informing me of what happened. I was told about the chase and the agent dying. I was told you shot Johnny. I was told all of this by Tom."

Jack looked shocked. The thought quickly ran through his mind, *How did Tom find this out?* "Thomas how did your son know all of this?" Jack asked.

"Jack, I have business across the state. I have offices in Warner Robins, as well as Atlanta. I have friends in those places also. Someone in a place we know shared it with him, and he in turn, called me."

Jack started to think that maybe his angle was wrong. Steve must have been thinking in the same manner. He asked the question that Jack was thinking. "Is Tom around so we can talk with him?"

Thomas looked concerned about this line of questioning. "He is not at this time; he is in Atlanta handling some of our business matters there and talking with some clients."

"When will he be back? I would like to meet with him and ask him some questions also." Thomas hesitated as he listened to Jack's question.

"Well, he is scheduled to be back tomorrow, but I think when you talk with him, I want a lawyer present. It seems that you are heading down a road of questioning I don't think I like."

Jack continued watching him and noticed a slight wrinkle above his left eye when Tom was mentioned. "Thomas, I am just asking questions, but tomorrow I will be in Atlanta myself. Maybe he can stay a little longer, and we can talk there?"

Thomas looked at Jack with contempt. "I will call him and plan for your meeting. Besides, our lawyer is there with him, and it will probably be more convenient." Thomas got up and motioned for the butler. Jack stood up and motioned to Steve. The two were escorted out of the front entrance and to their car.

"We will need to brief the sheriff and Danny," Steve said sheepishly.

"We will, Steve, but I think we need to leave out the part about meeting with Tom. I think that the sheriff may have some real reservations about pushing this matter any further with the Rygaards."

Steve looked at Jack after his comment. He disagreed and shook his head. "I don't think this is the time to start lying to him, Jack. He has been behind us every step of the way. I mean, he supported our meeting with Thomas, a man who donated massive amounts of money for his campaign."

Jack looked straight ahead and then rubbed his brow and eyes. "Steve, I think we need to start tightening the circle on this matter now. Think about it. We have powerful businessmen involved. Remember what happened in Atlanta when they got involved? I lost my job, and you were forced down here. No, I think we need to play it close to the vest until we unpeel this onion a little further." Steve looked at Jack and nodded.

When they arrived back at the station, they walked into Sheriff Jackson's office.

"Hey, sheriff, we are back from talking with Thomas Rygaard," Steve said. Jack walked over and sat on a bench stationed at the side of the Sheriff's desk and leaned back against the wall, waiting for the sheriff's response.

"How did the interview go?" Sheriff Jackson asked nervously.

"As well as expected. He was hesitant but honest. I think he did not have anything to do with Johnny's death."

The sheriff leaned back and exhaled a long breath. "Well, that is good news. I was worrying about the backlash if the meeting went badly. But in the end, it is what it is. When are you heading to Atlanta, Jack?"

Jack leaned forward and stood. "I am going to call Danny and get the specifics. I will let you know as soon as I do. Thank you again for allowing us to talk with Thomas. I know it took a lot of trust in us."

Sheriff Jackson looked at him and then rose and shook Jack's hand. "It is easier when I am trusting in a man of your character, Jack."

Steve looked at the sheriff and asked about Stacy. "Where do you want to keep her? She must be in a spot no one can find her, and she needs a guard twenty-four seven."

The sheriff looked at Steve. "I want you to pick your team and put her up in the house on Millpond Road."

Steve nodded. "I will take Anderson, James, and Strickland. They are good men." The Sheriff nodded. "I will go ahead and get her settled in. I will have one man posted for eight-hour shifts."

The sheriff walked back to his desk and sat down. "It's your baby; handle it." Steve walked out, and Jack went to see Stacy.

"How are you, Stacy?"

She looked up from the old couch she was sitting on. She was wearing a thick duty jacket, one that the deputies had given her. "I have really had better days. What is going to happen now?"

Jack walked over, looked at the neutral-colored gray paint, and thought it matched the mood. "Well, we are going to put you in a safe place and make sure nothing else happens to you."

Stacy looked down and put her face in her hands. She looked back up. "Why did this happen to me, Jack? What did I do to deserve this?"

Jack put his hand on her shoulder. "You did not do anything, Stacy. You were targeted, and that is it. You did nothing wrong." She shook her head as he said this.

"Then why am I the one who has to be watched and kept in a place where I can't be seen or see anyone?" she proclaimed.

Jack looked at her warmly. "Because we want to make sure nothing like this ever happens to you again." She seemed to calm down a bit. "Do you remember anything else that happened from the time you woke up until we recovered you from the trunk?"

She wiped her eyes. "Not really. Just road noise and feeling nauseous."

Jack paused and refrained from talking to give her a minute to think. "Did you hear the man driving talk to anybody?" Jack asked.

She became agitated. "Jack, I told you I don't remember anything." She looked at him with frustration.

"OK, Stacy. No worries. You are doing great through all this. But now you must go with Steve, and he will take care of you. He will watch over you at the safe house. When I get back into town, I will stop by, and we can talk some more." They both got up from the couch, and she gave Jack a hug as Steve entered the room.

"Thank you for helping me," she said as she turned back to look at Jack. Then she sighed and left with Steve.

Jack walked over and looked out at the congested office, with its desk and deputies sitting behind them answering calls and taking notes. He then pulled out his cell and called Danny.

"Hello, Jack. How did the meeting with Rygaard go?"

"I will tell you about it on the drive. Have you got things set for Atlanta?"

Danny sounded enthused. "I do, Jack. I will pick you up in about five minutes. I have some good news too. I think you will find it interesting."

Jack became curious. "What is the good news?"

"Oh, no. If I must wait, so do you. See you in five," Danny said and ended the call.

FOURTEEN

Oliver left his house and walked the perimeter of his estate, sipping on sweet tea. He looked out at his neighbor who was working in her flower bed. He wondered why someone with the money she had would work like a common person. He thought back to his upbringing. His foster father made him wake early and go to work with him at the grazier. This was the term used in his country for a place where cattle were raised. He remembered the stench of the cattle and the hard work it took to repair the fences. He also remembered the beatings he would get when he did not move as fast as his foster father thought he should.

Oliver could only watch so much and walked back inside his palatial mansion. He looked around at the possessions he was able to afford now. He thought, *I have certainly risen from the dust*, and almost laughed out loud. He heard the doorbell ring and waited for his butler to announce the person he was expecting.

"Sir, Mr. Winston is here to see you." The butler then waited for a reply.

"See him in." There was a small lapse of time before the average-sized, barrel-chested man was received into the spacious living room. Oliver noticed his tailored suit and leather shoes. He motioned the man to come and sit down on the expensive leather chair, which he had procured from Ralph Lauren when he had designed the interior of his house.

"Well, what do you have for me?" he said snidely.

"Sir, Johnny has been taken care of. I made the call, and we have nothing to worry about from him," the man replied timidly.

"Did you handle the problem, or did our friend perform the act as requested?" the man asked with a hint of aggravation.

"He saw the benefit in handling the matter after a bit of, let's say, persuasion."

Oliver walked over and looked out the window. "Did you see my neighbor as you entered?"

"Yes, I believe that she was pruning her rosebush as I drove in," he replied.

Oliver smiled. "Yes. She seems to find satisfaction in manual labor on this warm day. There was a time I would have admired her for her effort. Now I think the real effort is learning to apply pressure on people to do our labor for us." Oliver turned back to the man and walked toward him. He reached down and picked an envelope up from the table before them. He handed it to Winston and said, "Take this to our friend and tell him to follow the instructions to the letter. Call me when it is finished." The man got up and exited the room.

―――――――――

Steve was mulling around the sheriff's office and feeling aggravated as Jack and Danny headed to Atlanta. He picked up a magazine and sat down at his desk to read about the newest fishing lures. He was hoping to take his mind off not being with them. He heard some shuffling around in the adjoining office, looked up, and saw Shelly. He put the magazine down, got up, and walked over. "How are you doing, Shelly?"

She turned toward him, and he noticed a file in her hand and became curious. "I am fine. Just reviewing the results from the strand of hair left at the scene from Justice's murder."

Steve got excited. Stacy the waitress had been excluded when her DNA had not matched. "Let's open it up and see." Steve opened the file. He was shocked when he discovered the results. "I did not see that coming," he remarked.

The two walked into Sheriff Jackson's office quickly. Steve

noticed that the sheriff was sitting at his desk, reviewing a file of a case regarding a local man who was arrested for drunk and disorderly conduct.

"Sheriff, can we talk to you for a minute?" Steve asked as Sheriff Jackson looked up.

"Why not? Y'all are already in here."

Steve walked in with Shelly nervously following him. She was a newly hired CSI tech and not that used to working around the sheriff. "Sheriff, Shelly has some interesting information about the strand of hair found at Justice's murder scene. I was quite surprised when I saw this."

The sheriff looked at Shelly. "Go ahead and spit it out."

Shelly exhaled and spoke timidly. "Um, well it took a while because I sent it to a national database, and well, it takes some time for the results to come back."

Steve looked at her. "Come on, Shelly, tell him."

"OK. Sir, the hair was matched to a local lady. Her DNA was on file due to her having an issue when she was a juvenile. She was kidnapped when she was a teenager, and her parents submitted it to the authorities to help find her. Her name is Anna Lee Stewart."

"Steve, what do you think this means?"

Steve looked puzzled. "I don't know Sheriff, but I think we should find her and bring her in for questioning at the very least."

"Well, you might be right there, but I think we need to wait until the guys get back from Atlanta. I know that they will want to ask questions of their own." Steve sighed, knowing that his suggestion was being shot down. "I do think, though, that you should keep tabs on her until that happens. Find one of the other guys whom you trust, and you work out a schedule so we can always have eyes on her," Sheriff Jackson said.

Steve thought that this would be better than sitting around the office or patrolling his usual beat. He thanked the sheriff, and he and Shelly left his office.

Shelly walked to her desk and pulled out a second file. "This is what I pulled when the results came in. I know I am only a tech, but I am curious." She handed Steve the file.

He looked at it, noting that Anna Lee was born in Savannah, Georgia. Her father was dead, but her mother was still alive. He also noticed their old address and wondered if her mother was still living there. Steve looked at her. "You will make a good detective one day. Your mind sure works like one. Good job," Steve remarked as she blushed and thanked him. Steve decided that the best course of action was to call Jack and inform him of the recent discovery. He picked up his phone and pushed the autodial button for Jack.

"Hey, Steve, miss me already?" Jack answered and then laughed.

"You know it, buddy. Hey, I've got some news for you that I think you will find interesting or closer to closing the case anyway." Steve walked to the window and looked out.

"Is it good, bad, or ugly?" Jack asked.

"I don't know at the moment, but it could lead us closer to the truth." Jack laughed again.

"The truth isn't always pretty, and it doesn't always lead you to resolution, but lay it on me," Jack said as Steve shook his head.

"Always sunny. Right, Jack. But Shelly found a nugget. She finally matched the hair we found at Justice's murder scene. You are never going to believe whose it was," Steve remarked. Then he paused for effect.

"You going to tell me, or am I going to have to drive back and buy you a steak first?"

"A steak will be good, and I expect it when you get back. The hair belongs to Anna Lee, Tom's girlfriend. You know, the nurse that took care of you in the hospital." Jack then relayed the news to Danny.

"Steve, how did Shelly match it?"

Steve looked around and noticed Shelly working away in her office. "She found it in a national database. Apparently, Anna Lee was kidnapped when she was young, and her parents submitted a sample to help with the investigation. You know the FBI keeps those files forever," Steve commented.

"And I am glad they do. That might just be the link we are trying to connect. How is Stacy holding up, Steve?" Jack hated to ask after Steve's revelations, but he just couldn't help himself.

"My men are always watching her, Jack. We have a counselor who is going to talk with her later today. She seems to be holding up well."

"I never thought to ask her, but if you have a chance, would you see if she knows Anna Lee, or if she ever had any dealings with her?" Jack asked.

"I am sure she had to know her from the diner. I saw Anna Lee in there several times over the years," Steve said.

"Yeah, but you never know what someone knows until you ask," Jack stated.

"You are right about that, Jack. When I see her again, I will ask her. How is your trip going? Are y'all in Atlanta yet?" Steve asked.

"Tell him we are about an hour away, and we will keep him in the loop about everything," Danny said in the background.

"Got to let me know when you are on speakerphone, buddy. What if I talked badly about Danny? I wouldn't have wiggle room after that," Steve stated wryly.

Danny laughed and then replied, "Tell him goodbye, Jack." Jack did just that.

FIFTEEN

Jack and Danny pulled into a satellite GBI office building in Atlanta. Jack was a bit nervous because the building space was operated in conjunction with the Atlanta police department, which was a gesture from the state political parties after there were complaints that the two agencies were not playing well together. He knew that if he was seen by the wrong person, his presence would be known by the wrong people, which would make things a little bit difficult.

Captain Samuel Smith was more of a political figure at this point. Jack remembered sitting across from him when he was being railroaded out of the Atlanta police department. The man was cold and calculating. Jack was never able to respond in that meeting. He just sat there and listened to the man berate him. *If this man learns of my presence,* Jack thought, *any chance of solving this case will be in danger.*

"Danny, you better find a way to sneak us to the elevator and shield my presence," Jack said, slumping in the seat slightly.

"There is an elevator at the side of the building that no one uses. It was left over from some construction, and it is old and slow. Everyone tries to avoid it out of fear it will get stuck. We will use it. It leads straight to the top floor, which is where our side congregates. No other agency is allowed in there."

The two men drove up to the closest parking spot to the elevator and hurriedly got out. They headed into the old elevator. Danny pushed the button for the top floor, and the elevator, true to Danny's word, slowly started to rise. As it went, it creaked and made terribly uncomfortable noises until finally, the two men arrived at their destination. The door slowly opened. Jack looked up and down the hall, making sure that no one would recognize him. They stepped out onto a tiled floor, and Danny led Jack into an office suite in the corner. It was an unassuming office suite with light-beige paint. Cheap blinds covered windows. There was a nice mahogany table in the middle of the largest room.

"Jack, I have called a few friends and explained our situation. They have similar thoughts about Captain Smith, and his dealings. They are anxious to help us out. They really want to see him go down."

Jack took a seat at the conference table. "Danny, I want us to stay focused on the task at hand. We need to find out everything we can about Oliver Stansby. We need to know about his business, his day-to-day movements, and if possible, anybody in his employ whom we can turn. Bringing down Captain Smith will be the icing on the cake."

Danny took a seat across from Jack. "I have a place we can start. When I called to let my lieutenant know we were heading this way, I asked if we could start surveillance on him. We've had a man placed on him since last night. He will rotate with a couple of other guys until we find something. They will report in about an hour. The other agents will be here with us in about twenty minutes. I am headed to get a cup of coffee while we wait. Do you want one?" Jack nodded.

Danny came back with a colorful Styrofoam cup full of steaming coffee. "Thanks, Danny." The man handed Jack his coffee and sat down. They sat in silence for a few minutes until the door opened and two men in suits walked in.

Danny stood up with his right hand out. "Good morning, guys." He shook both men's hands and turned to Jack. "Jack, this is Sam and Donald. They will be helping us out." Sam was an older man with graying hair. He was dressed in a polo shirt and khaki pants. Donald was younger. He had broad shoulders, and he was muscular looking. He was dressed in an off the rack suit with no tie.

Jack stood and shook their hands. "Good to meet both of you."

The two men responded in kind and walked to the far side of the table and sat down. "Lieutenant Stinson is on his way up," Sam said.

When they were sitting, Jack noticed a couple of yellow manila folders, which they placed on the table. "You guys seem to have been busy. What have you got to share?" Sam reached for one of the folders and opened it.

"We searched for some information on Stansby, which wasn't that hard. We have been looking at him for some time." He pulled some pictures out along with a stack of papers. Jack reached out, and Sam handed him the pictures. There were pictures of six men, whom they stated were in Stansby's inner circle.

"We know three of the men. The other three we haven't been able to identify yet." Jack looked over the pictures, and he was not surprised to see one of Captain Smith.

"I was sure you would be interested in that one," a voice from behind Jack boomed. He turned to find a tall, muscular, middle-aged man looking back at him. "Greg Stinson. Nice to meet you, Jack." He walked closer and shook Jack's hand.

"Yes, it interests me very much. How do you think he is tied to Stansby?" Jack asked.

The lieutenant took a seat. "We think the two men met when Stansby first came to Atlanta. Smith was still working on the major crimes' unit. The two seemed to have joined forces around the time a shipment of drugs, which were scheduled for destruction, went missing. After that, Stansby's fortune grew. He then started making huge donations to some councilman, and shortly after that, Smith made captain," Lieutenant Stinson stated.

"Can you tell me about the other two?" Jack asked.

"The short man with the thinning hairline is Carl Fairly. He is suspected of being a middleman who brokers deals with different cartels. The other man is Vitaley Kermosh. He has had dealings with the Russian mob over the years. He makes the deals and has a direct line to their assassins."

Jack looked surprised. "This is just getting better and better. We have a truly international crime ring going on." Stinson smiled. "This is the biggest case we have ever worked on." Jack paused and looked at the other three men.

"These three have not been identified. What does that tell you, guys?" Danny asked.

"I think it tells us that they most likely are working or have worked for some intelligence agency from some foreign government," Stinson remarked.

"We believe that if we are going to take down Stansby, we need to start small. We need to find someone who takes care of small tasks for him. Then we find something on that small fish, which will send him to prison for many years. Then we can put pressure on that person to flip him." Stinson handed Danny some paper as he talked.

"Danny, we have determined there is a person named Winston Turner. Here is his file. He was spotted at Stansby's yesterday, leaving with some papers. We think he may be the gentleman we are looking for to give us our break." Stinson handed him the file.

Danny read his file. He was born in London and was an orphan. He was eventually placed in a foster family. He came to America at the age of eighteen and attended junior college. Then he attended Georgia State University, where he obtained a degree in business administration. He started a small company that imported clothing products from his native England. He soon found himself in financial trouble. Oliver Stansby then stepped in and bought him out. Stansby then put him in charge of the day-to-day management of the company. Then he became Stansby's go-between in his more illegal type of business.

"Good. That is where we will start. Let's get a good night's rest, and we will start tracking his movements tomorrow. Hopefully, we can follow him all the way up the ladder," Jack responded. Sam laughed. "Danny said you would be motivated, and we welcome that attitude." Jack started to leave but then turned around. "Also, from here on out, I think it will be smart of us to meet somewhere far from here. The risk is too great if someone notices me."

The lieutenant thought for a minute. "We have a safe house about thirty minutes from here, and it's not being used." Sam gave them the address of Buley House. "We will meet there from now on."

Danny and Jack pulled into the driveway of the Buley House on Peach Avenue. It was a quaint house with a small front yard and backyard. In the neighborhood, there were several other houses that were similar. They were mostly cookie-cutter constructions with single-level floor plans—two- and three-bedroom houses with garages. They were true slices of Americana, with their white-picket fences. Danny reckoned that this would be a good place to hide if someone was looking for you because it was so nondescript and plain. He also hoped Stacy had similar accommodations while Steve and his crew were looking out for her safety.

Jack walked in slowly and carefully, making sure the coast was clear. "Danny, I would like the bedroom on the right if that is OK with you," Jack said. The window was toward the east, meaning that the sun would shine into the room early in the morning. Jack found that it comforted him to look at the sunshine when he first woke up. This really seemed to help him come back to reality after the disturbing dreams he had been having.

Danny peered into the one on the left. "I think that will be satisfactory, Jack."

Jack walked into the kitchen and opened the refrigerator. The eggs and bacon were inside it. "Looks like someone thought of us. You want some breakfast for supper?"

Danny smiled and rubbed his belly. "There is nothing wrong with a full stomach," Danny replied.

Jack scrambled the eggs and fried the bacon. Danny found some bread, made some toast, and buttered it. Jack ate his meal and pondered the day's events. After a while of sitting there in silence and letting their meal settle, Jack yawned. "I think I have had enough for one day. I am going to call it a night. Hope you sleep well," Jack told Danny as he left to go to bed.

Jack found himself in the midst of a shootout. He was pinned down and quickly running out of rounds in his nine-millimeter Berretta. *What can I do to get out of this mess?* he thought. Suddenly, he felt a sting in his upper right arm. He looked down and noticed a stream of red liquid flowing quickly down his arm. He spotted a dark alley to his right. He had no other move because the shooters were closing in on him. He turned toward the alley and ran. He had just about made it when he tripped over something and tumbled onto his side. He looked back and noticed a young girl with blond hair. He looked closer and noticed her lifeless eyes. He shouted, "Stacy!"

Jack then felt someone put a hand on his shoulder and shake him. "Jack! Jack! You all right?" the voice said. Jack sat straight up in bed with sweat pouring down his face. When he realized where he was, he understood it had been another nightmare.

"You Ok, Jack?" Danny was hovering over him.

Jack rubbed his eyes and ran his hand through his hair. "Yeah. I just have been having these dreams. I'm OK though. Just give me a second to get ready, and we can get started." Jack's phone rang. When he looked at it, he saw that it was Steve. He looked at Danny. "It's Steve." Danny smiled and walked out of the room.

"Hello, buddy. How is life this morning?" Steve chuckled a little after saying this.

"If it were any better, I would not be able to live with myself. What can I do for you this morning?" Jack asked with a little sarcasm.

"Well, everything is going well with Stacy, but there are some unexpected developments," Steve replied.

"What do you mean unexpected developments?" Jack asked with some concern.

"Some guys showed up in town, and they were asking around about Stacy. They wanted to know if she was here. They told people they were her cousins from up north," Steve replied as Jack stood and looked out the window.

Jack thought this was not a good turn of events. "Where is up north?" Jack asked.

"Well, they weren't that specific," Steve replied.

Jack walked into the kitchen with Danny. "Steve this isn't good. Someone must think she heard or saw something. The people we are looking at here in Atlanta would not like that!" Jack exclaimed. "Steve, please keep someone on her at all times," Jack said as Danny looked at him.

Steve agreed. "I have bumped the watch up to two people each shift."

"Good. Now you have a good day, and I'm going to eat breakfast," he said as he clicked off the phone.

"Is everything OK?" Danny asked as Jack shook his head, trying to clear some more of the cobwebs from his dream.

"I don't know. Some new guys showed up in Moultrie. They were asking around about Stacy."

"We need to stay focused on our job ahead. Steve and Sheriff Jackson are good law officers, and they will take care of her," Danny said calmly as he handed Jack a cup of coffee.

Jack looked at him. "I know, but this whole thing keeps growing, and the level of confusion and complexity does too."

Jack and Danny finished their coffee and got dressed. They left the house and got into an unmarked, blue Chevy Camaro. Danny insisted on driving because Jack seemed different since the call. He was almost unfocused.

Jack was trying to focus on the task before them as he rode, but his mind kept shifting to Steve and praying that nothing would happen to Stacy. He felt a connection to her that he had not felt in a long time. He was not completely comfortable with this realization, but it was what it was. He knew that if something did go wrong, he would be devastated.

They pulled up a building downtown and drove into a parking garage. They stepped out of the car. Jack looked at the graffiti spray-painted on the concrete walls. All the scribble was so random and out of place. He considered that his thoughts seemed as confused as the poorly conceived artistic expressions spray-painted everywhere. Jack followed Danny to a shop, and Danny rang a bell on a locked, heavy steel door. There was a brief pause, and then they heard a buzzing noise, and the door opened. They walked in and noticed an area down a small hallway that lit up. They walked in further and noticed a collection of modern state-of-the art monitoring equipment.

Several people were moving various pieces of equipment into position. Jack noticed that Lieutenant Stinson was sitting at a small round table in a side room. Sam was there in the room, and he was monitoring footage from surveillance cameras, which had been planted in multiple locations. When Jack inquired, he was told the locations were known to be used by Oliver Stansby, one of which was Winston's shop.

He heard Donald, who was standing above Sam and looking over his shoulder, say, "How could we get so lucky."

Jack walked over, looked at the monitor, and smiled. The man was playing back footage from early morning. Jack noticed that the time stamp on the footage put the delivery at 1:30 a.m. This was from one of the first cameras that the team had set up. It was just now able to get a peek at what was happening at the clothing store. The camera had a perfect angle on a truck, which pulled in a back alley. It stopped outside the back door of Winston's shop. A short heavyset man got out of the truck and started to unload some boxes from it. When he turned to walk in, one of the boxes dropped, and several handguns fell onto the ground. There was a feeling of unbelief as the men who were gathered looked at one another.

"Winston deals in clothing, not handguns, right guys?" Jack said with a smirk. "This, I believe, is the first break we have had in this case. I think Winston is going to be the key to unwrapping the organizational structure of Stansby's criminal organization," Jack commented as the lieutenant looked up at Jack.

"I am picking up the phone now to call a judge in this district. Hopefully, we will have a warrant shortly," he replied. Jack sat down and continued to watch the video stream. They counted a total of twenty-nine boxes.

"This must be some of the weapons that were stolen from the armory," Sam said.

"Was it just pistols?" Jack asked as Sam looked over at him.

"Several boxes of AR-15s and ammunition were stolen also," Sam replied as Lieutenant Stinson hung up the phone.

"Guys, the warrant is being signed as we speak; we need to get an entry plan started and go over it with the team," Lieutenant Stinson stated.

"I am getting the floor plan for his shop now. I think we can enter from the side of the building, and to the left of where the truck delivered the boxes. We will need a second team to cover the front of the building and one man on the roof across from the shop watching the roof and the front street," Donald a former SWAT team leader replied.

"How many men do you think we need?" Jack asked, looking at Donald.

"Four for the entry, two to watch the front, and of course, one for the roof."

"There are four of us, and I have two men on standby. We only need one more," Lieutenant Stinson replied.

"I have a man I worked with on the team. He is solid," Donald answered.

"Call him and brief him. We want to move into the building at 0600. Winston comes early, usually at 5:45 a.m., according to intel. He will be by himself, and that means he will be on the hook for the guns."

Jack was hopeful that the case was leading somewhere for the first time. He felt something inside that he had not experienced in quite some time: hope!

SIXTEEN

Steve was drinking his morning coffee and getting ready for the day. He was heading into relieve the night-shift guys who were watching Stacy. The last few nights and days had been relatively slow, but the new arrivals to town worried him. The stakeout on Anna Lee revealed nothing at this point, so the sheriff decided not to pursue it any further. The good thing about it was that he got more people to double their efforts in surveilling Stacy.

He stood up and left his house to head over to the safe house. When he got in his car, a call came over the radio for immediate assistance. The officers who were coming to the end of their shift and whom he was getting ready to relieve had made the call. He could hear the nervousness in their voices on the radio. Sensing the urgency, he floored the gas pedal.

When he reached the road heading down to the safe house, he heard gunshots. He reached over and got his AR-style long gun out and ready for use. When he reached the front of the house, one of the officers on guard was on the ground motionless. He cautiously approached the downed officer and searched for a pulse. He had one, but it was faint. He heard the sirens from approaching cars, but he almost simultaneously heard a young woman screaming from around back.

He pointed his weapon in that direction and walked to the side wall of the house for cover. He eased along it until he reached the corner of the house. Then he peered quickly around the edge of the house. His heart was racing, and adrenaline was pumping. He noticed a man pushing Stacy into a black SUV and another person opening the driver's door. He aimed his rifle and squeezed the trigger. The man fell. He looked at the driver trying to fix his rifle sight on him, but the man turned and fired at him before he could. Steve felt a sting on his left thigh. His weapons' training kicked in, and he pointed his weapon to the dead center of the man's chest and shot. The second man fell.

Steve tied a makeshift tourniquet around his leg and approached slowly, limping from the pain of the wound. He focused on the bodies lying around the truck. He checked them both. Both were lifeless. He searched the men and removed their weapons. He was correct in his assumption—both men were dead. Now he needed to clear the truck. He walked over and checked it, noting it was clear except for Stacy hunched in the rear seat.

"Hold on Stacy. I need to check the house. Then I will be back for you," Steve stated as he looked at her and noticed her frantically nodding.

He went into the house to clear it and see if the other deputy was alive. The deputy in the house was conscious but holding his head. He had been struck in the back of his head with a solid object. He cleared the house and then returned outside to the truck. Stacy was lying in the back seat and crying almost inconsolably.

"You, OK?" he shouted to her.

"I think so. I don't know. Are they dead?"

"I got two down. Did you see any more?"

She looked at him and shook her head in disbelief at what she had just witnessed. "I just know about the two."

"This is the sheriff's office. If someone is there, make yourself known!" Steve heard from the front of the house.

"In the back. I have the girl, two deputies are down, and two suspects are dead!" he cried with as much energy as he could muster.

A small group of deputies and Sheriff Jackson walked around the house. Then the men secured the scene.

"You two all right; either one of you hurt?" one of the approaching deputies asked.

Feeling the pain from his leg starting to throb, Steve answered, "I took a round to the leg." He then eased to the ground. Stacy got out of the SUV with no injuries other than emotional ones. She walked over to Steve, bent down, and put her arms around him, giving him a huge hug. He felt her squeeze and then his eyes closed.

Winston left his upscale apartment and headed toward his shop. He was anxious to go in and make sure the shipment was safe. As he drove, he thought about how he never really wanted anything but to be a success at business. Over the last several years, he had made a lot of money handling and shipping weapons. This criminal enterprise had treated him well. But now he started thinking that maybe it had treated him too well.

Jack watched as Winston arrived at the shop. He pulled his car into a spot right up front. He walked to a side door, unlocked it, and went in. Jack gave the thumbs-up sign to signal them to be ready. They waited until a light turned on in a small room on the back right side of the building.

Jack and Danny approached the side door. There were two other two-man teams covering the front and back doors. They were all informed of any movement from their man on the roof. They had waited for Winston to make it to the shop, anxiously awaiting their opportunity to make an arrest.

Jack opened the door and entered first. He walked down the hallway with a Glock nine-millimeter pistol in his hands ready for use. He approached a hallway running perpendicular to the entrance they had used. He looked back to make sure Danny was in place and set. He then pointed to Danny and motioned in the opposite direction, as if to say, *Let's check the back room first.* Danny nodded in confirmation, then looked down the hall, and headed to the back room.

When the two men reached the back, they checked to make sure that no one was in the room with them. They looked around and then spotted the boxes. They walked over and looked inside one of them. They were surprised to find the pistols and AR-style rifles.

Danny whispered to Jack, "We got him." Danny called on his radio, and the other members of the team breached the front and back doors. Jack and Danny made their way to the front, clearing rooms as they went. When they arrived at the front of the shop, Winston was lying on the floor and was handcuffed. Sam and Donald were checking the front room for anyone they might not have accounted for.

"Guys, we have what we need in the back room. There are several boxes of weapons, some of which were AR rifles. I bet when we check their serial numbers, they will match those stolen from the armory. I love it when a plan works," Jack said excitedly.

"Me, too, but there is still a lot of work to be accomplished. Call it in, and let's secure the building and the weapons," Danny replied.

Jack walked toward Winston, helped him to his feet, and sat him in a chair. "I think we are fixing to get to know each other very well. In fact, I am going to be your best friend. You just do not know it yet."

"Well, Jack. I would not count my chickens before they're hatched," Winston responded. Jack looked at him with surprise. "Yes, I know you. I know your partner over there as well. Danny is his name. You got fortunate to be granted a job with the GBI, but it still will not help you in the end," Winston said as Jack looked at him with incredulity.

"I am not the one facing gun charges—possible Federal gun charges at that." Winston smiled a little as Jack stated this.

"Yes, well it does seem to be a tight spot I find myself in, but situations like these are planned for, Mr. Jack." At that moment and like clockwork, Jack's phone rang. When he looked at the phone, he was concerned, noting that it was Sherriff Jackson. "Like I said, Jack, these matters are planned on. Why don't you go ahead and answer that? I think your friend from Moultrie wants to chat."

Jack looked stunned and then answered the call. "Hello."

"Jack. I want to let you know there was an incident this morning. Steve was involved. He was shot."

"Is he OK? Is he hurt bad? Please tell me." Jack did not know what to think. He had just gotten an arrest and possibly a link to infiltrate Oliver's operation. Now his friend had been shot.

"Jack, he will be fine. He was shot in the leg. I reckon he wanted to do one better than you in that area. Here he is. I'll let him talk to you."

Jack heard a ruffling sound and then Steve's voice. "Jack there was ... um, well, Jack, I shot two men this morning. They were going after Stacy, and I ... well, I had to shoot them. I had no choice." There was a pause.

Jack spoke up. "It is OK, Steve. Are you all right? Are you hurt? Is Stacy OK?" Jack glanced at Winston who sat there with a smirk on his face. Jack walked outside of the building so that Winston could not hear the rest of the conversation. "Tell me, Steve, are you both all right?" Jack heard a deep sigh over the phone and then thought the worst.

"Yes, we are both all right. It was a close call, but we are OK. How did they find us, Jack? How would they know where she was?" Steve exclaimed.

Jack thought about that for a second. "I do not know, Steve, but I have a man in my custody at this time, and I think he may be able to spread some light on the situation. I am glad you and Stacy were not hurt."

"I am too, Jack. It all happened so fast!"

"I know. It happens in the blink of an eye, buddy. You did an awesome job. You kept your word and kept Stacy safe."

Jack heard a voice from the other end. "Hang the phone up. We are about at the hospital. We need to start an IV and get some meds in you." Then he heard Steve trying to refuse the request.

"Steve, let them work on you. I need to go anyway. I will call you back later today," Jack said.

He heard his friend say, "Crap." Then the line went dead. Jack rubbed his eyes, not wanting to show any emotion. He took a second, inhaled, and walked back into the building.

"You were saying, Winston?" Jack asked as he entered the building.

"I was saying, sir, that situations like this have been planned on. I think you realize now how far our reach has gone. Why don't we sit and talk about how you are going to let me go."

Jack looked up and thought that he witnessed actual arrogance dripping from the poor man. "If you are referring to the attempted kidnapping of a young lady from South Georgia this morning, I think maybe you need to reconsider the situation. Notice how I said attempted," Jack said as Winston looked at him with a new expression—one of concern.

When they arrived at an undisclosed location with Winston, he was placed in a room with nothing on the walls but paint. Jack thought that the color must be called putrid green because looking at it made him want to throw up. A two-way window covered the left wall and had a camera recording the room behind it. There was no ventilation in the room, and Jack watched as Winston sweat more than a long-tailed cat in a room full of rocking chairs.

"Let's give him a few minutes to stew, and I think he will be ready to cooperate," Danny said as he smiled.

"If we give him too long, he will admit to shooting Kennedy," Jack replied.

"In all seriousness, Jack, we don't have long before we could get in real trouble. After all, he hasn't been booked officially. So we better get started," Danny said in a serious tone.

"OK, who is the best interrogator on the team?" Jack asked.

"Well, of course, it's me. You are too straightforward, Jack, and the other guys are inexperienced in these matters." Jack watched as Danny entered the room with Winston.

"You supposed to be the good cop," Winston stated when Danny walked in.

"I am the cop who is going to save your life. I may be the man to save you from doing some real time in a prison cell with some redneck who is proud to be called Bubba."

Jack watched as Winston glanced at him spitefully. "I think you do not know the score. If you did, you would not have raided the shop," Winston stated.

Jack watched and listened carefully as Danny pulled a chair up, which had been placed in the corner, letting the legs scrape across the floor as he did so. He sat down, pulled a bottle of water out, and took a sip. "I think I know exactly who I am dealing with," Danny replied as Jack noticed that Winston squirmed in his seat a little.

"What does it take to get a drink around here?" Winston asked.

"A list of people and places that can lead us straight to Stansby." Jack smiled as he heard Danny say this.

"You know my name. What is yours, detective? Oh, I am sorry. You are the great friend of Jack Blackmon. Mr. Danny, right?" Jack sat forward in his seat and peered at the screen.

"First of all, it is not detective. I am not a local yokel. I am Agent Danny, and I am a GBI special investigator." Winston flinched a little. "That is right, Winston. You are dealing with the big boys now. No one is going to get you out of this mess." Jack watched as Danny eased back into his chair.

"What sort of mess am I supposedly in, agent?" Winston asked. Jack noticed that Winston had a steady stream of sweat running from his forehead.

"Gunrunning for starters. Then there are the robberies from the armory. You already know the armory stores weapons for the Atlanta PD, but did you realize the FBI uses it also? So now there will be some federal charges added."

Jack was almost glowing as Winston licked his lips a little. "Is there another water available, agent? It is hard to talk with a dry mouth."

Danny walked out and into the room with Jack. "See, Jack? Sometimes honey attracts more flies than vinegar, but federal time breaks rocks." Jack was brimming with the recent developments. He gave Danny a bottle of water and watched as he walked back to the room.

"Come on in. I think our little birdie is ready to sing." Jack quickly walked into the room with the two men when he heard Danny state this. Jack sat down in the chair where Danny had been sitting. Danny walked around the table and handed the man the water. He sat on the table by Winston. "This is Jack, but you know this already, don't you."

Before he could say another word, Winston chimed in. "Yes, I know Mr. Blackmon. I mean, we have not been formally introduced, but I have known him." Jack let this comment go but wondered why this man would know him.

"Tell us about the operation from the top down," Danny demanded.

Winston took a swallow of water. "Not until I have a deal in writing from the US attorney for the southern district. When I get that, we can talk."

Danny shook his head. "Boy, you are going for the top of the heap. Why do you want to take it that far? I have a DA ready to sign a deal for you now," Danny informed him.

"Because where we are going is further than you could ever imagine, Danny."

SEVENTEEN

Steve was on his way to the hospital after receiving a leg wound from the shooting. One of the deputies had been shot, and he was hanging onto his life. The other had suffered a concussion from being struck with what appeared to be a blackjack found on one of the assailants. Stacy was back at the sheriff's office, being watched by two deputies after the attempt on her life. The sheriff had no choice; he needed outside help to investigate. He picked up the phone and called Jack, who had been newly hired at the GBI, which was the agency with jurisdiction in these types of cases.

"Hello," Jack said as he was awaiting the district attorney to make a deal with the man they had just arrested.

"Hey, Jack. This is Sherriff Jackson."

"Is Steve doing all right? Has something happened?"

"No. He is fine. He is at the hospital recovering now."

"Good. Is there something I can help you with?"

"There is one thing, Jack. I need someone from your side to come down and help with the investigation into this shooting tonight. Can you help?" he asked.

Jack motioned for Danny, and when he walked over, Jack informed him of the request the sheriff had made. "Sheriff, Danny told me he had put a call out to a friend right after I talked with Steve earlier. He said he will be there within the hour. He was in the area on another matter. His name is James. Danny said he is highly trusted and great at his job."

"Thanks, Jack. I appreciate all y'all's help." The two men said their goodbyes and ended the call.

Sheriff Jackson walked around the scene and looked at the carnage that had been left behind. He thought back on all that had happened in his quiet county over the last bit of time. He wasn't sure how this was going to end, but his resolve had been tested. He wondered to himself if he and his department could withstand any further burdens. At that moment, he noticed the light from headlights that were approaching. After a small sedan pulled in, the sheriff watched as an older man with salt-and-pepper hair stepped out.

"Are you Sheriff Jackson?" the man said as he walked over to him, showing his credentials.

"Yes, I am. Are you the one Jack and Danny sent?" he asked.

"Yes. My name is James Towns. I am here to help with the investigation. Can you tell me what has happened so far?" he asked. The sheriff brought him up to speed, and James got to work. After some time and a lot of pictures and notes, he walked back and sat down beside the sheriff.

"Sheriff, I believe this is going to be a straightforward investigation. I will need to take the rifle your deputy used. I will stop by the hospital later and talk with him also," James said.

"That won't be a problem. I need to head to the hospital myself. If you want to, you can follow me over there."

James nodded. "We can head that way now if you like. One question though. What person on your team would you say is the most likely suspect to give away the safe house location?"

This question rankled the sheriff, but he refrained from saying anything crass. "I do not know. Time hopefully will tell all."

<hr />

"Jack, I have some news." Jack turned quickly, thinking that the deal from the DA had been nixed if the response was this quick.

"Did they approve the deal?"

Danny put his hand on Jack's shoulder. "The deal will come, but right now, there is news from Moultrie," Danny replied. Jack looked at Danny. "I need you to go back and help the sheriff watch over Stacy. I think she is going to be the key to help us unravel this mess. But I just cannot figure out why just yet."

"I agree she is important, but I can't figure out why. This shooting at the safe house tells us she needs protecting. I just don't want to let Winston out of my grasp though."

"I know, Jack, but we are a team and a good one. I will handle this, and you go back and handle that. Together we will solve this."

Jack didn't want to leave until he knew what information Winston was going to give them, but he oddly seemed drawn to the thought of seeing Stacy and making sure she was all right. There was also his buddy Steve. "I really want to stay, but you're right. I need to go," Jack said.

Jack gathered his thoughts and then collected his belongings. He walked out of the building to begin his journey back. He opened the door to his car, got in, and turned the key. Before he put it in drive, a thought occurred to him. He seemed to feel a way about Stacy that he had not noticed before. He had had some short-term relationships in his life but nothing too serious. He had a different feeling about this woman. He really didn't know if it was even feasible to think about her this way. He was considerably older than she was, but there was just something about her. She had been through a lot lately, though, and he may just be assuming she had feelings for him too. He decided to just focus on the case and her safety. He then headed out.

Jack drove down I-75, straight through and as fast as he could. He was intent on making sure that his friend was doing all right after being shot. In fact, he remembered well that Steve was the one who had visited him in the hospital just a few short weeks back.

Jack drove down Veteran's Parkway and pulled into the hospital's parking lot. He got out of his car and made his way into the hospital. When he walked into the lobby, he noticed a man talking with several county deputies. The man was older, of average height, and with salt-and-pepper hair. He looked like a man who was confident by the way he held himself. He thought this must be the man Danny had mentioned.

He walked over and introduced himself. "I am Jack Blackmon." He held out his hand as the other man did the same. *He has a firm handshake,* Jack thought.

"Jack, I am James. Nice to meet you. Sorry to do so under such circumstances."

Jack nodded. "I agree, but I seem to meet a lot of people these days under such circumstances." Jack then guided James away from any ears that might want to listen in and found a quiet spot. "Have you been able to ascertain any information about how these hitmen were able to find the safe house?" Jack asked.

"I haven't learned anything much yet. Is there anybody in the sheriff's office you were ever suspicious of?" The two men moved down the hall further to a small cafeteria. They both grabbed a cup of coffee and sat at a small table. "Jack, I was asking about anyone you may think of who might have been a leak inside the sheriff's office."

Jack took a long breath. "I really haven't thought of anybody I can put my finger on. There is one thing, but I hate to mention it right now," Jack stated as he noticed James's eyes squinting and the brow on his forehead wrinkling.

"If you are half the investigator Danny thinks you are, it means your gut is good. What is it telling you?"

Jack was still hesitant, but he decided to take James's advice. "James, the only odd feeling I have gotten is the way the sheriff was originally hesitant for us to approach Thomas Rygaard. He was nervous when I mentioned approaching him. Thomas was a client of mine, and I was trying to find his daughter's killer, which I did. But I suspected Rygaard was involved in the death of that man. I wanted to talk to him, but the sheriff was hesitant. He finally agreed to let us have the meeting. I just sensed something was off."

Jack was musing on the thoughts he had shared with James. He looked and noticed the sheriff getting off the elevator. He must be there checking on Steve. The sheriff glanced over and saw Jack. He headed over to the table where James and Jack were sitting.

"Jack, surprised to see you here," the sheriff said.

"Hey, sheriff. When I heard the news about Steve, I had to get down to see him. I am also concerned about Stacy. How is she holding up?" Jack shifted back in his seat.

"Well, Steve is doing as well as can be expected. You know, as well as anybody else with a leg wound feels like. Stacy is at the station. I have several men watching her," the sheriff stated.

"Can you sit for a minute, sheriff?" James asked.

The sheriff sat down at the table with the two men. "What would you like to discuss?" he asked.

"There are some things that just do not add up. First, how could someone find out the location of the safe house? Do many people know about it?" James asked.

Sheriff Jackson rubbed his eyes and thought. "The safe house was seized during an investigation into a financial fraud case several years back. We haven't used it very much. In fact, we were going to put it on the market several months back but decided against it. There are only a handful of people who know its location. I will get you a list," he replied.

"Thanks. Second, who knew about the details of scheduling for the watch? I mean there had to be a schedule of movement for the deputies—when they left, who would pick up food, and similar things." James noticed a look of frustration on the Sheriff's face.

"The deputies and I—oh, and my secretary. Her name is Sue. She has worked for me for the last two years."

James was writing this on a small pad. "Do you trust her?"

The sheriff's face started turning red as James finished. "I haven't had a reason not to at this point, James. Now if you will excuse me, I have some families to visit." The sheriff excused himself and left.

Jack looked at James and gave him a sheepish smile. "I am heading up to visit Steve," Jack told him.

"Go check on your friend. I will come up later," James responded.

Jack got off the elevator and went to the nurse's station to check if it was OK for him to visit his friend.

"Well, I be doggone if it isn't Jack. What is it with you and your friend? Do y'all just attract bullets?" Jack saw that it was Anna Lee. She had taken care of Jack while he had been injured. Now she was taking care of Steve. Jack also was reminded of the single strand of hair found at the murder scene. It had matched her DNA.

"Well, the friendliness at this place is irreplaceable. So I guess Steve had to test it out for himself." The two laughed. "How is Steve?" Jack asked her.

"He is in about the same physical shape you were. He will make it. Mentally, though, he is suffering."

Jack winced at hearing this. "These events have taken a toll on us all, but having to discharge your weapon and take a life takes it to a deeper level. Is it OK for me to see him?" Jack asked.

Anna Lee looked at him and smiled warmly. "He needs a good friend right now. So of course you can. Just keep him as calm as possible." Jack nodded, turned, and headed to his room.

"Is this monkey see, monkey do?" Jack asked when he entered the room.

Steve was peering out the window, and he appeared to be in deep thought. He jumped a little when he heard Jack's voice. "Oh, hey, Jack. Sorry, I was just, well anyway. What are you doing here? I thought you were in Atlanta?"

Jack pulled a chair next to Steve's hospital bed. "I was, but when I heard the news, I had to come and see if you were doing OK." Jack noticed Steve look down.

"You didn't have to do that. I am tougher than the average bear."

Jack grinned, knowing his friend was using humor to deflect. "I know you are, but everybody needs someone like me to come and aggravate him just to make sure." Steve let out a little chuckle. "You want to talk about what happened?"

Steve looked up at Jack. "I don't understand how they found the safe house, Jack. I can't imagine anyone of my guys slipping up or being on the take."

Jack thought for a minute. "Have you talked to James, the investigator from our office?"

Steve shook his head in aggravation. "Yeah, I talked with him some. He gave me the fifth degree on procedure. He ticked me off when he asked about the guys and Stacy. It was as if I was a suspect."

Jack put his hand on Steve's shoulder reassuringly. "He is a good man, Steve. He is just doing his job and being thorough."

Steve nodded. "I know, Jack, but it has been a long day."

"I know it has, Steve. Just sit back and relax. I am just going to sit with you for a while."

Steve lowered his hospital bed and eased into a deep sleep. Jack sat by his bed and drifted into deep thought. He wondered if the sheriff could be involved in this. *Was he involved in giving the location of the safe house to the men who tried to take Stacy? Would he allow his deputies to be injured in this way?* The gravity of it all weighed on him. *How am I going to solve this and put Stansby and his cronies in prison? How am I going to approach the sheriff?* He wondered about Danny and how things were going with Winston. Before he realized it, he also had drifted into sleep.

EIGHTEEN

Jack walked into a room filled with smoke. The light was very dim, and it was difficult to see his hand in front of his face. Nevertheless, it was where the screaming was coming from. He tried shining his flashlight to locate the direction, but it was useless. It only made his vision worse. He heard a noise; maybe it was her. He walked toward the sound and suddenly fell. He looked back and noticed someone lying on the floor. He moved toward the person. He noticed the long blond hair and looked at the face. He could not tell who it was. It was as if the face was blurred. He noticed blood and felt a pulse on her neck.

"Jack, Jack," someone called from beside him. Jack felt a hand on his shoulder, and he jumped out of the chair. He realized that he was in the hospital room with Steve. He noticed he was covered in sweat and breathing hard.

"Jack, are you all right?" a woman said.

"Yeah, yes, I am good," he stated.

"That did not seem like good to me," Steve said.

"Yeah, you were having some kind of nightmare."

He looked over at Anna Lee, who was standing there looking worried. "I umm, I am good," he restated.

"OK. I was checking because I heard you from the hallway. Do you need something?" she asked.

Jack sat back down in the chair. "No thanks, but I appreciate the offer." Jack rubbed his eyes.

"You can bring me a coffee," Steve said. "I am the patient."

Anna Lee smiled. "Sure, I will be right back." She turned and walked out of the room.

"Jack, that seemed like some dream you were having. Do you want to talk about it?"

Jack rolled his eyes. "You sound like the preacher at Justice's funeral," Jack said.

Steve smiled. "Maybe we both need to have a conversation with him."

Jack wondered why he was having these dreams. He had never had this happen before. He wondered if he needed a vacation and then wondered where a single, middle-aged detective would go on vacation. *Maybe a sci-fi convention.* Then he chuckled to himself. "Well, anyway, if you are fine, I think I am going to go and check on Stacy. She probably needs a break from that stuffy office of the sheriff's."

Steve looked at Jack. "You seem to have taken a shine to her, buddy."

Jack looked shocked and thought, *Is it that noticeable?* "Don't be ridiculous. I am just concerned for her welfare."

"Is that what the kids are calling it these days?" Jack looked at him, shook his head, and left the room.

When he left the room, he saw Anna Lee heading back in with the coffee. "Hey, when it is possible, and you have time, we need to sit down and talk."

She looked surprised. "Why? Do I have some parking tickets I haven't paid?" She walked past him and turned back.

"No. That is the purview of the man in the hospital bed. I just have some questions about our investigation that need to be answered. No big deal."

Her eyebrows furrowed. "We can meet later after my shift. Can we do it at the diner?" she asked.

"That will work, and you will get a free meal." She laughed and walked into Steve's room.

Jack walked toward the elevator as the door was closing and noticed a hand come out, holding it open. He got in and told the person, "Thanks." He looked over and thought, *This must be my lucky day.*

"Mr. Blackmon, how are you doing this fine day?" It was the preacher, Marvin Shiver, whom he had met at the funeral.

"Well, I am doing pretty good, Reverend," Jack said.

"Oh, no, just call me Marvin. Reverend sounds so official, and this isn't official business."

Jack squirmed a little. "No, not official at all," Jack replied as he started feeling uncomfortable in the man's presence.

"Would you mind having a cup of coffee with me, Jack?"

Jack looked at him, and he could tell that he wasn't going to take no for an answer. "Sure. Why not? I need some caffeine to get me charged up."

Jack led the man into a little café, which was sponsored by the Pink Ladies Auxiliary, and ordered two cups of coffee. Jack walked to a corner table and motioned for the man to sit down.

"Jack, as I recall, you were having some trouble the last time we talked."

Jack shrugged. "Well, we were at a funeral where a young man who died was being laid to rest. Doesn't that seem troubling to you?" Jack watched him take a sip of coffee.

"Haven't you dealt with death before? I mean, you are a detective. Death is something you should be familiar with."

Jack looked gobsmacked. "Well, you cut straight to the point, don't you, Marvin?" Jack said, being caught off guard. Jack then thought, *This isn't the time for this conversation.* Then a voice popped into his head and told him to have the talk. "To be honest, Marvin, I have been in a bit of a struggle lately. I am not being an adolescent, but to say that the evil and maliciousness I have witnessed in this world has not affected me would be an understatement."

Marvin listened intently and seemed to truly understand what Jack was trying to express. "You think that life is designed to be fair, Jack?" he asked.

"Not really, but the level of suffering for some, especially those who are basically good people, is far from what I would call being just. In fact, I would say there is no justice," Jack replied.

"Jack, have you ever studied or heard messages from a Christian perspective?" Marvin asked.

Jack looked at Marvin strangely. "I have not. I never really had the opportunity. But I think if you are going to tell me that this world, which has so much evil in it, is run by a loving Creator, I am going to say, 'Do not waste your breath." Jack straightened as he spoke.

"Jack, this world is full of evil. The Word of God tells us that. Satan has been granted full authority here on Earth to rule it. Granted, that is by our sin and letting him have the authority," Marvin calmly replied.

Jack became aggravated. He did not want to be rude, but his anger had reached a boiling point. "Marvin, I thought this conversation would give me some understanding, but I am more confused now than before. You are saying that all this suffering and anguish is caused by people, some of which are very good people. How does that make sense?" Jack slapped the table.

"Jack, I know that is a lot to take in at one time, but this is not what God designed for us. We, as humans, were designed to have a relationship with Him. He designed us in His image. We didn't want to be ruled, so sin happened, and this madness we deal with is a result of our sin."

Jack could not understand what he was hearing. He could not comprehend that man was the creator of his own pain. "Marvin, I think we have reached an impasse now, and I think we should probably leave the conversation here. I must go and see one of the sinful people who brought misery upon herself. So please excuse me." Jack got up to leave.

"Jack, it is all right. I understand the place where you find yourself. Please, when you want to talk some more, come and find me. I will be praying for your answers and you until then."

Jack walked away from his encounter with Marvin a little flustered. He had never heard the bad situations in life explained that way. But the words he heard were running around in his mind. He got in his car and focused on his upcoming meeting with Stacy. He was looking forward to seeing her. He got into his car and turned onto the road. His cell phone rang.

"Hello."

Danny was on the other end. "Hey, Jack. How are Steve and Stacy?"

Jack was anxious to hear what Danny had to say about the debriefing of Winston. "Steve is good, just a little shaken and sore. I haven't seen Stacy yet."

"Jack, that is good to hear about Steve. Tell Stacy we are thinking about her," Danny remarked.

Jack was impatient. "What has Winston revealed so far?"

There was a pause and a chuckle. "Jack, you always have your mind on business, don't you?"

Jack thought, *If you only knew.*

"Winston has given us small bits, but he says he is waiting for you to give us the real juicy details—the last being his words."

"I am going to get things set up for Stacy. I want her to be as safe as possible, and then I will head back up," Jack said as he took the last turn before the sheriff's office.

"Has James found out anything about how the safe house was breached?"

"No real breakthroughs yet. I will brief you more when I am back."

"All right, friend, be careful," Danny replied.

"You, too, Danny."

Jack arrived at the sheriff's office. He got out, and as he was walking in, he felt something in his stomach. He had only felt like this in situations that usually led to arrest. It was butterflies. *Can a man who has faced bullets and bad guys really be nervous?* He walked in, and the sheriff happened to see him.

He walked toward Jack and greeted him with a handshake. "Hey, Jack. Good to see you."

Jack looked at him and nodded. "Good to see you. How are you holding up?"

The sheriff had a worried look. "All this mess is putting a lot of stress on me and my men. Steve being shot has shaken all of us a bit."

Jack saw Stacy sitting in an office, looking out the window. "It appears as if she might say the same thing too."

"Yeah, she has been through a lot too. Maybe you should go and check on her."

Jack performed a double take on the sheriff.

"Well, if you say so." He then walked into the office where she was. "Hey, Stacy, how are you holding up?"

When Stacy turned to him, she had tears in her eyes. She hurried over to Jack and put her arms around him and squeezed. Jack was taken off guard. He wrapped his arms around her and returned the favor. "I am so scared, Jack. What is happening? What have I done to deserve all this madness?"

Jack grabbed her shoulders, gently eased her back, and then pushed some loose hair away from her face. "You did nothing wrong, Stacy. You do not deserve this. This whole mess just appeared on your front doorstep, and no one knows why." Jack wiped a tear from her face. "We will work this out, and I will keep you safe. I promise," Jack said as Stacy smiled.

"You sure do know how to make a girl feel better, Jack. Thank you."

"We need a plan that will keep you safe. I think I may have one, but we will need everyone to agree to it," Jack said.

"What kind of plan, Jack?" Stacy asked.

"I think you will be safer with the team in Atlanta. How do you feel about heading there with me? Then we can meet up with Danny. There are more places to hide there with less chance of you being spotted."

Stacy looked down, went, and sat on the small gray couch along the wall. "I don't really want to leave after all that has happened. But if you think it will be safer, I would be OK with going there."

Jack was excited that she responded this way. He thought it showed that she trusted him. "I need to go and talk with the sheriff and see if he will be accepting of what we have discussed." Jack walked out of the office and found the sheriff.

"Everything good, Jack?" the sheriff asked when he walked into his office.

"I think so. I have a plan that I would like to discuss with you. I think it would be safer for Stacy and would make me feel a lot better." Jack watched the sheriff smile like the Cheshire cat.

"Does this plan include Stacy traveling with you back to Atlanta?"

Jack returned the smile. "Do you have the office bugged, or are you just a mind reader?" Jack said as the sheriff chuckled.

"Well, it does not take a brain surgeon to figure out you have a little crush on her. It also makes sense to me. Atlanta is a larger city with more places to hide a person." Jack couldn't disbelieve how smoothly this was going. "It's also convenient for you having her in closer proximity. I somehow think you will function better knowing her whereabouts. Go ahead with your plan. It will give us a little time to recover from the disaster that has happened here."

Jack thanked the sheriff. He turned and went back into the other office, where Stacy was still sitting on the couch and staring into space. "Well, get yourself prepared to visit the Big Peach."

Stacy jumped as if caught off guard and then looked at Jack, smiling nervously. "The sheriff agreed to let me go?" she said as Jack held out his hand to help her off the couch.

"Yes, he realized the best way to keep you safe is to put some distance between here and you. I believe being up there with me will help—help with your safety and help you recover emotionally." She smiled. "Along the way, we can stop and pick up some things you may need. I don't want to risk you being out in public around this town. Too many prying eyes, you know." She nodded as they walked into the sheriff's office.

"We are going to go ahead and head out now, Sheriff. The quicker we leave, the probability of something going wrong goes down. Tell Steve I will call him in a few days to check in."

The sheriff stood and shook his hand. "Sure. Well, you guys keep safe and let me know if I can help in any way."

Jack and Stacy left the office, got into his car, and drove off. Jack picked up his phone and dialed Danny.

"Hello," Danny said.

"I have Stacy, and we are heading your way. I figured we could keep her safer up there," Jack said as he was scanning the mirrors for any signs of a tail.

"I believe that is the right call. I will have things arranged here, so don't worry; just drive safely."

"Thanks, Danny. I will let you know if anything comes up between here and there." The two men ended the call. Jack looked at Stacy, and he knew for the first time in a long time that he was on the right track. He even thought he was on the right track with Stacy.

NINETEEN

Oliver Stansby was in the solarium of his sprawling Atlanta mansion, watching the rain. He liked the vegetation from his native Australia. His fancy greenhouse provided that advantage. He was admiring the reddish tint of his favorite bottlebrush plant when his butler walked in. He motioned in a manner that let him know there was a phone call for him. Oliver picked up the phone and answered, "Yes" in his thick Australian accent.

"It's Carl. Is this line safe?"

Oliver waived his butler away. When he was out of earshot Oliver answered, "Yes, it is protected. What do you need to tell me?" Walking away from the bottlebrush, he found a padded bench and sat down.

"I have not been able to contact Winston. I made several calls, and now I am concerned." Oliver heard something in his voice that he did not like; it was fear. Oliver despised fear. Fear was for people who did not have the testicular fortitude to handle situations in life that caused them to turn to that emotion.

"Have you gone to the shop and checked on the shipment?"

Carl said, "Not yet."

Oliver sighed. "Well, I think that would be the next logical step. Send one of your guys by posing as a shopper or something and let me know what you find out. In the meantime, I have some friends who might be able to help shed some light on things."

"This doesn't feel right. Something is wrong, Oliver."

Oliver stood and looked down at the utricularia plant. He thought,

I would like to consume this man's doubt like the mosquito larva my plant feeds on. Then he gently poured more water into its pot. "I do not care for your feelings. Just do as you are told, and if something is wrong, I will fix it as always."

"Yes, sir. I will do as you ask." Oliver hung up the phone and went back to admiring his garden.

―――――――――――――――

As Jack and Stacy were driving into Warner Robins, they noticed a new gas station, which looked like a warehouse. "Buc-ee's!" Stacy remarked.

Jack pulled up to a pump to fill up the tank with gas. "Give me a second, and we can walk in to get a snack." Stacy nodded. Jack started pumping the gas and scoured the parking lot for anything that might be out of place—an odd person sitting in a car looking nonchalant or someone appearing not to be looking but looking. But he spotted no one who could be a threat. "All right, let's go in. I do not see anything suspicious." Stacy got out, and the two walked quickly into the store.

When they walked in, they were very surprised. They quickly found out that they could buy anything from soap to a slab of ribs in the monstrosity of a store. "This is the best idea since sliced bread," Stacy remarked.

Jack chuckled at her excitement. "You get toiletries. Then we can go and get one of those steak sandwiches if you would like," Jack said as Stacy nodded, walked to the other aisle, and grabbed the needed items. Jack searched his aisle, looking at the oddities.

"Jack, Jack!" Stacy said as she quickly made her way to him and grabbed him by the shoulder. "See that man!" She pointed in the direction of a middle-aged, White man wearing a cheap suit. He was in line paying for a drink and what looked like a side of ribs.

"Yes, I see him, but stop pointing in his direction before he sees us." Jack put his hand on her shoulder and turned her away. They moved to the furthest side of the store from the man who had frightened her. "Now tell me what in the world has gotten you so upset about seeing this man."

She was still visibly upset. "I remember his face from when I was kidnapped. He was outside the trunk and talking with Johnny about something."

Jack looked in the man's direction to see if he had noticed them. Thankfully, he had not. He walked out of the store.

"How could you have seen him from the trunk?" Jack asked.

She looked at him with angry eyes. "Because there was a hole in the trunk, and he stood in the spot where I could see him."

Jack changed his facial expression to one of understanding. "I am sorry. I did not mean to sound doubtful. Did you hear any of the conversation when the two were talking?" Jack wanted to make sure to turn her attention back to the night of the abduction.

"I could not really make sense of the conversation, but he had a weird accent," she replied.

Jack looked around to make sure that the man hadn't reentered the store. "What kind of accent? Northern, midwestern, maybe something from out west?" Jack inquired.

She looked confused. "No. I mean like German or Russian. I have never heard an accent like that except in a movie."

Jack put his arm around her and pulled her in close. He led her as they walked around to scan the store and parking lot. When he had determined the man was gone, he loosened his embrace, headed to the counter, paid for their things, and then headed out of the store.

They got back into the car and headed north on the interstate. Jack was quiet. As he glanced around, he noticed Stacy's body language. She seemed withdrawn, and she was almost guilty looking.

"Jack, you are very quiet. Did I do something wrong? Have I made you mad?" Stacy commented.

Jack, who had been in deep thought about what had just happened, realized he did seem a little sulky. "Of course not. I am sorry. I was thinking about what you told me."

She looked out the window and then glanced back at him. "By

your reaction, I am tending to think this situation is worse than what everyone originally thought."

Jack sighed and reached out for her hand without realizing it. "I am not sure, but I am not going to lie. The man we are investigating is suspected of having ties to the Russian mafia. What you have told me just reaffirms that notion."

There was silence during the rest of the drive to Atlanta. Jack was trying to figure out the best way to protect Stacy. He was also considering how to proceed with the investigation. They both jumped when Jack's cell phone rang. Jack picked it up and answered, "Hello."

He heard a familiar voice on the other end. "Hey, Jack, have you made it up there safely?" Jack took a breath and told her it was Steve.

"Tell him, 'Hey,'" she told Jack.

"Not quite. We have about another thirty minutes. Stacy says, 'Hello.'" He looked at her, and she smiled at him. "How are you feeling?"

There was a little silence, and then Steve said, "Physically, I am feeling OK; just a little soreness in my leg. Mentally, not so well."

Steve sounds different, Jack thought. "You want to talk about it?"

Again, there was a pause. "I am struggling with the senselessness of the ... Why has all this happened, Jack?"

Jack thought about that question for a second. "Steve, I can't rationally explain it. I asked the same question to a wise man earlier. He told me that there is a God in heaven who loves us and that He did not want life to happen this way." Jack paused, listening carefully to what his friend would say.

"I sure hope that is true because this is some ugly stuff," Steve said sharply.

"It is ugly, but because of your actions, a good person is sitting beside me now. That is a great outcome, Steve."

There was another pause. "Thank you, Jack. I need to go."

Jack smiled at Stacy. "Anytime, my friend."

A frail man wearing an Adidas jumpsuit and carrying a cane was walking down the sidewalk across the street from Winston's shop. He was in his late fifties, and he looked as if a strong wind would blow him over. He stopped at the coffee shop across the road and ordered an espresso. He needed something to give him the energy to make it back home after his journey. He was checking on things for Carl. He originally thought this was a great way to earn a quick hundred bucks. But his stamina had left after taking the long walk.

At first, he did not notice anything strange. It looked like a normal shop that was closed. Then he noticed something on top of the building. It was a quick flash of light. Upon further examination, he noticed a man on the building searching the block using binoculars. He also noticed after more looking that an unmarked police car was parked at the end of the street. He decided it was time for him to report back. He got up and slowly walked out of the store. Then he went down to the end of the street and got into a small car with tinted windows.

"Well, what do you think, Burt?" Carl asked.

"I think that I am getting too old for this kind of work. Can you buy me a scooter next time?"

Carl had peered at Burt when he had responded in such a crusty manner. "Cut the foolish talk, Burt. Tell me what you saw," Carl snarled.

"At first, nothing. But given time, they gave themselves away. There was a man on the roof. After some more time, I noticed an unmarked police car parked down the road."

Carl turned to him as he shifted in the seat. "That was an easy way to make a hundred bucks." Carl handed him the crisp hundred-dollar bill. He motioned to the driver, and they left, dropping Burt by his house. After several minutes went by, Carl's phone buzzed.

"Tell me what you found out!" Carl heard Oliver's voice.

"The shop was not open, and there were some cops hanging around." he replied.

"That is not good! Get over to the warehouse. I will contact you in a bit." Then Oliver hung up and quickly made another call.

"Hello," a voice on the other end answered.

"Winston has been taken off the board. Find out what happened and where he is. I want to know before the end of the day tomorrow," Oliver stated firmly.

"Good as done," Oliver heard. Then he hung up the phone, walked to his bar, and poured himself a drink. He walked back to his couch, flopped down, and took a sip of the elixir.

Jack finally arrived in Atlanta with Stacy in tow and pulled into the parking deck of a nondescript building, which the bureau had set up for this operation. The two got out of the car and walked into the building. Jack guided Stacy to the door, and they entered it.

The two greeted Sam, who was sitting in a side room, going over video footage from Winston's shop. They walked through the room, saying, "Hey," to Donald and Danny as they were going over some files.

"Here is the man of the hour," Donald said.

"Nice to see you, too, Donald," Jack replied. "Meet Stacy and be nice!"

Donald grinned at Jack's comment. "Military men are always nice to beautiful women," he said, putting out his hand to shake hers. Jack felt a little jealous over this comment and cut his eyes at the man.

"Jack, good to see you. Stacy, you too," Danny stated.

Jack moved toward Danny and patted him on the shoulder. "Looks like there is a lot of work happening here," Jack commented as Donald looked over.

"The work is just beginning. The gunrunner said he would not talk until you came back. Hopefully, things will pick up now that you are here," Donald said as Danny motioned Jack to sit down. He did.

"We have been watching the shop with no success. They must know by now that their man is either on the lamb or in lockup. The sooner we can get actionable intelligence, the better."

Jack agreed with Danny's statement. "You are right. We need him to talk. If they know Winston is compromised, they will start covering their tracks. First, though, we need to make sure Stacy is safe. Do we have somewhere to keep her?"

Danny looked at Jack, waved his hands, and looked around the building. "I think here is the best place. There are some extra bedrooms and a comfortable living area upstairs."

Jack consented, but Stacy looked uncomfortable as she gazed at the gaggle of men. "Stacy, this gives us time to work on the case and keep you safe. Please be patient," Jack said coolly.

"Since you think it is best, I will," she said sweetly.

Danny waved Jack to another room where the two could talk in private. "I've got to say that this case is the most in-depth one I have worked in a long time. There are so many moving parts. A local sheriff's agency and their witness protection have been compromised. I also need to tell you that your former captain has made a call to our lieutenant inquiring about the raid as well."

Jack looked with concern at Danny. "What did you tell him?"

Danny waved in a manner to let him know not to worry. Jack's facial expression didn't align with his wishes though. "Nothing. We froze him out for now, but there will be some pressure applied soon."

Jack rubbed his chin like an old miser pondering deep thoughts. "Stacy remembered something or rather someone on the way up here." Jack told him about the encounter at the store.

"Well, the dots continue to connect. Why would she be a target of this group though?"

Jack couldn't think of a good answer. "Let's put first things first. I am ready to talk with Winston," Jack said. Danny agreed, and they brought the man up from the room they were keeping him in and set him up in the putrid-colored interrogation room again.

Jack walked to the door where Winston was. He stopped and took a deep breath, trying to relax his mind. He did not know what to expect from this interrogation. *Is this just going to be a jousting match for Winston to work a deal, or is he really going to give up some pertinent information? Is this just another cleverly disguised plan from the mastermind, or do they really get lucky?* Jack thought that this was a dangerous game he had been playing blindly for years. He took one more deep breath, exhaled, and opened the door.

TWENTY

Steve was lying in his hospital bed and thinking over the case. There was really nothing else for him to do. TV shows were boring him, and crosswords really were not his thing. He realized that there were still some loose ends that had not been tied up. There were lingering questions. *Why was Anna Lee's hair fiber found at the barn where Justice was murdered? Did she know Stacy? Why was she kidnapped when she was a teenager? This couldn't be chance, or maybe it could?* He knew that he had to find out.

The good news was that she was back at work today, and she was going to be his nurse. *Killing two birds with one stone*, he thought. *Killing boredom and working a case;* although he knew boredom really wasn't his biggest issue. There was still the gnawing thought of the dark emotions building in him after being shot and having been forced to take another person's life.

Anna Lee finally came into the room to check on Steve. "Well, hello, sunshine," Steve remarked as she walked in.

She gave him a sassy smile. "Yeah, yeah. I figured that as much as we have seen each other over the last few days, it wouldn't be that big of a deal if I came in a little later to check on you."

Steve laughed a little at her sassiness. "Never can get enough of you, girl. You are like sunshine in a poop factory. You bring relief."

She gave him a wry look. "If it is relief you are looking for, I can go get one of those suppositories. They work really well and quickly."

Steve gave a belly laugh. Steve, all kidding aside, was in a little pain. He requested that Anna Lee bring him some relief in the form of a pain pill. She went and got what he requested.

"Thanks for the pill. While you are here, can I ask you a few questions?"

She looked at him wearily. "You aren't going to ask me on a date or something, right? Because you know Tom can be a jealous man."

Steve shook his head, continuing to like her verbal jousting. "No, no, it is nothing like that. I have been sitting here with nothing to do and remembered a few loose ends I need to tie up. These loose ends have come from some questions we have about you," he replied. "We know that you questioned Jack when he was being treated here. We know Tom or Thomas put you up to it," Steve said as she looked at him in a funny way.

"You already know that because Thomas told it to Jack during a conversation they had."

Steve held his hand up in a manner to show his understanding. "Yes, I know you were just doing them a favor, but did you know that your hair fiber was found at the murder scene in that country barn a few weeks back?" Steve stated as she looked at him incredulously.

"No, I didn't. What does that mean? Am I a suspect? Because you know I help save lives; I do not take them," she stated with passion.

"Not I or anyone else thinks that. But doesn't that seem odd too you?" he asked.

She was in full-attention mode at this point. "Yes, that is very odd, but my hair falls out like any other person's. Maybe we shopped at the same store or something."

Steve nodded. "It was a single strand of hair, and that is very unlikely," he said as she shrugged at the thought. "I do not have an answer for that."

"How did you determine that it was my hair? I haven't been arrested. How do you know it was mine?"

Steve was trying to think of a good way to say it but finally just blurted it out. "We know that you were kidnapped as a teenager. Your DNA was submitted to help the police find you at the time. And it was on record with the FBI." Steve noticed that she looked dumbfounded, and then a tear ran down her cheek. "I know, and I am sorry. This is a bad situation, but it is necessary," Steve said as humbly as he could.

Anna Lee wiped the tears from her eyes. "I am sorry. I knew one day someone would find this out. I knew I would have to relive it but not in an active murder investigation. Yes, I was kidnapped as a teenager. How does that play into this?"

Steve did not know either, but he had time, and he needed answers, so he went on. "I am not sure if it does play into anything, but the more information we have, the clearer the picture becomes. Can you or will you tell me what happened with your kidnapping?" Steve paused.

"After all this time why should I let that situation still have power over my life? Sure, I will tell you my story. The fact is that I really do not remember much. I was in Savannah, walking on River Street with some friends, and we got separated. Someone put a rag or something over my face, and the next thing I knew, I was waking up in a warehouse with my hands tied to a chair."

Steve looked at her with compassion. "That must have been very frightening for you—especially at such a young age."

"Yeah, it certainly was. The guy wasn't very good though. He wore this childish mask like he was Jason from that horror movie. I noticed him bump his head a few times while walking around the warehouse that he kept me in. I guess because he couldn't see or something."

Steve let a laugh out. "Sorry, it must be the pain medicine." His face turned red because he was more than embarrassed laughing at such a traumatic event.

"Well, I am glad such a tragic event in my life is funny to you. If you want to know the truth, though, I have thought about this more than a few times over the years. The questions just kept on popping into my mind. Why? Why me? Why him? Why that warehouse?"

Steve noticed her expression change to one of frustration, and she appeared to be more tense. "How did you escape?" Steve inquired.

"I told you he wasn't that good of a kidnapper. He also was not a sailor because he could not tie a knot to save his life. The next day, I got my hands free because of it; the ropes just came free after some manipulation. If I wasn't so scared, I would have thought of that earlier. I probably would have been back in my bed before midnight."

Steve looked at her, noticing her mannerisms as she relived the moment. "He must have never gotten his knot-tying badge. Did they ever catch him?" he asked.

"No. I couldn't remember which way I ran. I left out of there so fast, and I never thought to look at any landmarks. When they finally found the place, it was cleaned up. The only thing he did right, I guess. It made me fear life for a long time. Every shadow and every bump in the night almost gave me a panic attack."

Steve watched her take a deep breath and then heard the matching sigh as her shoulders dipped slightly. Steve looked at her and said, "I think your bravery and smarts played a bigger role in those events than you give yourself credit for."

Her shoulders lifted, and her face brightened. "A bigger role is the right comment. I believe God had a bigger plan for me than to be lost to a nitwit who could not tie a knot."

Steve smiled at that comment. "You know, that is the second conversation I have had lately that has tied events of life to God. Do you believe there is a God out there in the universe somewhere?" Steve asked as he watched her not being able to contain herself.

"I believe in the God of the universe. I believe Jesus came to earth, fully man and fully God. I believe he hung on a cross, and all my sins were put on Him. I believe He died, was buried, and then was resurrected."

Steve looked at her, surprised. "Wow, you came with both barrels blazing on that, Anna Lee."

She walked to him and grabbed his hand. "Hey, you asked, and I wanted you to know. He wanted you to know. That is how much He loves you."

Steve pulled his hand back from her gently. "I um ... I can't really understand that right now. It sounds good and all, but I just don't know."

Anna Lee smiled softly at him. "I understand. I was in the same position. Tom has had the same response too. I am going to be praying for both of you." She fluffed his pillow and poured him some water.

"You mentioned Tom. How is he doing?" Steve noticed that she curled her lip a little.

"He is doing fine. He travels so much sometimes that it is hard to keep up with him."

Steve followed up. "I know he helps his father in the investment business. Is that the reason for all the travel?"

She shrugged her shoulders. "Sometimes Thomas has some international clients, but they usually travel here. Well, I mean the Atlanta office. Tom is trying to start his own business though."

Steve nodded with some interest. "What kind of business?"

She looked at her watch. "It is some kind of import-export thing. I really don't know much about it because he keeps it close to the vest. All right, I need to go check on my other patients. If you need anything, press the call button." She then left the room.

James was in a motel room. He had made his rounds throughout the sheriff's departmental offices. He had met with everyone. He just couldn't put his finger on the culprit who would betray his fellow deputies. His suspicion kept going to the sheriff himself because of Jack's statement, but he felt that in the grand scheme of things, the sheriff was an honorable man. He was just plain uncomfortable, which was a feeling he did not like. He had found moles, turncoats, and just plain greedy cops in departments across the state. It was more common than one would think. There was always someone disgruntled or in debt, but there was no money trail or any sign of unrest in this department.

James was so in tune with his thoughts that he didn't hear the knock on his motel room door. Then the person on the other side knocked again—this time with a bit more enthusiasm. James jumped a little and came back to the present. He walked to the door and looked through the peephole. He was surprised to see the man who was outside the door. He opened it, and Thomas Rygaard was there. James recognized him from his picture in the case file.

"Hello, I am Thomas Rygaard. I would like to talk with you if you have some time."

James nodded and motioned him inside. "Thomas Rygaard, I presume, from the pictures I have seen. How are you today?"

Thomas stepped inside, and James motioned him to a chair. Thomas obliged his request. "I know this may be a surprise—I mean my presence here with you today."

James sat down on the edge of a full-size bed, which had a mattress so firm that he thought they had stacked bricks and covered them with a comforter. "I am a little surprised to see you here for sure. What can I do for you, Mr. Rygaard?"

"Well, I am hesitant to just blather here tonight, but I do have a concern I thought I might discuss with you."

James pulled a small yellow notepad from his luggage bag, which was stationed by his bed. "Well, in my business, hesitation is not a bad thing. I will let you know I am one of the most experienced investigators the GBI has on its roster. I have handled cases so large that if I mentioned some names, you would recognize them. So let's start like this. Tell me the specific concern you have, Mr. Rygaard."

Thomas seemed to want to just spill the beans, but he held back. "I do want to help, but in the process of helping you, I may hurt someone I do not really want to hurt."

James motioned his hand in a circular manner to himself as he was taught in one of his body language classes at the bureau. "I can understand that. Can you tell me at least who or what this information could affect?"

Thomas started rubbing his hand in a nervous manner. "You must understand I have lost a daughter to a monster. I do not want to lose my son," Thomas blurted out, and James noticed the tension in his voice.

"I am sorry, sir, but I am a bit lost in this conversation. Why would what you have to say to me affect you or your son in a negative way?" James kept eye contact as he asked this question.

Thomas rubbed his hands a bit harder, and a tear gathered in the corner of his right eye. "I think my son may have been responsible for giving away the location of the house where that girl was being kept." As soon as he let the words out, he began to sob uncontrollably.

James walked over to the bedside table, grabbed some tissues, and then handed them to Thomas. "Please tell me, Thomas, why would you think your son would do such a thing?" When Thomas turned, James could see his face in the light coming from the light fixture. He looked like a man who had been made haggard by life.

"My son has been groomed to be able to take control of the business I built. I was determined he would take over ever since he could walk. In fact, he has exceeded my expectations time and time again. He is the one who expanded our footprint overseas. His acumen for business and money management is far superior to mine." Thomas spat out these words quickly.

James knew that the man in front of him was starting to waffle a bit. If he let him stray, he might talk himself out of telling him something important. "I understand your son is an excellent businessman, but you came here to tell me he was responsible for telling someone about the location of the safe house. Please, sir, tell me why you would think that." James was in full interrogation mode.

Thomas cleared his throat. "Well, in the last two years, he met a man who wanted to invest a lot of money in our company. I really did not want to take him on as a client. Tom, well Tom could only see the money. He engaged this man, and we took him on."

James was taking notes on his pad and looked up at Thomas. "What is this man's name, and what kind of business was he in?"

"His name is Oliver Stansby. I could never ascertain his business. All I can tell you is that he has invested a boatload of money with us."

James almost fell off the bed when he heard Oliver Stansby's name. He inhaled a long breath and then slowly exhaled, refocusing his mind. "Tell me more about what your company does for Mr. Stansby?"

Thomas stood up and looked over at a picture on the wall of a simple pasture with a wood fence, which was surrounded by several leafless trees. "That is the place where I imagined my life when I started this business. All I could see was a peaceful place where I could spend time with my family. Now I wish I never hadn't had the dream. I have lost my wife, my daughter, and now my son." Thomas started choking up a bit.

"Please, Thomas, finish telling me why you think your son has done this."

Thomas turned back to James. "My company owned the house where all this took place. I made a business move and saw I could make a profit one day from its purchase. The profit came when I sold it to the county."

James looked confused. "It is on record that they collected that house from a drug dealer after a bust there." James looked oddly at Thomas as he laughed.

"Yeah, not so much. That was the sheriff's idea. He did not want it to look like a favor was being repaid for supporting him in his election."

"That is surprising. The sheriff seems like a stand-up guy."

James was surprised as Thomas quickly interjected, "He is one of the most stand-up men you will ever meet."

"OK, I will accept that on face value. Now let's get to the part about your son again," James said.

Thomas sighed and took a deep breath. "Tom was home the week the matter happened. We were finishing up some work on our taxes. The sheriff came by to talk with me after that detective Jack came to question me. He was making sure I was not too flustered. Anyway, we were having a conversation, and the house was mentioned. I asked him if he was getting good use out of it. He said he used it in a few operations. When I looked, Tom was outside the room listening."

"And you think he told Stansby this?"

Thomas nodded, took a long breath, and sighed loudly. "I do, but I did not realize what Stansby was. I didn't understand until I confronted Tom. He told me what he was doing to make his money and said that we were tied to him and that we would go down if

Stansby went down. The company and all that we had worked for would be gone." There were a few moments of silence.

"You are telling me that your firm is laundering money for him?" James was trying to draw him out more.

"You must understand that I had no idea. I had taken my eye off the day-to-day functioning of the business. I was obsessed with getting and hype-focused on Emily's killer." Thomas cradled his face in his hands. He stood there silently.

"Thomas, thank you for sharing this with me. I will talk with my superiors about this. I think we can strike a deal with you and your family if you can supply us with the details of Mr. Stansby's money. You know, by now, that Stansby is involved with some major crimes. Tying his money to his actions will go a long way in bringing him to justice." James watched the man as his head slowly lowered, and he looked at the floor.

"I do not know the details of his money. Tom handled all his business. But I am honest and above board. I want to get out of this, and I want Tom out of this too. Whatever it takes, I will do it. I just want Tom to be OK also. He is all that I have left."

James reassured him that he would do his best to help him and Tom. "I will need to make a few calls. I also need you safe. I want to put you in protective custody."

Thomas walked back and sat down. "I think I can help more if you let me go back home. No one knows I am here, and I can operate better if I am around the business."

James thought about this for a while and then came to the same conclusion. "OK, you go back home, and I will contact you tomorrow about the next steps." Thomas got up and shook his hand. "I will talk to you tomorrow."

James took a deep breath and thought of the conversation. This was such a tangled web of deceit. He wondered how such an upstanding family could go so far off the tracks.

TWENTY-ONE

Jack opened the door and walked into a five-foot-by-seven-foot room. The paint was peeling from the walls. It was an ugly greenish color. Jack noticed a stench that smelt a bit like sulfur. *Perfect.* Jack thought this would make Winston think of the prison cell he would be inhabiting soon. Winston appeared to be sitting patiently in the room, ignoring his surroundings. His hands were clasped together, and his elbows were resting on the table.

"Winston, I hope you're enjoying your stay in our fine establishment," Jack said.

"Jack, it is nice to see you again, but the accommodations are lacking, to say the least." Winston replied. Jack became a little uneasy. This man, whom he did not know, continued to speak to him in as if he knew him. "You walked in here thinking I was off guard and put out by this environment, but I kind of surprised you by showing knowledge of you, didn't I?" Winston said while wearing a wry smile.

Jack calmly took a seat across from him. "You seem to be in a talkative mood. Let's start with you telling me how you know who I am."

Winston straightened in his seat. "I have heard about you for years, Jack. You are almost a pinup model in my ranks."

Winston smirked as Jack looked at him in confusion. "It is nice to know I have garnered so much attention. The question is how I pulled that feat off." Jack eased back in his seat and crossed his arms on his chest.

"Well, you have an admirer who has been watching you for a long time. He is, let's say, a genius with a bit of a vengeful streak."

Jack thought that he needed to feed his pretentiousness. "Are you close with this admirer of mine?"

"Oh, you can say I am on a first name basis with him," Winston said.

"Would you mind sharing that name with me?" Jack asked.

"All in due time. I haven't anywhere else to be. Besides, Jack, we need to get to know each other better. I need to know if I can trust you. Because I do not think I can go back home."

Jack felt an odd sense of admiration toward the man for accepting his fate. "So you are going to tell me all about Mr. Stansby. Is he this genius you are proclaiming?" Jack was pushing this a little hard, but to have a man in front of him talking was almost irresistible.

"I said, Jack, all in due time. I promise I have a story to tell that you will be interested in. First, though, there is the issue of mutual trust I was talking about."

Jack thought this might be a very long night, so he asked Winston if he wanted some coffee. He agreed and Jack motioned to the camera. "What would you like in return for this information—maybe immunity?"

Winston smiled and leaned forward slightly. "Yes, let's start with that. Immunity from the crimes I have been immersed in. I am sure your DA is cooking that up right now."

Jack nodded his head. Winston folded his arms as Jack said, "How would we know the information is good enough for that?"

"Well, Jack, there is, of course, the issue of guns. You have in custody a very small fish, but a small fish with a lot of knowledge."

Jack was interested, but he did not want to give in too quickly. "I think calling you a small fish is a bit of an understatement."

Winston picked up his coffee and took a sip. "What if I tell you this is a multinational operation with some very interesting players involved."

Jack wasn't surprised by this. They already knew of the Russian involvement. "There is more to this than Russian influence too."

Jack was fishing in deep waters at this point. This interrogation was somehow leading to a multinational crime syndicate. Jack heard a knock on the window and stood up as Winston smiled.

"Your masters are calling you," Winston commented. "Take your time; I am sure there is a lot for you to discuss." Jack held his tongue and walked out.

"What are you stopping this for?"

Danny put his arms up to signal Jack to calm down. "We must get the DA here and possibly a deputy US attorney. I believe we may be in over our heads."

Jack didn't want to do this. He wanted to go in and push forward. "Well, why don't we get the DA down here and let him listen in. Then he can make the call." Danny agreed to this and made the call to the DA

While they were waiting, Jack decided to go and check on Stacy. He walked down the hall and up a set of stairs. He came to a very pleasant-looking room with a full set of living-room furniture and a big-screen television. Stacy was sitting on a love seat watching reruns of her favorite soap opera.

"I was going to ask if you were comfortable, but it looks like you have made yourself at home," Jack said, noticing her face turning a little red.

"I can't help it. I just love cheesy romance. Besides, there is nothing else on but sports." She took the remote and paused the show. "Come and sit. Let's talk a bit." She scooted to one side of the love seat. Jack was a little hesitant, but he decided to oblige her. "How is the interrogation with that man going?" she asked.

"It is going well, but I wanted to see how you are doing?"

She motioned to the television. "This has been therapeutic. I am not in danger. And I am not on the run, so this is enjoyable. I hope that this can come to an end soon." She laid her head on Jack's shoulder after her comment. "This feels good. You make me feel safe, Jack."

Jack felt butterflies in his belly, but he was still hesitant. "Yes, it does, and I hope you do feel safe around me. I really want you to feel that way. I also want you to know that I will do everything in my power to keep you safe." Before Jack could start his next sentence, he felt her lips on his. He returned her show of affection.

"Wow, that was good, Jack. You are a good kisser." Jack felt hot all over, and he felt himself wanting to kiss her again.

"Jack, hey, Jack." He heard Danny calling from the other room.

"Yeah, I am coming," he shouted back. "Looks like I am needed in there. Can we talk more after we finish?" Jack really did not want to leave at this point, but he was compelled by the thought of getting a full confession from Winston.

"Yes, I would like that," Stacy replied. He got up from the love seat and walked back.

When Jack entered the room, he noticed a well-dressed man in an expensively tailored suit sitting at the table with Danny. "Jack, this is Brian Tolbert. He is the District Attorney."

Brian stood and shook Jack's hand. "I understand there is some informant here that has some major news for us."

Jack thought, *This man is behind the eight ball*. "The man we have is not just an informant, but he is a mid-level player in a major crime syndicate. We caught him in possession of weapons that were stolen from the armory." Brian's face lit up.

"Well, I figure since I am here, he is wanting some kind of immunity deal?"

Jack put his hands on the table. "Yes, he does want immunity. We think that if he gets his immunity, he may lead us to the major players." Jack could tell that this man was almost hooked. "I think that when you hear his story and think of the headlines this prosecution could give you, you will be onboard," Jack said, coaxing the man.

"Well, you don't have to sell it any further. Who are the people he is going to lead us to?"

Jack knew he had him hooked. "One of the men is Oliver Stansby. He is an Australian immigrant who has been masquerading as a multinational businessman." Brian moved back a little and had a concerned look on his face.

"Do you mean the Oliver Stansby who has donated thousands to the Atlanta police department? The same Oliver Stansby who rubs elbows with the mayor himself?" Jack was caught off guard by this comment.

Before he could speak Danny replied, "What better cover than to put yourself in the lap of the political elite? I know he has a lot of friends in high places, but he is a big fish." Jack watched as the wheels in Brian's mind seemed to be turning so fast that he had to wait for a second to respond. "If this man can give us credible information and if I can act on it, the deal for immunity is approved." Jack nodded, got up, and walked toward the room where Oliver was being held.

"Well, if it isn't the man of the hour!" Jack exclaimed.

Winston smiled. "Did you get the deal for my immunity?"

Jack sat in the chair across from him. "It was hard, Winston, but I think I persuaded the DA to your terms." Jack noticed it for the first time. When Winston heard the response, his left eye opened just a bit wider. It was a tell—something Jack had learned to look for over his years of interrogations.

"That is good, Jack. I really appreciate your efforts. I think I can give you a little nugget. Stansby, as I told you earlier, has had his eye on you for a while."

Jack was taken off guard. *Why would he want to reveal this so quickly?* Jack wondered if this was part of Stansby's game or something real. "Yes, you mentioned that, but why?"

Winston looked like a kid who just couldn't hold his secret any longer. "He wouldn't give many details, but it had something to do with an investigation many years ago. You interrupted his plan. You noticed him too close to a crime scene in which he was involved. Apparently, you cut it short because he was looking at another member of that family to attack also. One thing you will find out about him is that he hates intrusive people. No, the right response is becoming obsessed with people who stand up to him or interrupt his desires."

Jack watched as Winston grinned, knowing he had sucked Jack into this well-weaved story. "You make it sound like he is Geppetto, pulling the strings of all the people of Atlanta," Jack said.

"You are going to be surprised when you hear whose strings he is pulling, but I must see this agreement before I go any further." Winston put his hand to his lip and motioned like he was zipping them.

There were several minutes of awkward silence, and then Danny entered the room with the agreement for immunity. Winston took a few minutes to read the paper and then signed it.

"All right, let us get this party started. Let's start with the organization," Danny stated as he took a seat.

"Well, it is going to take some explaining and some imagination on your part. But it is an interesting web of money, guns, human trafficking, and to top it off, maybe espionage." Winston was really becoming a Chatty Cathy.

"You do not need to spin tall webs, Winston. I know there is a multinational crime consortium, but espionage is a bit far. Let's start with the local stuff first," Jack stated with a smile on his face.

"All right. It will take some time, but you will see," Winston replied. Winston started to sing like a canary. He told the two agents how he had met Oliver Stansby and how he had become part of his organization. He gave them details of the street-level criminals who were under his control. Winston was part of several heists of government weapons from supposed secret and not-so-secret storage facilities.

Danny kept pumping him for any and every detail that he could give him. Jack was waiting patiently for a moment when he would lead him to an opening—an opening that would shed light on why and how he was part of Stansby's list of people to terrorize. After all, this sordid affair had been going on for several years. It had led to many murders and he and Steve being shot. There were also the Evans and Rygaard families, who had suffered untold misery at the loss of their loved ones. He even thought about Justice, even though he was a conman and small-time crook. He replayed the images of pain that were on the faces at the funerals he had attended.

"Then there is the money, and I am talking about billions that this organization controls."

Jack tuned back in when Winston stated this. "Well, that is how we can track it all. Let's talk about that for a while," Jack said intently.

He heard a knock and watched the door as a man walked in with a cup of coffee. "This is for Winston to keep him going." Danny took the coffee and handed it to Winston.

"Good. I always need caffeine to keep me going." Winston took a sip. "Wow, this is the good stuff—not like that mud you gave me earlier, Jack."

"Tell us about the money," Danny said impatiently.

"Yes. The root of all kinds of evil. Well, the money is given to a middleman, who takes it and launders it. From what I understand, it is an elaborate undertaking. Of course, my shop takes in $30-$40,000 a month for that purpose. But there are numerous businesses across this state that are owned for that purpose." Winston paused a second and cleared his throat. "Excuse me. There is also some money being laundered in Western Europe, but I do not know much about that."

"Can you give us the name of the money guy?" Jack asked.

Winston nodded. "You know him, Jack. You worked for his father. His name is Tom Rygaard. He is Stansby's main financial guy." Winston coughed and tried to clear his throat, but he coughed again.

"You, okay?" Danny asked.

"I am sorry it has been a long day." Winston coughed again, then stood up. His face started turning a dark shade of red. He took two steps to the side and reached out for Danny. Jack watched in astonishment.

"Winston, are you all right?" Jack asked knowing something was wrong. Winston fell to the ground, reaching for his throat and struggling to breathe. Danny called out for help. Jack went to the man and loosened his shirt collar. Winston tried to speak, but he was struggling so much to breathe that he couldn't.

"Jack, be careful. I think he was poisoned!" Danny said.

By the time the emergency medical technicians arrived at the building, Winston was long dead. Jack and Danny sat at a table in disbelief. They were joined by the district attorney.

"Who handed you the coffee, Danny?" Jack asked in a low voice.

"I thought it was one of the new guys. I never dreamed someone could penetrate the security we had in place. I should have known. I should have known." Danny shook his head and placed his face in his hands.

"Have we locked the building down?" Jack asked.

"Yes, we have, and we've swept it also. There is no sign of the guy who brought the coffee in," Danny replied.

"We have a mole. There is someone who has turned this into a fiasco. Do we have an idea who that may be?" Jack asked.

"Not now, but we are investigating. We will catch the person responsible," Danny said in frustration.

"The person responsible is Stansby, and we must get him, Danny. He thinks he is above the law. What about Captain Smith? I know he was involved. He was bought and paid for," Jack said with a raised voice.

"Jack, we know. We are on the same team here. Let's take a deep breath and figure it out."

Jack stared at him, knowing he was just pulling the reins slightly. "I know, Danny. I know. We must end this and put them all in a cell." Jack walked to a window and looked out.

Danny walked over and put his hand on Jack's shoulder. "You have been one of the most levelheaded investigators I have ever known. Please let's just not turn on each other. I have a thought on who the rat is. I have my guys going over that. I will go and talk with Brian. Hopefully with the video, we can cause some damage."

Jack took a deep breath. "You are right. We are a team. Let's go find Brian, and then we can figure this out together." The two men left in search of the district attorney.

"Where do we go from here?" Jack asked when they found Brian sitting in a chair outside of the interrogation room where Winston had been poisoned.

"We have the footage from Winston. There is a chance we can take all that information and make a case against Stansby's organization," Brian responded.

"Yes, we can, but the only road to Stansby now is Tom Rygaard. We need to go after Rygaard," Jack said with conviction.

"Well, if you want to kill a snake you have to cut its head off," Brian responded in a quiet tone.

"So we will work the details out and get it done," Danny responded.

Jack got up and walked down the hall. Thankfully, Stacy was safe. She knew that something bad had happened from all the activity and the general somber mood of all the people around her. Jack entered her room and sat down.

"You all right, Jack?"

As Jack listened to her soft voice, he found it oddly soothing. "The most important thing at this moment is that you are safe," Jack said as he smiled at her. She walked toward him, and he stood. She gave him a hug. "Thank you for being patient. I know it is hard to wait with everything that has happened," Jack told her. He felt closer to her than before. Then he thought that it was not the time to let his thoughts go down this path. Too much was happening, and he wanted to make sure that lines weren't getting blurred due to the danger of the situation and the emotion tied to it.

TWENTY-TWO

Oliver Stansby stood in his town house, watching a spider that had spun a web. A fly was buzzing around the web as if something about it was drawing it in. He watched as the fly flew into it and suddenly found itself trapped. The fly struggled and struggled, but the spider web was too strong. As if to further horrify the fly, the spider slowly walked down the web, repairing tiny strands as it moved toward the helpless insect. When the fly had gotten to the point where it could not struggle anymore, the spider pounced on it, piercing its helpless body with its fangs and finally putting it out of its misery.

Oliver thought, *I am the spider, and all who stand against me will end up playing the role of the helpless fly.* "You did good, Smith," Oliver said.

The man standing behind him smiled when he heard the compliment. "Thank you. Your leadership and planning make it easy." The man walked to Oliver's side. He was wearing his captain's uniform with the Atlanta police department's insignia on it and his midway cap tucked on his left side.

"Smith, one of the best moves I have made was partnering with you in these endeavors. How did you plant the man in the bureau's safe house?" Smith took a puff on his expensive Cuban cigar.

"Once you alerted me, I knew that they would go after Winston. I had a man on the team they used to arrest him. From there, he arranged to have our assassin in the building, and he slipped poison in the coffee he drank." Oliver turned and motioned for the man to sit. Smith walked to a chair and did as was requested. "I need to step things up to a faster pace, Smith. We need to move the operation to our new location. Can you promise to contain this issue with the GBI?" Oliver then took a puff off his cigar.

"We can maneuver them in such a way that your plan will be safe," Smith replied confidently.

"What about Jack Blackmon? I want his head." Oliver's cheek turned a shade of red.

"Sir, why can't we just bypass him like with the GBI?"

Oliver quickly rose from his chair and walked toward Smith, who seemed to lose his confidence as a long finger pointed in his face. "I do not need your suggestions. I need you to do what you are told. I said I want Blackmon's head, and you will give it to me!" Oliver watched as Smith slumped and cowered down to him.

"Sir, if you want him, I will get him for you. I just want us to be careful. These are perilous times, and the others seem to be questioning things."

Oliver knew the man was trying to divert his anger. "The other questions will be answered soon enough. Now go and get me what I desire." After those marching orders were handed out, Smith quickly stood up and hustled out of the room.

Stansby walked to his window and peered out. He smiled. He looked at a beautiful house where a tedious gardener had lived. After some masked men broke into the woman's house and threatened to kill her and her family, she decided that it was best to move. Now, Stansby owned the property. He bought it for pennies on the dollar. He thought that he would enjoy the view after he flattened it and bulldozed the garden.

||||||||||||||||||||||||||||||||

Jack was sitting and thinking over the events that had just occurred. Winston had lost his life after his arrest. Fortunately, they were able to question him and get information about the lower levels of Stansby's organization. He gave them information about the weapons and other pieces of the intricate organization. But Jack was focused on what

Winston had told him about Stansby's obsession with his demise. *What is the next move?* he thought.

"Jack, come with me. The DA wants to talk with us." Danny was in the room, and Jack did not even realize it.

"I have got to get better, Danny. This man is running circles around me. Every time I think we are making some headway, the rug gets snatched out from under us." Jack stood and rubbed his head.

"I know how you feel, Jack, but let's go in and discuss this with Brian. I think he has a sound idea." The two men walked into a semi-arranged conference room where Brian was ruminating.

"Well, I have more than enough to start an investigation into the smaller-level guys. It could take me months to build a strong case against Stansby, but for some reason, I don't think I will ever get what I want if I pursue the case that way." Jack watched as the man looked crestfallen. He was an ambitious lawyer who realized that a golden goose had been lying in his lap and then had suddenly been taken away.

"I want the top guys, and I want Stansby. I have some friends on the federal level. I took the liberty of calling them and calling in some favors. Since 9/11 there have been some new laws that may help us infiltrate the banking system and see where all the money is being transferred to and laundered. All we need is a direction." Jack wished he could simply kick the man's door in and put him in cuffs. The financial crime direction had been effective in the past though. In fact, Al Capone served his time for tax evasion.

"It is quite simple, guys. You will always know who a person is and what a person is up to by looking at the money trail. We need to follow the trail," Brian said.

"It just so happens that the firm that handles the money is based in a place that Jack knows well." Jack looked at Danny as he told Brian this information.

"Yes, I was hired by Thomas Rygaard to solve the murder of his daughter. I could use that. Stansby hired a conman to trick and then kill her. I think if Thomas understood that, he would help us." Jack's mind started racing. "We will need to head back that way. We will also need to make some arrangements for Stacy. She needs to be kept safe."

Jack could feel Danny staring at him as if he was a cheap palm reader. It seemed the man knew what he was thinking. "Jack, I know you have developed feelings for her. I promise she will be safe. I will make sure of it. You need to focus on the case. I want to take Stacy somewhere no one will ever think to find her. I have a family cabin off the coast. It is on a small, quiet island. I can take her there and watch her myself. In fact, I think she is an important piece for us. At least, I think she is. Why else would these people go to such lengths to try to kidnap her?"

Jack wanted to be the one with his eyes on the woman, but he knew that Danny was right, so he relented. "You are right, Danny. Please take care of her. I do not think I can take too much more loss in my life. Give me some time to let her know."

Jack's friend smiled. "Go ahead. I will get everything set."

Jack went in, and Stacy ran to him and grabbed his hands. "What is the next move?" she asked.

Jack looked into her eyes, noticing how they sparkled like diamonds reflecting the sunlight. "I wish I could say that we could go somewhere quiet, sit down, and talk about us—"

"We can, Jack. We can simply leave now and be far from here in a matter of hours."

Jack put his finger to her lips and put his head on hers. "I wish it were that simple, and I do want that so bad, but I must end this. This man I am after will never let this end until either he or I comes out on top. Neither you nor anyone else around me will be safe until that happens."

Stacy gave him a hug. "Is this truly the only way this madness will end?"

Jack squeezed her tight in his embrace. "It is, Stacy. Danny is going to take you someplace safe and watch you until then. He is one of only a handful of people I trust with everything. Please go with him without argument, and when this is over, I will come to you."

She returned to his deep embrace and then kissed him. "Please,

Jack, be careful and come back for me," she said warmly. Something inside Jack changed when he heard those words. He felt like a butterfly that had just escaped the cocoon. His struggle started to seem worth the effort.

"Jack, I hate to pull you away, but can I speak with you a minute?" Jack looked over and saw his friend standing in the doorway.

"Sure, Danny." Jack walked out of the room to talk with him.

"Jack, I wanted to call James and talk with him before we left. I feel like it is easier for us to listen together." Jack nodded in agreement as Danny made the call.

"Hey, Danny," Jack heard him say over speakerphone.

"Hey, James. I am here with Jack and wanted to get an update about anything you may have stumbled onto." Jack was anxious to get back to Stacy, but Danny tapped him on the shoulder and pointed to the phone.

"I have had an interesting conversation with Thomas Rygaard. It seems he knew the county owned the safe house. He was involved with the sale of it to the county and overheard the sheriff at an event talking about the house. He came to me and let me know that his son Tom had that information also."

Jack's ears perked at this information. "Tom knew of the safe house? What about anyone from the department? Did you find any link to a staff member?" Jack asked.

"Thomas told me know about his son knowing because he was scared for him. There is no link to any staff member."

"Why would he be scared for Tom?" Jack asked, thinking of the information that had been shared earlier by Winston before his untimely demise.

"That is the million-dollar question. Turns out that Tom has been courting Oliver Stansby and has been involved with his business—you know, managing the money," James replied.

Jack looked at Danny. "James, that has confirmed something that was brought to our attention up here. Usually when two sources of information agree, it's believable. I think at this time, Thomas should be fearful for his son because usually where there is smoke, there is fire. We need to talk with him about these new developments. Keep working things down that way. I will be down there soon. It has become clear that we need to focus on the Rygaards," Jack stated.

"I am going to take Stacy and perform a witness protection mission. I am taking her to a secret location and keeping her out of sight until we know that she is going to be safe. You guys be careful," Danny said as Jack looked over his shoulder and into the room where he had left her.

"I am like a dog with a bone; I will keep working. Danny, be safe. Jack, see you when you get here." Jack heard Danny thanking James, and then he ended the call.

"Danny, this is solid. Tom will be the key to the door that opens on Stansby and his organization."

Danny shook Jack's hand. "You use James; he is solid. I will take Stacy and watch over her. Do not let your mind wander from the case. We will not have any more chances. We must have Tom and his knowledge. Now go tell Stacy goodbye and get started." Jack did just that.

Steve was home eating a bologna sandwich and trying to ease his conscience after the shooting. Cheap food seemed to be the salve to coat his emotional pain. He had tried alcohol when he was a teenager and had decided that if he was going to be sick the following day, it needed to be from something he enjoyed. He noted that alcohol was not something that made the list.

Steve heard a knock on the door. He grabbed his sidearm just in case it was a wolf knocking on his door. He peeped through the hole in the door and saw that it was James. He opened it and greeted him. "You come here to interrogate me again?" Steve said wryly.

"No, I came to tell you that I figured out who gave up the safe house. I also want you to know what the plan is from this point on and ask for your help," James responded.

Steve waved him to a chair in his living room, noticing that he needed a maid. His house looked like a hurricane had made its way through it. The two men sat and talked over all that had transpired.

"You mean Tom found out from his father and he told the location? That is good to know. I was so worried it was going to be one of the staff who wanted to put a few dollars in their pocket," Steve said as he worked the soreness out of his leg.

"I know this has been tough on you. We want you to know that you are still part of the team, and we want you to be involved. You deserve the chance to help bring this crew down." Steve looked at James and nodded in appreciation of his comment. "Jack is a good man and a better detective. If he needs me, I will be by his side," Steve said with conviction.

"How well do you know the Rygaards, especially the son? Is there something that you can tell me before we start this?" James asked.

"I tell you what, let me think a bit and get some rest. When Jack arrives, I will tell you both what I know," Steve said.

"That sounds fair. Get some rest, and we will do that." James got up, shook Steve's hand, and then left.

||||||||||||||||||||||||||||||||||

Jack was on I-75 headed back to the place where this had all begun for him. He was tired; he felt worn down. There was also a feeling of excitement in knowing that through all of this, he had found Stacy. The thought of finishing this because it affected her negatively drove him now. It was late, and as much as he wanted to drive straight on to Moultrie, he knew he needed some rest. He pulled into the parking lot of a Best Western hotel. He rented a room and went inside. As soon as he entered, he crashed onto the bed and fell into a deep sleep.

"Clickety-clack." Jack heard a noise. *What is this? Is someone trying to break in?* He reached for his gun, but he felt something wet. *What?* He noticed the red-tinged color on his fingers. He stood and then he heard the noise again. It was coming from the closet. His heart was pounding. *This isn't right.* Jack noticed his eyes wouldn't focus. He wondered if he had been poisoned like Winston. *This just isn't right,* he thought. "Clickety-clack." There was the noise again. He looked, but he couldn't see where the blood had come from. He walked over to the closet and reached for the handle. He pulled the door open, and to his surprise, he looked into his own eyes. His hands were tied together, and he had bruising on his head. He reached for the figure that resembled him. Then he had a strange feeling of falling.

Jack awakened with sweat pouring off him. These nightmares were getting worse and more personal. He was still tired as if he had never slept. The case and the misery all around him were taking a toll. He knew that he had to end this matter. He remembered the conversation that he had had with Marvin, the preacher who tried to counsel him. Then he had a strange feeling. It seemed as if a small voice was inside his consciousness trying to tell him something. *What is it trying to tell me?* He listened quietly. Then he shook his head and thought, *These dreams really are driving me to a breaking point.* He looked at the clock on the bedside table and noted that it showed 6:00 a.m. It was time to go. He got up and showered. As he walked by the closet door, he peered at it and then shook his head. *I have to get a hold of myself,* he thought. Then he walked out and got into his car.

TWENTY-THREE

Stacy found herself riding a ferry to Cumberland Island. *It is very beautiful,* Stacy thought. The birds were flying across a scenic blue sky, and the smell of the salt water lowered her stress level. "How did you manage to have a house in such a beautiful place?" Stacy asked as she looked over at Danny.

"I come from a long line of island dwellers. The house has been in the family for ages. The best part is that if anyone comes here to cause trouble, I will know about it long beforehand." Danny looked around and felt that this was the right decision. He could keep Stacy safe, and Jack could finish his work.

When the ferry finally arrived at their destination, Stacy found herself in a small but well-kept cottage. It was located on the beach and was surrounded by small hills and a few trees. She thought it odd that there were not many houses around the area, but she liked the calmness. She watched as Danny left to walk the property. She was a bit unsettled at him doing this, but she felt safer on the secluded island.

Danny finished putting out the cameras and went back to the cottage to check on Stacy. When he walked in, he found her kneeling on a rug by the couch and praying. When he closed the door, she gasped and jumped.

"Sorry I did not mean to scare you. I just finished with some last-minute security and wanted to make sure you were OK."

Stacy had her hand to her chest, and her eyes were wide. She took a deep breath and smiled. "Sorry, but with all that has happened, I am a bit on edge."

Danny walked to the kitchen and poured them both a glass of sweet tea. "I am sure you are nervous. I would be too in your situation. I wanted you to know that if something happens, there is a secret location in the house." Danny walked to the south side of the living room and pulled a book away from the shelf. When he did this, an area on the wall popped open, and there was a small entrance to a tiny one-person safe room.

"Wow, we are really getting James Bondsy now. What in the world is that?" Stacy walked over and looked in.

Danny walked over beside her. "Well, if you really want to know, my mother worked for an unnamed spy agency, and she built this room for me when I was young. It was to keep me safe in case something went wrong at her job. If you ever feel threatened, pull the lever, go inside, and wait. When everything is cleared, I will come for you." Danny closed the opening, walked back, and sat on the couch. Stacy followed suit and sat down in a comfy chair. "I want to ask you something, but I do not want you to get offended," Danny said to Stacy.

"You are keeping me safe, so do not be afraid to ask me anything," Stacy replied.

"When I walked in earlier, I saw you praying. Are you a religious person?" Danny had not been around someone who prayed before, and he was curious.

"When I was younger, my family went to church, and my father would tell me about Jesus and praying. I was too young to really understand such things. Now that I am older and especially with everything that has happened, I thought I would ask Him to show me the path for my life. I do not know if it is the correct way, but I do know what my earthly father showed me. My hope is that there will be a response from our heavenly Father," she stated as Danny nodded his head with some understanding.

"I really appreciate your faith. It has been hard for a man like me to even consider such thoughts. I hope you find the answers you are looking for."

Stacy smiled at what Danny had just said. "I only know that since I have started praying, there has been a calmness in my spirit that was not there before," Stacy said as she noticed Danny looking out the window.

"Well, the heavenly Father sure created a beautiful place when he created this island," Danny stated, looking back at Stacy and gesturing to the view. "Do you think there is some kind of afterlife—something that awaits us after our brief time on this earth is over?" Danny asked and then watched Stacy ponder his question.

"I do know there is life after death. Just look at a tree that has been chopped down. You think it is dead, but soon after, life springs out of it. You see a new sprout coming up from the dead wood," Stacy stated.

"Maybe I need to find someone to talk with about my questions. A preacher or something," Danny said.

"I think we both do. When this is all over, maybe we can talk with a guy I know. His name is Marvin."

Jack arrived in Moultrie after his long night and another nightmare. He parked his car in the lot at the sheriff's office. He was still feeling tired and worn down, but he needed to push forward. Jack called his friend Steve to check on him.

"Hello, Jack, it is nice to hear from you." Steve answered.

"It is nice to hear from you too, friend. How are you feeling?" Jack asked.

"I am rip-roaring and ready to go. James stopped by last night, let me know what was going on, and asked for my help."

Jack was glad to hear his response. He was also glad that James was so motivated to help. "You better believe we need your help, especially me. I seem to be on a losing streak, and having someone like you can only help."

Steve's voice perked up. Jack knew he had been in a funk ever since the shooting and hoped this would help him. "Let me call James and we can all meet up at my house," Steve said.

"That sounds good. We need to sit down and develop a good plan of action. We need to take advantage of this opportunity because it may be the last good one we ever get," Jack told him. Jack's mind started racing over the way they should approach the Rygaards. Jack had worked for Thomas and knew him to be a decent man, but after the information they had learned about his son Tom, he understood that he was not like his father. He knew Tom was the point man for his father's company in dealing with Stansby. He assumed Oliver's influence had swayed the young man. *Is this simply a business relationship? Or has Stansby sucked young Tom into his fold?* Only time would tell. He put the car in reverse, backed out of the parking lot, and headed to meet his partners.

When Jack pulled into Steve's driveway, he noticed that James had already arrived. He got out and was greeted at the door by Steve. Jack smiled. He was glad to see that his friend was looking better. "How are you, my friend?" Jack asked.

"I am good, but you look rough, buddy. This case is wearing on you bad, isn't it?" he asked.

"Yes, it is. We need to stop this man," Jack said intently.

"Well, you are with the A-Team now, so hold on to your hat because we are going to put a hurting on them," Steve remarked as Jack grinned a little.

"I like your fire, Steve. You seem reinvigorated."

"You know, it sometimes takes a horrible event to help you realize that you have a purpose and that the purpose is the reason you are alive. If that doesn't motivate you, there is no helping you." Jack nodded at Steve's epiphany. The two then walked into the house.

"Jack, you are looking rough. You look like you need a good eight hours of sleep," James said to him.

"That is what everyone seems to be saying to me these days. What I really need is a plan that will get Tom Rygaard to tell us where Stansby's money is located. Then we need to find out how to follow the money-laundering trail," Jack replied.

"I think that if we approached his father and put pressure on him about the trouble his son could be potentially in, it would persuade him to help us. After all, by now, he knows we are investigating Stansby. He has also lost his wife and daughter. Hopefully, he will see it best to tell us all he knows to save his son. I do not think he will want to even take a chance of losing another member of his family," James said.

"If it were me and if I were in his position, I would do whatever it took to see that he was safe. Oliver Stansby, from what we have seen, is a very cold and calculating man. Once we show Thomas that, I think he will persuade his son," Jack said, more hopeful than realistic.

"If not, we can beat it out of him," Steve said with a smirk.

"Man, someone has been feeding you gunpowder for breakfast," Jack said jokingly.

"Someone filled both of us with gunpowder, you mean," Steve shot back.

"All right, guys, let's get serious and get down to business. How are we going to approach this man?" James said snippily. He was trying to get them focused on the matter at hand.

"I think Steve and I will go pay him a visit. It will be under the premise of following up on his daughter. When we get into the details, we will bring up the matter of Tom helping Stansby invest his money," Jack replied.

"That sounds smart, Jack. Put him on edge and then bring it all back to Tom. Then the money trail," James said and then looked at Steve. "You going to be all right?"

Steve looked at him with a steely gaze. "Don't worry about me; I will be ready for anything," Steve said as he watched Jack pick up the phone and call Thomas Rygaard. The meeting was confirmed for later that afternoon at Thomas's house.

"Why don't we stop by the café and grab a bite to eat, Jack?" Steve asked.

"What about it, James? Do you want to grab a bite with us?"

James shook his head. "You two seem to be the type who can eat anytime, but my stomach gets twisted. I think I am going to stop by and talk with Sheriff Jackson. I will prepare him in case he gets a call from Thomas."

<hr />

When Jack walked into the café, he realized it was the first time they had been back to the place since Johnny had fired shots at Steve. Jack realized his flesh was like goose skin. He walked in, spotting a booth near the back. A new waitress came over and took their drink order. She came back with some sweet tea and took their order. Jack nervously kept up the small talk, trying to avoid serious conversation about all they had been through and the struggles he knew Steve was having after the shooting. Then just as they started to relax a little, Jack saw the preacher, Marvin. He had not wanted to meet him this soon after their last conversation. The man looked around and headed their way. Jack suddenly became uncomfortable.

"Hey guys. How has everything been going?" Marvin asked.

"Preacher," Steve stated in greeting, "it has been going."

"Do you mind if I sit and visit with you both a little while?" Marvin asked.

Jack really did not want to let him sit down because he did not want to face the questions he knew were about to be asked. But he was a little curious about how the man would answer them. "Sure. Come and sit for a while," Jack said as he slid over.

"What did you guys order?" Jack knew Marvin was trying to be inconspicuous with where he wanted to take this conversation.

"I ordered the catfish, and Jack got the burger," Steve answered.

"Well, the burger will not swim in my stomach all afternoon, so I think I will get that." Marvin ordered when the waitress returned. "I am not a person who is shy, so I will just ask. How are you two doing after everything that has gone on?" Marvin asked bluntly.

"Well, you don't beat around the bush, do you?" Jack asked.

"No, I am pretty steadfast in what I do, just like the both of you." Steve looked confused. Jack looked at Marvin and knew he was reading Steve like a book. "Anna Lee mentioned the conversation you two had in the hospital, Steve. Jack and I had a similar conversation a little bit ago. So I want to follow up with both of you about those questions." Jack glanced at his friend and realized they both needed to hear what Marvin had to say.

"OK, my question is this: Why does God allow so much suffering in this world if He created it?" Steve blurted out quickly.

"Wow, you are kind of quick to the point also," Marvin replied. "OK, I will grant that there is a lot of suffering in the world. That goes back to Adam and Eve and their sin in the garden. Then—"

"I understand that, but do we suffer for acting like humans?" Before Marvin could go any further, Steve had cut him off.

Marvin put his hands up to try and slow him down. "All right, let me say this. Do you know God's plan deals with suffering. He sent Jesus to take our eternal punishment for us, not to take away the sin but the punishment for the sin. It was prophesied in Isaiah 53. He even called him the suffering Servant."

"Can you explain that in more detail?" Jack asked.

"Yes, I can. God created us, and He knows our, as you call it, human nature. God calls that sin. He is so holy He cannot be around sin, so He needed a way to take the sin from us. That is where Jesus comes in. He was born of a virgin, sinless, falsely accused, beaten, and hung on a cross. Our sins were placed upon Him. Then He died, was buried, and was resurrected on the third day. With all of that, he conquered sin and its effect, which is death." Marvin paused then took a breath.

"Wow, that is a lot to take in, but what does it mean for us here and now?" Jack asked next.

"It means that He loves us. He wants a relationship with us. He wants us to come to Him and ask Him for forgiveness so that He can then start working in and through us to make us what He intended us to be all along—His children," Marvin explained.

"So He wants to be a father to us?" Steve asked doubtfully.

"In a sense, yes. He created us with a hole in our heart that only He can fill. He created us to want Him like an earthly father wants his children to come to him. He wants us to seek the relationship like little children seek the love of their father," Marvin said.

"But to use suffering to draw that out of us is sadistic, isn't it?" Steve said passionately.

"We suffer because of our choices. You are affected by someone else's choices, whether you like it or not, and others are affected by your choices, whether you like it or not. You need to realize that your choices are influenced by the sin you and others commit. When you read the scriptures, you see that because of Jesus's choices, storms are calmed like when He walked on the water to His disciples, who were in a small boat in the sea during a sudden storm. They got very frightened and called out to Him for help. He commanded calm, the weather cleared, and He stepped into the boat," Marvin stated.

"I just cannot make that leap right now. There is so much to unpack in those statements; it will take a lot of time to figure out. I feel like I have been a punching bag for so long," Jack told Marvin.

"Yes, it is a lot to think about, Jack. I also have watched and heard some of what you have had to live through. So please just do that. Please just think about it. In the meantime, I will be praying for you both." As Marvin finished his statement, the server brought their food out. "I tell you guys what; let's enjoy this meal and talk about whatever you choose. I will get the tab. Then if you need further answers, you can call me later, and we can then discuss this some more." Jack rubbed his head and looked at Steve, who was sitting in stunned silence. "I really hope and pray that God will use this situation to open your spiritual eyes," Marvin said as he watched the men pondering all that he unpacked for them.

TWENTY-FOUR

Jack and Steve were traveling to see Thomas Rygaard. Jack was driving as Steve was looking out the window and watching the clouds, deep in thought. Jack was pondering the conversation they had just finished and the one that was forthcoming with Thomas. "Jack, what do you think about Marvin?" Steve asked.

"I think he is a good man. But what you want to ask me is what do I think about what he said?" Jack looked at Steve with an eyebrow raised.

"You know me too well. So what did you think?"

Jack looked at Steve, looked back out the window, and took a deep breath. "I think that I like the idea of what he was saying. I've never had anyone explain it to me in the way he put it."

There were a few minutes of silence, and then Steve said, "I think I need the peace that Marvin shows in his life. Anna Lee, Tom Rygaard's girl, spoke in much the same way."

"You mean you spoke with her about this subject?" Jack asked.

"She caught me in a weak moment," Steve replied.

"I have been having those lately myself," Jack said as the silence returned.

When Jack turned into Thomas Rygaard's drive, he looked at the scenery—a manicured pasture and well-maintained fences. He also noticed some horses galloping inside those fences on the manicured pastureland. He had an overwhelming thought of how relaxing this beautiful place could be. He looked at the big yard and the big house and then thought about what this man had accomplished. He had worked so hard to acquire the finest possessions of this world.

Then he thought about how miserable his life must be. His wife had passed away, his daughter had been murdered, and they were in business with a man who was a criminal. *How could things have gotten so offtrack?* Jack asked himself. Then he thought about his own life and all its twists and turns. Hopefully, they would lead to a better place and outcome than the misery he had watched Thomas Rygaard go through.

"I hope you are ready for this, Steve," Jack stated.

"I do not think anybody could ever be ready for this," Steve said sharply.

The two got out of the car and walked up to ring the bell, but before they could, the butler opened the door and beckoned them in. This caught Jack off guard, and he became unnerved. It was as if he were heading into the belly of the beast, and the beast was prepared. The butler showed them to the study and told them that the master of the house would see them shortly. Jack looked at the fine woodwork that some master craftsman had created—handcrafted tables, built-in shelves, and expensive leather-clad furniture. It appeared that no effort had been wasted while creating a persona of elegance.

Thomas Rygaard walked in. He was looking more kempt and upbeat than the last time Jack had seen the man. His face was clean-shaven, and his clothes were pressed to perfection. *Thomas must have been like this before the tragic death of his daughter,* Jack thought.

"Hello, gentlemen." Thomas walked toward them and shook their hands. "It is good to see you, Jack. Steve, it looks like you are doing better after your incident. Please have a seat," he said as he motioned to two smaller wooden chairs.

"Thank you, Thomas. I am moving slowly, but I do feel better," Steve replied.

"Thomas, thank you for letting us meet with you. I know you are a busy man," Jack said cordially.

"No problem. What can I help you guys with?" Jack looked at

Steve and thought, *Here we go.* "Thomas, we need to address the circumstances around the death of Emily," Jack said cautiously.

Thomas looked at him, piercing him with his steely blue eyes. "But you caught the man who killed my daughter, Jack," he said sharply.

"Yes, technically he was the man who performed the actual act, but someone else was the mastermind. This man was ultimately responsible," Jack stated.

Then Thomas interjected, "Mastermind! This is not some Sherlock Holmes mystery. This is the death of my daughter at the hands of a very sadistic monster!" Thomas looked beet red, and he was starting to become unhinged.

"Thomas, I know this moment has caught you off guard, but you need to listen to us. We are not here to upset you further. We are here to bring a man to justice," Jack stated.

"Justice was served the day that man was killed!" Thomas angrily exclaimed.

"Johnny was the pawn used to do the actual act, but there was someone behind him who gave the order. He was ultimately responsible for your daughter's death and a lot of other heinous murders." Jack was trying to make him think instead of reacting with emotion.

"You have lost too much, Thomas, and we know that, but there are others out there who have lost people too. If you could stop that from happening again, wouldn't you want to do it?" Steve asked.

"You have no idea what I have lost. You think this is some grand conspiracy, but it is not. It was simply a soulless man who murdered a young girl, who was trying to deal with the pain of losing her mother. She was trying to scream for attention. It was a cry for help. Then he turned that into her death. He is gone now, so I am not interested in any further dip in this pool of shame." Jack watched as Thomas waved his hand as if to banish them but then turned to exit the room.

"I think you need to stop and think a minute, Thomas, because whether you want to bathe in this pool of shame or not, you are involved," Jack said with firmness. Thomas stared at him with his steely gaze. Jack knew he was not accustomed to someone being this blunt with him. Jack watched as he walked to his window and looked out for several seconds. He turned around, looked at Jack, walked back, and sat down.

"Like I said, there is a man at the head of this; let us say at the head of the snake. He has maneuvered people into spots like Johnny on other occasions. One of those happened in Atlanta years ago. I told you about that case when you hired me. He has used people to accomplish his means over and over—"

"Yes, but what does this have to do with me, here and now?"

Jack put his finger in the air. "It has everything to do with you, your business, and your son." Jack thought that Thomas was going to jump out of his seat and attack them when he said this, but then he noticed him take a deep breath.

"This has something to do with that Australian businessman, doesn't it?" Thomas asked almost with a whisper.

"Yes, it does, Thomas. Can you shed some light on anything you know about this man? How do you know he is Australian? What business ties does he have here in this state?" Steve asked.

"I have done the research on him. He seems to have done well in the import-export business. His business seems to be a sham though. I could not convince Tom he was a criminal, but that was the only thing that made sense to me," Thomas replied.

"We have done some research too. We know he invested a lot of money in your company," Jack said, fishing for a response.

"Yes, he has invested in us—against my better judgement. Tom had been spending time in Atlanta for years, and he met Stansby there. The man has a forked tongue, and my son became a little enamored with him. I told your friend James this already," Thomas said, shaking his head.

"Thomas, you know we are investigating Stansby. We know that he has a vast criminal network. This network runs on money. Your firm has dealings in investing and managing his money. We need access to these networks of money to figure out his ventures. Would you be willing to help us?" Jack asked.

"Well, Jack, if I do something like that, how would this affect my son and my business? I know that James already shared my apprehensions with you after our conversation the other night," Thomas said nervously.

"Thomas, I promise we will be fair to you and your son. If Tom has not done anything illegal and was just conducting the firm's usual business, we will not go after him. We want Stansby, and that is all," Jack answered, giving a reassuring look to Thomas.

"Jack, all I have left is my son. My business is of no consequence to me anymore," Thomas said as he put his head in his hands.

"I really can't even begin to understand your pain, Thomas, but there are other families that do know that pain. The man who should answer for that pain has a lot of money invested in your firm. So what do you say? Will you let us into his records?" Jack asked.

Thomas thought for a few seconds. "Jack, let me talk to my legal team about how this could affect Tom, and then I will decide," Thomas responded.

"Thomas, this is time sensitive, so please make this a quick decision before something else happens," Steve pleaded.

Thomas motioned for the butler to come in and show the two men out. They got up and shook Thomas's hand. They walked out and got into the car.

"Well, Steve, what do you think?" Jack asked as Steve shook his head.

"I do not know, Jack. I really could not read him. I know he loves his son. I just hope he realizes how dangerous Stansby could be."

Jack turned the wheel and pulled out of the drive. "I think we need to get ahold of the sheriff and start thinking about getting a warrant for the records," Jack said as Steve thought about that for a while.

"That would give Stansby too much of a warning, and he would be gone—like a shadow at noon," Steve said as Jack turned onto the road.

Jack and Steve called James and informed him of the conversation they had had with Thomas. They also told him of the plan to meet with Sheriff Jackson and to request a warrant for Thomas's business records.

"The sheriff is here with me. We have been discussing the way the safe house was infiltrated. He would like to meet with you, let's say in about thirty minutes at his office," James said. Jack agreed and headed that way.

Thomas was in his study, going over the conversation he had had with Steve and Jack. He played out scenarios in his mind, and he could not come up with any that would leave his son unscathed. He decided to investigate how deeply his son was involved and opened the computer files on Stansby's investments. After a little time of looking over the investments, he noticed several discrepancies. Tom was laundering money for this man. *How could his son do this?* He knew that Tom was too deep in this matter. Tom was way over his head, and he needed to talk to him. He needed to ask his son the reason and then hear for himself the answer his son would give. He picked up the phone and dialed Tom's number.

"Hello, Dad," Tom answered.

"Hey, Tom, are you home yet?" Thomas asked his son, knowing that he was supposed to have arrived home from a recent trip to New York.

"Yeah, Dad. I got home a few minutes ago. I am supposed to have supper with Anna Lee tonight, so I was trying to relax and get refreshed."

Thomas knew this was going to take some effort, but he wanted to confront this head on. "I need you to come over. There is something off with an account, and I need your assistance," Thomas told him.

"Could we handle this tomorrow?" he asked.

"No, son, we need to handle it today. The company's reputation depends on us figuring this out," Thomas said firmly.

"All right, I am heading over now," Tom said in a frustrated voice.

Jack walked into the sheriff's station and heard a lighthearted conversation taking place. It seemed the sheriff and James were both

Atlanta Falcons' fans and were consoling each other on the state of their affairs.

"Guys, let's get down to business," Jack said with a small smirk on his face. He had been a lifelong New England fan, and he took joy in their athletic afflictions.

"Sure, this mulling over football makes me want to go jump in a lake anyway," James answered.

"We had an interesting visit with Thomas Rygaard," Steve blurted out, not considering that Thomas was a big contributor to the sheriff's campaign.

Jack noticed the small wince that the sheriff's face made. "What Steve meant to say is that Thomas knows that Stansby is not the best of investors to have in his company," Jack hurriedly stated.

"Does he know that he is being investigated for the murders?" the sheriff inquired.

"Yes, we let him in on the crimes. We suggested that he might not want to be involved with that business. We also asked if he would let us peek into Stansby's investments. He was cautious about that idea," Jack said.

"Sheriff, what do you think would be a good course of action if he refuses to be gentlemanly, and he won't let us peek into his books?" James said.

"Well, Thomas has always been a by-the-book kind of guy, especially when it comes to his business. This situation, though, has far-reaching implications. If we present valid evidence to the district attorney, he may give us a warrant to search the records," he responded.

"I could have the DA from Atlanta place a call to him. He was there when Winston was poisoned and heard enough to start an inquiry into this matter," Jack said, floating a life raft to the sheriff.

"Now that would help us a great deal. Our local DA has not had a good run lately in trying the cases here. If he thought that he could endear himself to the Atlanta office, he would more than likely jump on the chance," the sheriff said with a little relief in his voice. Jack could see the team forming and growing closer. He knew this collection of men would be up to the challenge of taking down a major crime syndicate.

|||||||||||||||||||||||||||||||||||||||||

Thomas was at home awaiting his son's arrival. He had not left his study window since the visit from Jack. His butler had brought him some coffee and cookies, but he wasn't interested in food or drink. He wanted to find a way to unwind his son from any business dealings with Oliver Stansby.

"Hello, Father," Tom said when he had come alongside his father.

"Hey, Tom. How was your trip to Atlanta?" Thomas inquired of his son, trying to feel his young prodigy out. They sat down.

"It was productive. Business is good. Hopefully, we will continue to see the fruit of the efforts," Tom replied.

"How is Anna Lee? Everything going good with you two?" The impromptu inquiry continued.

"She is well, and things are going well. She makes me happy."

Thomas watched as Tom shifted in his chair. "Is everything OK? You seem to be a little more inquisitive than usual today." Thomas was really stalling. He was hesitant about approaching his son regarding what he had discussed with Jack and his sidekick.

"You mentioned there was something off with one of the accounts. What was so important that it couldn't wait until tomorrow?" Tom said as Thomas tried to watch his body language to judge his thoughts.

"Well, I was paid a visit this morning by Jack and his friend, the sheriff's deputy. They had some questions about our dealings with this Stansby account," Thomas said cautiously, knowing he had had disagreements with Tom about this same issue in the past.

"Stansby is a businessman, plain and simple. His money is no different than any other investor in our business," Tom said as he walked over and stood in front of the fire.

"They said that Stansby is being investigated for criminal acts, Son," Thomas said and then got up and stood beside his son.

"Criminal acts? This man came to this country with nothing, and he has built his wealth despite of his situation. He reminds me of you, Father," Tom proclaimed as his voice rose, and his body tensed.

"Son, I have looked at the investments, and it doesn't take much to see that this man is using this firm to launder money, and your name is all over it. Let's be smart here. It will not be long before a subpoena comes our way," Thomas answered, desperately trying to convince his son to change his mind.

"You are being led around like a child by these men with their accusations. We have a good partner in Stansby, and I will not stand here and have him lambasted this way!" Tom shouted.

"You do not realize, Son, that this is still my business, and you are a junior partner. You have made a mistake in getting us into bed with this man. Tomorrow we will call the sheriff and let them investigate the financial records they want to see, and that is final!" Thomas had not raised his voice to his son this way in years, and he regretted doing it.

Tom walked to the window. He did not say anything for several minutes. "Well, I guess I do not have a choice in the matter. Please, Father, sit down, and we will discuss the way you want to handle this henceforth," Thomas said calmly. Thomas sat down, knowing that the matter was settled.

Suddenly Tom grabbed an antique sword that was hanging over the fireplace. He turned and took two short steps toward his father. He raised the sword and then delivered a blow, which struck his father in the chest. Thomas tried to react, but the thrust was too fast. The sword was thrust between two ribs on the right side of his chest, which subsequently pierced his heart. Tom watched his father struggling for breath and unable to move. Thomas's last sight as he exhaled his last breath was of Tom smiling.

Tom thought back to his childhood and how his father was never around. He reminisced about how hard and cold he felt his father was toward him. It was always about achievement and tools to succeed. He noticed the way other fathers fawned over their sons. He resented his father because he was only interested in growing his business and grooming him to run it one day. He could not stand to see his mother feeling sad and lonely on all those days when his father was away on business. He really became enraged when he thought that his sister had gotten away with it all. She was able to rebel and live the way she wanted—no rules, no consequences. The whole time his father just doted on her, and it drove him mad. Thomas Rygaard was the root of his pain. His father deserved what he had received.

TWENTY-FIVE

Jack was on the phone with Brian, the district attorney he had met in Atlanta. The others were listening as they sat at the small conference table. The sheriff was looking at Jack, Steve was leaning back in an old leather office chair, and James was leaning against the wall and peering out a small window. Jack was trying to get the lead attorney for the state of Georgia onboard. He was also lobbying him to place a call to the local DA. Hopefully, this call would grease the wheels, or at least, that was the hope. Jack heard Sheriff Jackson's secretary knock on the large glass door before she walked in. When he looked, he could see her visibly shaken.

"Hold on, Brian, something is happening here, and I want to hear what is said." Jack then paused and listened.

"Sheriff, please answer line two. There has been an incident at the Rygaards' house!" the woman exclaimed with fear and sadness in her voice.

"Brian, let me call you back. There seems to be an emergency here that we may need to handle." The two men said goodbye and hung up. "Hello," the Sheriff said as he answered the phone. "Yes, this is him. What? Slow down and say it calmly," the sheriff said. "What? How long ago?" The Sheriff's squinted his eyes and looked very concerned. "Don't touch anything, and do not let anybody in the house. I will be there shortly." The sheriff slammed the phone receiver down and rubbed his face.

"What happened?" Jack asked.

"Thomas Rygaard is dead. The butler found him just a few minutes ago in his chair by the fireplace with a stab wound in his chest," the sheriff answered with a pained look on his face.

Sheriff Jackson headed toward the door as he motioned the others to come with him. Sherriff Jackson waved them to his SUV, and they loaded up as he jumped in the driver's seat, started the vehicle, and sped off headed to the Rygaards' home with the others in tow.

Jack wondered what had happened, or better yet, who had happened to Thomas Rygaard to leave him in his current state. "I knew we should have watched the house after the meeting we had with him. Stansby seems to have a step up on us always," Jack said with disgust in his voice.

"I don't think this is Stansby. Jerry told me that Tom was the only one at the house, and he watched him leave in a hurry," the sheriff answered.

"Who is Jerry?" Jack looked at the sheriff as he asked the question.

"That is Thomas's butler. He was in the kitchen when he heard a noise. He went to check on it and found Thomas." As he answered the question, Jack noticed a tear in his eyes.

"Thomas was a good friend to you, wasn't he, Sheriff?" Jack inquired.

"Everyone thought the relationship we had was based on the financial donations he made to my campaign. He only donated the money because he believed in me. He wanted this county to be a safe place, and he thought I could make that happen. Now looking back with everything that has transpired, I think I failed him," Sheriff Jackson explained.

Jack thought for a minute. "Well, we all have our responsibilities, and we have our failures too, but if the intent is getting up every day and making the world a better place, no one can judge us for that," Jack said.

Steve, who had been silent up to that point, said, "There is too much evil in the world. If it does not touch people, they must be on a mountain with no one else around."

"I wish I was on that mountain now," Sherriff Jackson said.

As they pulled into the driveway that led to the Rygaard house, Jack noticed the beautiful landscape again, wondering how such bad things could have happened there. When they pulled up to the door, Jerry the butler was waiting outside for them.

"Jerry, are you OK?" Sheriff Jackson asked as he stepped out of the vehicle.

"No, sir, I am not OK; I am pretty much the opposite. After Tom left, I went in to see if Thomas needed anything. To my horrible surprise, I found him lying on the floor unresponsive and left in a terrible manner." Jack noticed the emotion in his manner and face as he watched the man recount the events to the sheriff.

"Was there anybody else in the house? Jack asked, looking around and scanning the perimeter of the house.

"No one. I constantly walk through the house. It is a habit I picked up over the years when the children were around. People would occasionally show up unannounced, thinking they could talk with Mr. Rygaard and seeking money from him," he replied.

Jack noticed his hands trembling. "Tell me about your relationship with Thomas," Jack said.

Jerry looked at him with resentment as his lip curled. "Thomas was not only my boss, but he was my friend. I respected him for the person he was and his hard work. So I don't appreciate that line of inquiry," he replied with an incredulous tone.

"So what happened then, Jerry?" Jack inquired. "If no one was here but Tom, do you think he was involved?"

"I just don't know. All I can say is that he was talking with his son. Then the next thing I knew, I found him like a slaughtered sheep." Jerry looked pale, as if he were going to faint, as he told them his story.

"Did you overhear the two arguing or having harsh words?" Jack continued.

"Not really. I was in the kitchen, so I really could not hear much."

"Do you know where Tom might have gone?" Jack asked as he noticed the look of realization coming on the butler's face.

"He has a house on a small farm that is located on the north side of the county. He may have gone there. I do know that he was spending some time earlier with his lady friend," he answered.

"How do you know that he was at his lady friend's house?"

The man looked at Jack with contempt as he continued questioning him. "Because I was in the room when his father called him. He did not want to come over because he was with her. His father insisted that he needed to talk with him today, so he reluctantly came," Jerry said, looking at Jack as if he could strangle him.

Jack raised his hands in mock surrender. "All right, Jerry, we have questioned you enough. Go home, and I will handle things from here," Sheriff Jackson said.

Jack walked into the house, and the others followed. They walked into the study where Thomas Rygaard's body lay. The man was on his left side, and a pool of red liquid was on the wood floor in front of where he lay. Jack walked around and noticed Thomas's face was frozen in a horrified manner, as if he finally had realized his worst fear before his death. His eyes seemed to be focused on the picture of his late wife, which hung on the paneled wall across from the man's final resting place. It was as if he were looking at her and wondering what kind of monster the two of them had created in their son, Tom.

"This is so surreal. I would never have thought that Tom would kill his father. We need to find him before he escapes. If he does, it is possible we will never see him again," Steve said with concern.

"I will send some guys over to check out the farm. If he is there, we've got him," Sheriff Jackson said and then called out the order.

"I will put out a BOLO on him throughout the state," James said as Jack walked over and glanced at the sword stuck in the wall on the far side of the room near the door. He noticed that the blade was stained red.

"Jack, what do you think happened? How could a son do this to his father?" Steve asked as he stood by the fireplace staring at Thomas Rygaard.

"Well, I cannot imagine what was going through his mind. Marvin stated that when sin engulfs a man, these are the results. We have seen a lot of bloodshed since we began dealing with Stansby, but I think

Tom got to a point where he was just consumed with hate and greed." Jack couldn't believe that he had made that statement, but he had no other words to express the situation they were witnesses to.

"If money and power lead to this, I would rather be a poor man. This is possibly the worst thing I could imagine happening to a family," Steve replied with his brow furrowed.

"I have the crime-scene team headed this way," Sheriff Jackson told them.

James walked back in and let them know that he had put the BOLO out with the GBI and the state patrol. "All this money and accumulation of things led to the destructive actions we see here today. It makes me glad that my mother spent so much time instilling the values of Christianity in me as I was growing up," James told the others as Jack scoured the room for any clues that would put the twisted puzzle together.

"James, I did not know you believed in Jesus," Jack said.

"Yes, I gave my life to Him when I was young. It is what led me into the bureau. I wanted to help people in the roughest periods of their lives through the justice system. Everyone deserves help in these times, and he called me to this life."

"Look at this," Steve said after picking up a little lamp. He found a small camera attached to the area near the switch, which was pointed in such a way to cover the majority of the room.

"Thomas has video of this room. If we could find where the recording station is located, we have Tom dead to rights."

Jack walked around the house until he found a small room to the side of the kitchen. When he entered, he noticed a small recorder with a monitor. The monitor was on, and he was able to review the footage recorded. He watched the video in horror as it showed the actions of a prodigal son. He then called out for the others to watch the ghastly deed.

"We need to find him now. That was the action of a crazed and cold-blooded murderer. That was not the man I used to know," Sheriff Jackson stated.

"That was not the action of a man who killed because he was

mad. That was the action of a man who has killed before. He likes it," Jack stated.

"It makes you wonder if he is connected to one of the other murders that we contributed to Stansby," Steve said as the men looked at each other.

"After seeing that footage, I would not be surprised," James added.

The men spread back out and tried to locate anything in the house that would further help them. There were several other deputies who came to the scene, and they secured the entire estate. They swept the entire area. Inside, Jack found a little black leather book with what appeared to be passwords to business files. He placed it in a clear plastic evidence bag and labeled it.

"Come in, Sheriff!" Jack heard a muffled voice on the radio.

"Go ahead."

"I found a little area in the horse barn that has some strange things. You really need to see this," the voice responded.

"All right, secure it, and we will be down there in a second," Sheriff Jackson replied as Jack followed him out of the house.

Jack headed down to the horse barn with the nervous anticipation of what he might encounter. When they got close to the area, Jack noticed the bewilderment on the deputy's face who had secured the scene. "What did you find in there?" Jack asked.

"I really do not know how to explain it. You must see it for yourself."

Jack looked at the others and then entered the room. Jack immediately understood what was transpiring. The room was set up in the same fashion that the barn at the farm had been when Justice was murdered. It was like the scene in Atlanta when Jack had investigated the Evan's murder. It was staged like an apartment with a few antique-looking chairs and similar paintings hung on the wall. There was the same style of bed. The only thing missing was a body. Jack's mind immediately went to the location of Anna Lee. The logical thought would now be that Anna Lee was in trouble.

Stacy was in the yard, and Danny was on the porch watching over her. He understood that Jack had taken a fancy to her and wanted to make sure she was kept unharmed. He considered all that Jack had been through. If there was a sliver of a chance of these two coming together and being happy, he wanted that to happen. Stacy had enjoyed being on the island and the safety it seemed to bring. Danny felt warmth in his heart as he watched her enjoy her surroundings.

Stacy walked to the porch, and the two sat down. She poured them a glass of sweet tea. "It would be nice if we could walk to the beach. I haven't put my feet in the sand since I was a little girl." She smiled sweetly at him.

"I know you would like to do that, but it would be too risky to be in a place where so many people could notice you. One of those people could be a bad guy, and then you could be in danger," Danny said weakly.

"I know what you are thinking, but who would be looking for me here? Does anybody know about this place besides you?" Danny thought about this and knew she just wanted to enjoy the environment of the island.

"There are only a handful of people who should know about this place, but why take a risk? You are safe." Danny could feel himself weakening. Truth be told, the only reason he kept this place is because of his love of the beach.

"Just for one hour. That is all I am asking. Then we can come back, and I will stay put. Please?" She was using all her girlish charm by this time.

"All right, we can go in the morning but for an hour only. Then we come back here and hunker down." He knew he had caved too easily. She jumped up and performed a victory dance.

Jack had stepped out of the barn. He looked up at the sky and watched the clouds pass by. He was thinking hard about what had just happened. There was so much darkness in his world that it was hard to focus. He was conflicted about all the madness he had experienced, but then he turned his thoughts to Stacy and smiled. He felt warmth deep inside when he thought about the kiss they had shared. There seemed to be a ray of sunshine peering through the drabness he was mired in. Maybe God was smiling on him in some strange way. Maybe what Marvin had told him was true in some way. Maybe he just needed to realize that he did not have to settle for what sin had brought him in this world. Jack thought about this for several minutes and then decided that he needed to hear the voice of the woman who sparked this feeling.

"Hello," Jack heard after he had dialed the number of the burner phone he had bought Stacy.

"It is nice to hear your voice again," he said.

"Jack, are you OK? Is everything good?" she inquired.

"It is not good, but it is so much better now that I hear your voice. How is everything there?" he said as he longed to be there with her.

"It is beautiful here. Danny has a great place. I wish you were here. I miss you." As she said this, his heart fluttered a little.

"It will not be much longer, and then maybe I can come and enjoy some time with you in that southern paradise." She laughed a little as Jack said this.

"I look forward to that," she said enticingly.

"The main issue is keeping you safe," he said, wishing he was there at that very moment. "I just wanted to hear your voice. I need to go now," he continued.

Stacy could hear concern in his voice, but she did not want to pry any further. "Hurry up and do what you need to. I will be waiting for you." There was a pause that seemed to last as somehow their souls communicated through it all. Then came the goodbye.

TWENTY-SIX

The team was still at the Rygaard farm, processing the scene and trying to figure out the details of what had happened. The sheriff was still stunned and grieved over his friend's murder.

Then another call came over the radio. "Come in, Sheriff, come in," Jack heard an excited voice say as the sheriff reached for the radio on his side.

"Go ahead," the sheriff said.

"He is here, and he has a gun. He fired some rounds at us. We need backup." The man on the other end was loud, almost yelling as he informed them of the events.

"Stay back and keep an eye on his movements. Do not engage; just keep an eye on him. We are heading that way," the sheriff replied. Instinctively, they all headed to the SUV.

They drove to the farmhouse as fast as their cars would go. Jack could only imagine what they would find when they arrived. He was very afraid that the young nurse who had taken care of him and Steve in the hospital would be in danger. Tom Rygaard had shown a heart of evil when he had murdered his father. It was time for the killing to end, and Jack was going to do anything in his power to see that it did.

They pulled into the dirt driveway that headed up to the small farmhouse. Jack noticed that a perimeter had already been set up around the property. The area was surrounded by tall pine trees on three sides. It was perfect for snipers to hide in. He also noticed a small creek running through the back side of the property. He made a mental note that this was a means of escape for anyone wishing to do so. They pulled up short of the house and met with the deputy in charge.

"He is in there, sheriff. There is also a young lady in there with him. We cannot be sure if she is injured or not," the deputy told them.

"Has he made any demands yet?" Jack asked.

"He has not communicated any as of yet," the man responded.

"Let's get a secure line and call him. He must want something. He is still here, and Anna Lee is still alive," the sheriff said.

Jack looked at the sheriff and knew that he was thinking the same thing that he was. This was not going to end well unless they acted quickly. Jack then asked James to walk around the property and determine the points of entrance where someone might sneak to the house without being seen. He walked the tree line, looking at the yard, which was immaculately maintained. Bushes were clipped, and limbs were trimmed, but he noticed one area that seemed to be a blind spot for the inhabitant of the house.

He walked back to the crude base of operations where Jack and the sheriff were stationed. There was a small insertion team there as well, and a plan was developed. However, neither Jack nor anyone else believed that they could penetrate the house without the girl losing her life.

"That young girl in there is Anna Lee. We need to do everything to save her," Jack said emphatically.

"I know. We will do everything we can," Sheriff Jackson replied.

"Why would he do this? He has had all the advantages in life. He has money, possessions, and even someone who seemed to care for him," James said sadly.

"Money is a root of evil," the sheriff replied. Jack started reflecting on all the times lately when he had heard someone speak about God and His Word. *This*, he thought, *cannot be a coincidence*.

The staging area was set, and the sheriff decided to give Tom a call and see if they could end this standoff peaceably. He had talked with Tom on numerous occasions about investments and even campaign issues. He never thought he would be talking to him regarding hostage negotiations. The phone was turned to speaker mode so that everyone could hear him.

After four rings, an unusually steely voice answered the phone. "Well, it is about time you decided to reach out. What can I do for you today?" Tom answered. It was so casual that it caught the sheriff off guard.

"For starters, you could release Anna Lee and then come out with your hands on your head. This could be over before any other bad thing happens today. What do you say, Tom?" There was a dramatic pause as tension rose in the air. Then there was a surprising response.

"Ahaa, ha, ha. That was a good one. Do you think that this is going to end with a good outcome? Come on guys. You know as well as I do that this is not how the game is going to end." Then silence.

"It could end like that Tom. Anna Lee could be safe, you could be safe, and this could all end now." Jack listened as Sherriff Jackson looked hopeful that the situation could be resolved like he had laid it out.

"Sheriff, I knew how this was going to end when your deputy showed up here before I could leave. There are no rainbows and unicorns in this ending." They could hear Anna Lee crying and pleading with Tom. Jack could only think of Stacy and how lucky they had been to rescue her after she had been kidnapped. He hoped for the same outcome.

"Tom, we promise that if you just come on out, we will put a good word in for you and maybe get you a lighter sentence," the sheriff responded.

Again, Jack was surprised as he heard Tom laughing. "Lighter sentence? I am walking out of here a free man, and if you try to stop me, she will end up like my sister. Anna Lee is about as annoying as her, anyway," Tom snarled. This comment made the men look at one another in confusion as Jack started to fume with anger.

"What do you mean by that, Tom?" the sheriff asked as he noticed Jack start to pace back and forth.

"Come on, guys, keep up. You think that the boogeyman has an Australian accent, but he is not the one who is hands on. He is a good planner and enjoys influencing. He casts a long shadow, but I am the boogeyman." Then the phone line went dead.

This conversation left Jack and the others astonished. Jack felt a shiver run down his spine, which quickly turned to steely determination. The assumption was that Johnny had killed Emily Rygaard, but Tom was all but admitting to the crime. Tom had just murdered his father, and it had been captured on video. Now they realized that this cold-blooded killer had killed two of his family members. *How could a man get so twisted?* Jack thought. "We need to find a way in. If we rush in with force, Anna Lee is as good as dead," Jack said.

"I think I found a way," James stated. "When I was scouting the property, I found a blind spot where there is some shrubbery that blocks the window. We can follow a drainage ditch to them, which will give us cover. There is a window that we can slip a man into from there," James told them.

"Do you think that will work? I mean if one mistake happens, this is all for nothing," Steve said.

Jack was unsure of the plan. There had to be something that Tom wanted. They just needed to figure it out. "I think the best course of action is to keep him talking and to wait until nightfall. Then we can make our move," Jack said. He knew this was really the only shot they had to possibly get Anna Lee out safely.

"I agree, Jack. It is risky, but I think it is the only move we have," Sheriff Jackson said uncomfortably.

―――――――――――――――

Tom looked out of the bedroom window and knew he was surrounded. He looked around the room at the heavy wood dresser and thought he could use it for cover. He looked at the closet door and knew it was thick and heavy. If needed, he could scramble in there and be protected from gunfire. After all, that is where he had Anna Lee tied up and hidden for that very reason. He wanted to make sure his ticket to possible escape was safe. Then he had a moment of realization. *Who am I kidding?* He knew the outcome. He would not come out of this alive. Jack would make sure of that.

He thought back to when this had started years ago. He was fresh out of college and in Atlanta, trying to drum up business to prove to his father that he was worthy. He had never felt worthy before. His father made him miserable. He never could measure up to his father's expectations. That did not matter now though. He was happy that he had witnessed his father suffering through the death of Emily. In a way, Tom felt bad that he had killed her, but to witness his father shrink into oblivion before his eyes had been worth it.

The ringing of his phone brought Tom back to the present. He looked over at his onetime girlfriend, who was tied up in the closet. Tears were flowing from her eyes. *Quite a pity,* he thought. He had a grand plan in mind for her. He had thought and prepared for weeks to have her be the next muse in his play of death. After his emotions had gotten the better of him, and he had coldly dispatched his father, she was merely his pawn to further his wishes. Then the phone rang.

"So nice to hear from you again, Sheriff. Have you missed me that much already?" Tom said with his quirky smugness.

"Tom, let's talk to each other and see if there is something we can do to resolve this in a peaceful manner." Tom was surprised to hear Jack on the line instead of the sheriff.

"Well, Mr. Detective, I was not expecting you to be calling on me at this time. Did the sheriff have to go and take his afternoon nap?" He laughed as if he were at some niche comedy show.

"Tom, what do you want? What can we do to—"

"I want nothing from you. You have been ruining things far too long. There is nothing you have to offer me. Now either come and kill me or watch this sweet little flower die." Tom spoke with a furious venom coming from an insane man.

"Tom, is there anything we can do to change this situation?" Jack had to try again.

"I tell you what, Jack. Why don't we do this? I will trade her for you." Jack looked at the sheriff and then looked at Steve, who was shaking his head vehemently.

"Why would you do that, Tom?" Jack was trying to keep the man talking.

"You were there at the beginning, Jack. I think you should be here at the end," Tom replied slyly.

"What do you mean I was there from the beginning?" Jack asked, looking at the sheriff who was motioning for him to keep Tom talking.

"That is right, Jack; you were there at my first kill—you know, at the Evan's house after I had killed Carly. She was a lovely and delicate rose petal, whom I plucked the life out of all those years ago."

Jack was astonished at what he was hearing. He had always assumed that Oliver had committed that murder. He had even seen him close to the scene. He pursued him hard until he was railroaded by Smith. "Tom, that was you?" Jack continued, trying to keep him going.

"Yes, great detective, it was. I saw you in the lot that day. If only you had known that the man whom you were looking for was looking at you. Oh, great times, Jack, great times." Tom walked over and ran his fingers through Anna Lee's golden locks and then snapped her head back.

Jack heard her scream. He was startled by the guttural cry of her fear.

"Now I have your attention. Are we going to continue to play this game, or do I need to cut this short." Jack grimaced and listened as Tom laughed sadistically.

"Tom, this is not some game; this is real life," the sheriff stated.

"Hey, Sheriff. Now do not forget when this is over, there is a small sum of cash in my father's house under the sink. Please take it for your next campaign donation."

The sound of Tom's laughter sickened Jack. "Tom, let us get back to the trade. How would you have that transpire?" Jack asked, trying to refocus the direction of the conversation.

"What will happen to make this go smoothly is that you will walk to the porch and go up the stairs. I will be waiting at the door with

Anna Lee. When you get on the porch, lift your shirt up and turn around. That way, I will know that you do not have a weapon. Then you walk in, and I will let her go." Tom sounded calm and smooth as he laid his plan out. "If anything does not go according to my plan, she dies, and you die."

Jack knew there was no other way. He was willing to sacrifice himself for the young lady. He knew that his failures had let matters get this far. "OK, you have a deal," Jack said coolly and ended the call.

"There is no way that I will let you do this, Jack!" Steve cried out as the call ended. "If this goes down the way he is planning, you will be killed, and I can't let that happen."

Jack grabbed his friend by the shoulder and smiled. "The only one who will die today is him. I have a plan. We just need to get ourselves together and then execute it." Jack had an air of confidence in his voice as Steve listened. After thirty minutes of getting everything set, Jack was ready.

There was a pause, and James came over to shake Jack's hand. "Before you head in, Jack, I need to do something." He motioned to someone. Jack noticed a familiar figure walking toward them. It was Marvin Shiver. "Jack, we need to soak this in prayer, so I called Marvin." James smiled and welcomed the man.

"Jack, we meet again," Marvin said as he reached out and put his hands on Jack's shoulders.

"Yes, we do. I don't know how, Marvin, but it seems as if this has been constructed to fulfill a greater plan than the one the monster in that house has prepared," Jack said as he nervously smiled at Marvin.

"I know that you are fixing to partake in an untenable event. So let's pray and ask God for help." Jack smiled, and the men prayed. Marvin asked for safety on Jack and the others involved in the rescue operation. He prayed for blessings on Jack. He ended the prayer with a request for safety on Tom, which threw Jack sideways. The prayer came to an end, and they said their amens.

"Marvin, I must ask you something. Why did you pray for safety on Tom? We have found out that he is a serial murderer and is holding Anna Lee in there, threatening her life," Jack said.

Marvin could sense the confusion Jack was feeling. "Jack, Jesus died for every man and woman. He died for Tom as well. I know he is a bad person, but you never know how this will end. It may be God's plan to spare him. If he does, he will spend the rest of his natural life in jail, but his soul will live forever. If he lives, there is an opportunity for his soul." Jack couldn't understand this line of reasoning, but he knew that Marvin had his reasons, so he smiled and thanked him.

TWENTY-SEVEN

Jack was ready, and his team was too. Snipers were in place. The deputies were armed with AR-15 rifles. Body armor was in abundant supply, and there were even several pairs of night-vision goggles out and ready for use. Most importantly, there was a sense of comradery to stop the rampage of the man who had caused so much pain.

"Place the call and let us get this show on the road." Jack had not been this nervous but this sure in his entire life. It was late evening, and the shadows were cast heavily around the tree line and shrubbery. Lights were shining a little brighter in the house. The sheriff picked up the phone, turned the speaker on, and called.

"Hello. Tom's Bar and Grill. Home of the best little basket of loony in the county. How may I help you?" Tom let a sinister laugh out. It was a man who sounded like he had nothing to lose.

"Tom, it is time. Jack is heading up to the house. You better not try anything or—"

"Or you will do what, Sheriff? Will you come in with your guns blazing?" There was another sinister laugh.

"I just want this to end with everyone safe, Tom; that is all." There was a huge sigh from the county's top lawman.

"If Jack does what he is supposed to do, Anna Lee will be safe. Jack better play like a good little boy." Then the phone went silent.

Jack got the signal and started the long walk up the drive. It felt like one of those slow-motion walks—the ones that he had seen in cheesy old movies late at night. The closer he got, the more he could see inside the little house. It looked cozy and rustic. There was a porch with a covered roof, which was lined with tin. The windows were large. When they were not covered with curtains and blankets, the inhabitants would have a beautiful view of a gorgeous South Georgia farm. He noticed how well-manicured the bushes were as well as the outside of the house. Tom had invested a lot in this small country property, which just didn't fit the profile that Jack perceived about the man he was about to face. Something about this whole picture seemed off to him, but he did not have time to think about it. All he wanted to do was save this young lady, who had so much of her life left to live.

He took his first step onto the stairs that led to a porch. There were several chairs but nothing to really hide behind that would protect him if things took a turn for the worse. As he took his first step onto the porch, he looked at the door. He could see a partial figure looking out of the small pane of glass at him.

"Well, hey there, Jack. Are you alone, or should I just start shooting?" Tom said.

Jack moved toward the door a couple of steps. *Not enough for a sniper to shoot at me*, Jack thought. "No, Tom. I am alone. Now that I am here, please let Anna Lee come out, and this swap can be complete." Jack was anxious to set his eyes on her to make sure she was not injured.

"In case you did not understand, Jack, I am the one in control here. You do as I say and not the other way around. Are you clear about that?" Tom stated with a very firm tone.

"Let's just make this a smooth swap. That is all I am wanting," Jack replied.

"Pull up your shirt and let me see your waistband. I don't want any surprises later." Tom had opened the door slightly, and he was now peering at him. Jack put his hands over his head, reached back, pulled his shirt up, and spun around, letting Tom have a good look at his waistband. "No gun. That is good, Jack. Now pull up your pant legs." Jack looked at him wearily and performed his request.

"OK, Jack, come on in, and when you step in, I will let her go,"

Tom said with a wolfish grin. Jack took a few steps into the room. Jack noticed some of the furniture had been shifted as if moved during a struggle. All the windows were covered except the one that James had told Jack was in a blind spot. It was good for someone to sneak into. The fireplace had a little ash in it like someone had started a fire for warmth or maybe to be romantic.

Anna Lee must have been caught off guard and put up a struggle, Jack thought. "All right. Let me see her," Jack stated firmly.

"What, Jack, you don't trust me?" Tom replied and looked toward the back room. "She is in there. Let's go back and get her." With the pistol, Tom motioned to him to head in that direction. Jack walked cautiously to the room. He noticed a bed that looked as if it had been slept in and not remade. The canned lights in the ceiling shone dimly.

Tom must have dimmed them to make it hard to see, Jack thought. When he walked in, he found the closet door open and Anna Lee with her hands tied, lying on the floor. She looked tired and scared, but there was no physical injury. Jack took a breath and thought that it might just work. "Let me untie her and get her out to the sheriff," said Jack, trying to guide this along because he was getting a strange vibe that Tom had other plans for this swap.

Tom smiled as he kept Jack at gunpoint and pulled a knife from a scabbard on his side. Jack became increasingly nervous because Tom had used a knife to kill before. He walked toward Anna Lee, stooped down, waived the knife around her neck area, and smiled a devilish smile. Jack noticed a piece of cloth tied around her mouth and heard her try to say something, but it sounded muted. Her face was painted with fright.

"This is just how quick a beautiful girl can lose her life, Jack. Just a flick of the blade, and she is gone."

"Tom, if this goes wrong, there is nothing stopping the men outside with the guns from coming in and ending you," Jack said, wanting to put some doubt in this man's mind. "Let's just let her go, and then it will be me and you." Jack noticed a different countenance come over the madman as he spoke. His eyes turned dark, and his lips tightened. He wondered if this was the look he had given his father right before he had snuffed out his life. He knew it was time to act on the plan; he just needed to maneuver Tom away from Anna Lee.

"Jack, do you think that I am not a man of my word? You know, Jack, you are really starting to hurt my feelings." He took the knife and slowly cut Anna Lee's arms free and bent down and did the same with her legs. "See, Jack, I wouldn't lie to you." Anna Lee rose, straightened her posture, and stretched as if she had been tied up and put in the closet for several hours. Her eyes were red and teary. She was shaking as she started toward Jack. She started to take off the mouth covering that had kept her silent. Tom grabbed her arm, denying the motion, and then guided them both to the living room. When they were in the room, Jack motioned for her to exit through the front door.

"Hold on now, Jack. It won't be that much fun just to let her walk out, will it now?" Tom waved the gun at them to sit on the sofa. Anna Lee hugged Jack, and he heard her whimper loudly. Jack glanced at Tom, who was getting closer to them, and then knew that they were ready to proceed to part two of the plan.

"You want this to be like the others, Tom?" Jack was leading him in for distraction's sake.

"No, this is less personal, but you are here to witness it, so it makes up for the impersonal side." Tom took his eyes off Jack and looked at Anna Lee. "Sorry, baby. I know you were looking for a forever man, but on the bright side, forever will end in just a few short moments," Tom sneered and pulled the knife back out with his free hand. He still held the pistol in the other.

Jack nodded and held two fingers outstretched, which was the preplanned signal. There was a crash at the side window where the shrubbery was located. *The blind spot*, Jack thought. He noticed a large figure trying to make it through the window and into the room. Just then, Jack noticed a string attached to a circular device placed on the left side of the window seal. There was a bright flash and then just as sudden, a loud boom. Jack grabbed Anna Lee and dove behind the couch, covering his head and ears with a cushion just before the device went off. Unfortunately, he was unable to cover Anna Lee's. He hoped that she had been able to do that herself. Jack heard a bloodcurdling scream. Tom had rigged a flash-bang device in the window. Steve had been incapacitated before he could get all the way into the cabin. This was what Jack had felt wasn't right. The blind spot was intentional and a trap set by a devious mind.

Tom was prepared. As Jack looked that way, he noticed Tom had earplugs. But Tom was more concerned about the man coming through the window than Jack. This gave Jack his opportunity. He had to get this right, or he and the other two were goners. He reached between his shoulder blades, pulled out a small thirty-two caliber pistol, and pointed it at Tom. Before he could aim and fire, Tom turned, as if he had sensed something permanent was fixing to overwhelm him. As he did, Tom hurled the knife at Jack, and it struck him in the right arm—the one holding the gun. This was the only means he could think of that would free him and his friends from the deadly situation.

Try as he might, though, Jack could not use the arm any longer. There was a searing pain when he tried, and the gun slid from his grasp. Jack reacted the only way he could. He hurled himself toward the younger man. He hit him with the ferocity of a linebacker trying to sack a quarterback to stop a game-winning drive. They crashed into a side table and rolled onto the floor. Jack was trying his best to overwhelm the man, but he was stronger than Jack had anticipated. Jack yelled out, "Run, get out now." Jack watched as Anna Lee ran for her life. Jack was horrified when he witnessed Tom raise his pistol and fire. It whizzed past her and struck the doorjamb.

Jack was struggling and trying his best to somehow beat his assailant in this game of life and death. He grabbed Tom with his good arm and struck him with all the force he could muster. It didn't seem to have an effect. Tom, who was still holding onto the handgun, used it to club Jack on the side of the head. As much as he wanted to, Jack couldn't contend any longer. He had to let go. When he did, he rolled and tried to kick out to knock the man off balance. Tom was too fast, and he blocked the attempt. Finally, Tom, who was the younger, stronger man, had overwhelmed his opponent.

Tom stood over Jack with the gun pointing at him. Jack understood now that all the nightmares he had dreamed always ended before something catastrophic happened. This was real life, and he understood that as the moments slowly passed, he was not going to survive. He suddenly felt warm, and a strange peace came over him. He understood; he was ready. Jack watched as Tom's finger, which was on the trigger of the gun, inched closer to the release. Then Jack's eyes closed, and he heard the loud bang.

To Jack's surprise, he was able to open his eyes again. He tried to focus and then hesitantly looked around. What he noticed was one of the most amazing things he ever witnessed. There on the porch was Sheriff Jackson with his old-school, long-barreled, thirty-eight-caliber sidearm pointing at the place where Tom had been standing. He quickly glanced over and saw Tom lying prone and motionless less than five feet from him. He looked back as the sheriff made it through the door. He walked over to Tom and kicked away his side arm. He reached to feel a pulse. He looked over at Jack and shook his head.

Jack struggled to his feet and looked over at the window where Steve had tried to enter the house and asked, "Is Steve hurt?"

James entered the house and checked on Steve. "He is lucky. It seems that when he tripped the booby trap, there was a delay in it going off. He turned his head and absorbed most of the blast with his backside. He more than likely has a concussion and some splinters and glass embedded in him but nothing too serious."

Jack took a long breath and exhaled. "I knew something was off with that brush being overgrown. It made no sense that the rest of the grounds were so manicured," Jack said as he laid his head back down on the hard wooden floor. He had become woozy from the blood loss from the knife wound. "How is Anna Lee? Did she make it out without being hurt?" he asked, hoping for some more good news.

"She is frightened, but she has no major injuries—just some small cuts and bruises. She should be fine," Sheriff Jackson said.

"Maybe our luck is starting to turn for the better," Jack said as he noticed the EMTs entering the room. He then stared at the young man lying their lifeless. "Such a waste of a life. He had so much opportunity and promise. Do you think we could have—"

"He chose the master he served, Jack. Do not look on this thinking you, I, or anybody else could have changed the outcome."

Jack looked at the sheriff. "I think I need to call Stacy." He then slumped back down and closed his eyes.

TWENTY-EIGHT

Jack awoke and found himself in a bed that was about as comfortable as a cardboard box on concrete. "Hey, partner," Jack heard a familiar voice call out. He looked over and saw Steve with gauze wrapped around his head like a Civil War veteran.

"Well, I guess we should earn frequent flyer miles from the hospital as much as we use their services," Jack said. He looked around the area, making sure he wasn't hooked up to any wires. Other than an IV, he was electronics free.

"Yes, we do tend to be gluttons for punishment." Steve chuckled as he answered Jack. They both lifted the heads of their beds, which resembled a geriatric bed race. Jack felt a dull throbbing pain in the shoulder.

"How are you feeling? I was afraid that you wouldn't make it after I heard that explosion," Jack said as he looked over at his buddy.

"It takes more than a firecracker to hurt this piece of twisted steel," Steve remarked.

Jack laughed again. "I thought that I was a goner. He had me dead to rights." Jack rubbed his head and knew that he was very fortunate to still be above ground.

"Well, we were a step behind him all the way up until the end. I think our stick-to-itiveness paid off in the end though." Steve looked over with a big cheesy grin.

"That was cheap. Don't smile too much because I am paying the price for being so far behind," Jack said. Then he started reminiscing on the last several weeks and knew that the comment Steve made was right. If they were going to one day stop Oliver Stansby, they would have to step up their game. "I think I would like to call Stacy now." Jack was anxious to talk with her. The one good thing that had happened through all of this was her. He did not want to waste any more time. He witnessed firsthand how fleeting life was. He noticed Steve was grinning again. "What in Sam Hill are you grinning about now?" Jack knew that he was going to be the laughingstock and waited for the reply.

"Jack, it is just good to see that you have someone you seem to care about. You really deserve a shot at happiness. I am happy for you." These comments really knocked Jack off his rocker.

"You mean there are no snide comments coming my way?"

Steve smiled and pulled up his covers. "I figure I will have plenty of time for that later." Then he closed his eyes.

"Hey, Jack." The sweetest voice he could imagine was on the other end of the phone, speaking to him.

"Hey, Stacy. How are you doing?" Jack asked.

"I am good. Where are you? Are you all right?" Jack had a sunshiny feeling when he listened to her voice. "I do not want you to worry because I am fine—just a little banged up."

Before Jack could go any further, she quickly responded, "When people tell you not to worry, that is when you should start worrying. What has happened?"

Jack was impressed at her level of savviness. "Well, I am at the hospital. I have a shoulder wound but not a serious long-term injury." He paused.

"What happened? Why are you in the hospital recovering from a shoulder wound? Was it this man you have been chasing? Was it Stansby?"

Jack heard her questions, but he didn't want her to worry about him. "Hold on. Give me a second, and I will tell you everything. First, I want you to know that I have missed you and that I am glad to hear your voice." There was a pause, and Jack thought that the call may have been dropped. "Hello? Are you still there?" Jack asked.

"Yes, I am Jack. I am just so happy—happy that you are thinking of me at a time when you are in pain and that you would tell me that you missed me and wanted to hear my voice."

Jack smiled, knowing that she was happy. She needed some happiness. "I just wanted you to know that, Stacy. I have had you on my mind ever since you left with Danny," Jack stated.

"Tell me, Jack, what has caused you to be such a good man?" Stacy had never known a man who seemed to be so selfless and interested in her happiness.

Jack could feel her smile over the phone. "I guess I have seen such dark things in life that when something bright shines, I just want to make sure that I notice it and that the person knows I have taken notice." When Jack shifted, a sharp pain ran from his shoulder to his neck. He refocused.

"Well, I do. Now, please tell me what caused your injury." Jack smiled as she asked it. He took some time and explained all the events that had led up to the call they were now on. "Wow. You mean Tom killed Thomas? How could a person be so evil? How could he kill his father? What could cause someone to be in a mindset where murder is willy-nilly?"

Jack knew she was overwhelmed by all that she had just heard. "I do not know, Stacy. I have been trying to stop people who commit this act for years, but I have never been able figure out how some people get that twisted. I talked with a man lately who tried to explain it, but it just didn't make sense from his perspective either."

"What is that man's name?" she asked as Jack thought back to his conversations with this man.

"His name is Marvin Shiver, and he is a local pastor here," Jack explained.

"Yes, I know Mr. Marvin. He was a regular customer at the diner. He was a very nice man. He witnessed to me about Jesus," Stacy said.

Jack heard a different tone in her voice. "That is the man," Jack said as he chuckled to himself.

"You know, Jack, maybe there is something to what he is trying to tell us. I mean life so far without the things Marvin is preaching about has not been that good. Life just isn't what people say it's supposed to be when seeking pleasure from material stuff."

Jack thought to himself that Stacy was starting to go deep in her thinking. It kind of made him feel a bit intimidated, not because she was getting deep but because of the subject. "Maybe we can discuss this further tomorrow," Jack blurted out, trying to change the subject.

"Do you mean that this is over, and I can come back to Moultrie? That would be great." Stacy sounded truly excited.

"Well, I do not think this is over by a long shot, but I think that with all the heat on Stansby, you will be safe here with me," Jack said. He turned and looked out of the window. The sun seemed to be shining a bit brighter. "When we are finished talking, I will talk with Danny about the arrangements. Hopefully, you will be here in the morning before ten." Jack was getting excited about having Stacy around him. He missed her smile. He missed the way she smelled. He was also thinking about the sparks he had felt when he kissed her soft lips.

"That sounds good to me, but Danny promised that we could visit the beach in the morning. So we may be delayed an hour or two if that fits in with your plan." She was being coy when she said this.

Jack could sense her anticipation for the little beach trip. An hour of extra waiting wouldn't be a big sacrifice if she was happier when she got back. "I think your beach trip is deserved, and I will make sure Danny sticks to his word," Jack said as he began thinking of her there with him again. "Is Danny close by?" Jack inquired.

"He is outside on the porch. I will get him for you." Jack could hear the door creak as she went to get his old friend.

"How are you doing, Jack?" Danny sounded excited to hear from his friend.

"To be honest with you, I am in the hospital with another wound. We got Tom Rygaard. He was more or less a serial killer. He was so twisted; he killed his own father." Jack wanted to tell him the whole story, but he knew he had the time to explain it all on the following day.

"That sounds like a long story, Jack," Danny remarked.

"It is Danny, but can I tell you it later?" Jack was getting tired from his pain and the medicine to calm it. "You feel like driving back here tomorrow with Stacy?" he inquired.

"Jack, if you feel it is safe, I will be there. First, though, I have a young lady who wants to tour the beach first thing in the morning. Will you be good with us being back at around eleven thirtyish?" Danny asked.

Jack knew his friend would have a long drive back if the promised beach time was not given to Stacy. "Yes, I think that would do her good after all of this. Besides, neither of us would hear the end of the matter if we denied her request." Jack heard Danny let out a weak laugh.

"Don't worry. I know how beach fever feels," Danny replied.

"Let me tell her goodbye," Jack said, a little sad at having to end the call.

"All right, Jack. You get some rest, and I will see you tomorrow," Stacy said.

"OK. Be easy on Danny. Be careful." Jack said goodbye, and the line went silent. Then he started feeling a little lightheaded and looked over at Steve. He was fast asleep. Jack soon followed suit and rested snug as a bug in a rug.

There was a splashing sound, and Jack looked around. It was morning, and the sun was rising. It was beautiful; the sunrise looked like a canvas of pink and purple hues, making the most beautiful painting. He felt sand on his feet and a small breeze blowing. He heard whispers, and he looked for its source. He couldn't find it, so he looked harder with no success. Then there was an ear-piercing scream. He ran down the sugar-colored beach but went nowhere. The harder he ran, the more the sand seemed to go out from under him. He looked up again and noticed clumps of red sand. There was a figure. He tried running harder, but the sand slipped away faster and faster. He fell to his hands and knees and cried out.

"Jack. Jack. Wake up. Wake up!" Jack suddenly opened his eyes and noticed that he was covered in sweat. He had had another nightmare, and the voice was Steve trying to wake him.

He looked around and noticed the morning sun peeking through the window of his golden and brownish colored hospital room. "Sorry, Steve. It was just one of those dreams." Jack took a small rag that was on his over-the-bed table and wiped the cold sweat from his face.

"You have been having a lot of those dreams lately. Maybe you need to talk to a professional about that, Jack. It is not normal to have that many terrible dreams," Steve said to his friend.

"I think you are right, Steve. It really makes it hard to get any real rest. I feel as if I have run three marathons back-to-back." Jack looked like a different man than he had weeks earlier. He looked tired and even haggard. How could anyone who had been through so much in such a short time not look that way?

"When Stacy gets here today, I hope to be able to get out, have a good lunch with her, and just try to relax." Jack sounded hopeful as he spoke. He knew, though, he needed to talk to someone about his struggles.

"You know, I was doing some research, and Marvin is not only a pastor but a licensed counselor. Maybe since you know him, you could see him, and he could counsel you?"

Jack gave Steve a look that he had not seen before. It was a look of resignation. Jack knew he needed help. "All right, all right. Geez I got it. I will call him and see if he can see me. Maybe then you will get off my back," Jack said.

"I just want you to be the best you, my friend," Steve responded.

"Now, I think I want to eat some breakfast and get cleaned up. Then I will call Danny and Stacy to see how their beach trip went and when they will be here." Jack smiled as he said this. Then he thought that maybe she was the ray of sunshine on a dark day that God had brought to his life.

Jack and Steve had a meager hospital-style breakfast—toast that had been toasted too much and some kind of gray-looking meat that they were told was sausage. The best part of it was the fact that it was over, and their stomachs were full—somewhat. Jack looked at Steve, smiled, and then picked up his phone to call Danny. He dialed and the phone rang and then rang again and again until it went to voicemail. Jack repeated this multiple times over the next thirty minutes.

"They are just enjoying the beach," Steve said, but Jack knew that it was not normal for Danny not to answer his phone.

"Something is not right, Steve; I can feel it." Jack called the number one more time. He had gotten to the point where he was consumed with concern. Then there was a small knock at the door, and James walked into the room looking sullen.

"Guys," James said, nodding his head as he walked over and sat down, "I am not one to mince words and sugarcoat things, so here it goes. There was an attack this morning at the beach where Danny was keeping Stacy—"

"Are Stacy and Danny OK?" Jack's mind turned to the dream.

"Danny was shot. He is in critical condition at the local hospital. He suffered a wound to his chest and some head trauma." James paused, thinking about his friend for a quick second.

"What about Stacy? Is she OK?" Jack asked. He was afraid of the answer that he was about to hear.

"We don't know. All we know is that she is missing. She has been kidnapped, Jack," James answered with a voice that he had acquired after years of having to deliver bad news.

"Have you searched the island? Have you put out a BOLO? Do we know anything about how the people found out where they were staying?" Jack's mind was moving a hundred miles an hour as panic sunk in.

"Jack, we have over a dozen agents on the case along with local and other state agencies. There are no real leads yet, but there was a letter," James replied to Jack's questions.

"A letter? What kind of letter?" Jack asked incredulously.

"It is a letter to you, Jack. I have a copy of it for you to look over." James handed it to him. "I will let you read it and stop back by in a little while. Jack, I want you to know that we will do everything in our power to find her." James rose and slowly walked out of the room as if he were a defeated man.

Jack opened the paper and read the following:

You showed up like an unannounced guest many years ago,
Stumbling around and stepping on unknown toes.
You ruined a perfect crime,
And you almost stumbled onto a budding villain before his time.
You were shunned and told to go,
But you kept looking for what you did not know.
Now is the time for recompense
Because your head is hard and way too dense.
Will you ever see her again or will you not?
That is the question you will ask yourself a lot.
—Shadow

TWENTY-NINE

It had been almost two weeks since the day Danny had been shot, and Stacy had been taken. Jack and Steve were out of the hospital. Danny was getting out of the ICU that day. He had been transferred to Mercer Hospital, where his chest wound was treated. He had taken a turn for the worse on two occasions. One time, it was from severe anemia; the second was from pneumonia. He was a tough old bird, though, and Jack knew he would pull through.

Jack had traveled to the beach and looked around the house where his friend and the woman he had fallen in love with had been. He thought he could find a clue that no one else could, but his efforts were fruitless. It was really a needle-in-a-haystack venture. He had hoped that Stacy would have been found by now and that he could hold her in his arms, but that had not happened. He was hurting and was losing hope. Steve and all his friends encouraged him to talk to someone. Maybe they thought that would help him out of the hole he found himself in. Jack did not want that though. He did not want to talk to some headshrinker. He just wanted to find Stacy. Then he wanted to get the man behind the whole plot. He wanted to find Stansby and make him pay.

He had lost another ten pounds. He had not had a solid meal since he had received the bad news from James. He still had not had a good night's sleep, and he was looking older by the minute. The combination of events was wearing on him. He felt like he was sinking further and further into a black abyss. There was no end in sight, and he didn't know how much further he could go.

One day, he decided to walk. *Maybe the exercise and sunshine can give me enough energy so that I can formulate a thought and then a plan. Maybe, just maybe, I can find her.* As he walked, he noticed that he was at the diner, the place where he had first met Stacy. He thought, I haven't eaten all day. Maybe I will go in and try the special of the day.

He entered it and found an empty booth in the back. He sat down and took in the environment. He looked at how happy most of the people there looked. He heard the buzzing of numerous conversations. There were people planning trips and talking about weddings and their children. He just sat there and listened to the noise. He ordered the special, but he really did not eat; he mostly moved food around his plate. He took a drink of sweet tea and decided that he needed to leave. This was too overwhelming for his emotional state. He started to get up and leave but heard a familiar voice—one that he did not want to hear.

"Hello, Jack. I hope you are doing well. Do you mind if I sit and share a meal with you?" Marvin asked.

"Marvin, please sit and rest your legs." Jack had been thinking about this moment and wanted answers.

"Tell me, Jack, how are you feeling? You look like you have been through the ringer." Marvin looked at Jack. He had not shaved. His eyes were dark.

"Marvin, to tell the truth, I have been through the ringer. I have been pursuing an endless case against a ghost. I have seen multiple murders. I have been shot and stabbed. The worst is that the woman I have fallen in love with has been kidnapped by the ghost. I can't eat or sleep because of recurring nightmares. I feel like I am cursed. I am angry with God, and I want answers. I know this is a lot to drop on you, but you are the closest thing to a religious man I know. Please tell me how good God is now. Tell me why he has done this to me." Jack knew he had come to Marvin with both barrels drawn, but if he didn't then, he did not think he would ever ask his questions.

Marvin sat and looked at him without emotion. "Jack, I cannot understand where you have been or what you feel. I can see how much strain this has put on you, and I do want to help answer some of your questions. I cannot promise all the answers, but I can promise you that Jesus loves you and wants you to know that." Marvin spoke with empathy. Jack noticed the kindness in his eyes.

"Jack, I lost my wife to an insidious disease and my daughter to drugs. I came to God myself with anger, and I questioned his way myself. I had a conversation with Jesus one night, the proverbial come-to-Jesus meeting." Marvin laughed as he recounted it. Jack continued to sit there stewing in his anger. "I wanted to know why. Why did he take them from me? Why did he let this happen?"

Jack was listening harder than he had before as he realized that misery wasn't his alone. "What happened at that meeting?" Jack asked earnestly.

"He showed me his servant Job."

Jack looked confused as Marvin mentioned that name. "Who is Job?" Jack asked.

"He was a man who lived during the time of Abraham. Job was a righteous man, and one day, he lost all he had—his children, servants, cattle, and all but his life and his wife's. He was also stricken with boils from the bottom of his feet to the top of his head." Marvin noticed Jack tuning in.

"Why did he do that to a righteous man?" Jack asked as he leaned in toward Marvin a bit closer.

"For His glory. God knew Job was a righteous man and honored Him in all that he had done. Satan wanted to put Job to the test. He wanted to prove God wrong about Job. So he let Satan sift him like wheat," Marvin responded as Jack thought maybe this was how God was getting his attention.

Jack understood he had avoided dealing with God. "Is he sifting me like wheat now?" Jack inquired.

"I cannot answer that, Jack. Maybe he is letting you come to the end of yourself like he did with me."

Jack shook his head at Marvin. "Why would I need to come to the end of myself?" Jack asked as Marvin smiled, reached over, and put his hand on Jack's shoulder.

"Because He wants you to know that He is your Father in heaven and that He loves you. You are sinful like everyone else. You want to be the king of your life, but that will only lead you to eternal separation from Him. If you accept what Jesus did for you on the cross and His death, burial, and resurrection, you will be eternally with Him in heaven. That is His desire, and if He needs to take you through the fire to make you understand that, He will."

Jack cringed at that comment. "He wants me to spend eternity with Him in heaven? But He also wants to let me be sifted like wheat? Why?" Jack asked indignantly.

"You need to know, Jack, that you were born into sin. You are sinful. Have you stolen anything?" Marvin asked Jack as his eyes squinted.

Jack then put his hand on his face and rubbed his eyes as if he were trying to clear them. "Maybe," Jack responded as he started to squirm in his seat.

"Then you are a thief. Have you lied?" Marvin asked.

"Yes, we all have," Jack responded as he started feeling hot like he was under a heat lamp.

"Then you are a liar," Marvin said as he noticed Jack squirm.

"I get it, Marvin. I am a sinner. Can't I just do some good works to be forgiven?" Jack was trying to make an argument, but he knew he was losing.

"God says that man's good work is like filthy rags in His presence. So good works will not work." Marvin was leading him down the road, and Jack seemed to be following.

"Well, what about Job? Did he get restored?" Jack asked.

"Job did get restored, but he had to come to the end of himself. He needed to humble his will and submit to God's will, which he did in the end. But God told him he needed to man up and see if he could even think of what God did every day to support His creation. He realized quickly that he could not answer that." Jack felt a calmness start to come over his body as Marvin spoke.

"Jack, the bottom line is that God loves you. He sent His Son Jesus to the world to die for the sins of the people of the world. You simply must respond to His calling. Will you do that?" Marvin reached over and touched Jack's arm. For the first time, Jack felt that he needed a Savior. "Can I pray with you to accept Jesus as your Savior, Jack?"

Jack was overwhelmed with emotion. He felt a tugging on his heart and felt like he needed to respond. "Yes, Marvin, let's pray." Marvin then led Jack into the sinner's prayer.

Just as soon as Marvin and Jack finished praying, Jack heard his phone buzzing. He had a text message. It was only a few short words: "Jack, I am alive; please help. On plane. Stacy."

To be continued.

Printed in the USA
CPSIA information can be obtained
at www.ICGtesting.com
LVHW090816170824
788329LV00001B/57